At the top of the stairs, Ben hesitated.

Jessie felt a rush of recklessness. She turned and leaned her back against her closed door. His smile was wry as he flattened the palms of his hands on either side of her head.

"This isn't a good idea," Ben murmured, staring at her mouth.

"No, it isn't," she said solemnly, agreeing, but unable to stop what was happening between them. She had chosen him, back there on that lonely road. He just didn't know it yet.

Ben smiled. "Tell me you want this as much as I do."

Jessie couldn't deny it, didn't even try. She wanted him to kiss her, more than she'd ever wanted anything in her life. Slowly he drew her into his arms. She'd waited for this moment. She wanted to hold on to the sensation.

Her silence drew him....

Dear Reader,

Fall is to be savored for all its breathtaking glory—and a spectacular October lineup awaits at Special Edition!

For years, readers have treasured Tracy Sinclair's captivating romances…and October commemorates her fiftieth Silhouette book! To help celebrate this wonderful author's crowning achievement, be sure to check out *The Princess Gets Engaged*—an enthralling romance that finds American tourist Megan Delaney in a royal mess when she masquerades as a princess and falls hopelessly in love with the charming Prince Nicholas.

This month's THAT'S MY BABY! title is by Lois Faye Dyer. *He's Got His Daddy's Eyes* is a poignant reunion story about hope, the enduring power of love and how one little boy works wonders on two broken hearts.

Nonstop romance continues as three veteran authors deliver enchanting stories. Check out award-winning author Marie Ferrarella's adorable tale about mismatched lovers when a blue-blooded heroine hastily marries a blue-collar carpenter in *Wanted: Husband, Will Train*. And what's an amnesiac triplet to do when she washes up on shore and right into the arms of a brooding billionaire? Find out in *The Mysterious Stranger,* when Susan Mallery's engaging TRIPLE TROUBLE series splashes to a finish! Reader favorite Arlene James serves up a tender story about unexpected love in *The Knight, The Waitress and the Toddler*—book four in our FROM BUD TO BLOSSOM promo series.

Finally, October's WOMAN TO WATCH is debut author Lisette Belisle, who unfolds an endearing romance between an innocent country girl and a gruff drifter in *Just Jessie.*

I hope you enjoy these books, and all of the stories to come!

Sincerely,

Tara Gavin, Senior Editor

Please address questions and book requests to:
Silhouette Reader Service
U.S.: 3010 Walden Ave., P.O. Box 1325, Buffalo, NY 14269
Canadian: P.O. Box 609, Fort Erie, Ont. L2A 5X3

LISETTE BELISLE
JUST JESSIE

SPECIAL EDITION

Published by Silhouette Books
America's Publisher of Contemporary Romance

To my husband, Frank,
for his unwavering faith and support.
All my love.

SILHOUETTE BOOKS

ISBN 0-373-24134-8

JUST JESSIE

Printed in U.S.A.

LISETTE BELISLE

believes in putting everything into whatever she does, whether it's a nursing career, motherhood or writing. While balancing a sense of practicality with a streak of adventure, she applies that dedication to creating stories of people overcoming the odds. Her message is clear—believe in yourself, and believe in love. She is the founder and past president of the Saratoga chapter of Romance Writers of America. Canadian-born, she grew up in New Hampshire and currently lives in upstate New York with her engineer husband, Frank.

She'd love to hear from her readers. She can be reached at: P.O. Box 1166, Ballston Lake, NY 12019

The Silhouette Spotlight
"Where Passion Lives"

MEET WOMAN TO WATCH *Linette Belisle*

What was your inspiration for JUST JESSIE?

LB: "The idea came from wondering how people survive terrible events and heal themselves. Ben Harding is a burned-out veteran of the Colombian drug wars. I created Jessie for him. Touchingly full of hope despite many disappointments, Jessie's naive about the world, yet wise about her place in it—frightened of change, yet fearless when it comes to facing life's everyday challenges."

What about the Special Edition line appeals to you as a reader and as a writer?

LB: "I like the variety in tone and writing style in Special Edition, as well as the extra length to develop plot and minor characters. Since I like to write an essentially upbeat story about people recovering from some trauma, whether it's physical, mental or emotional, Special Edition is a good fit. I'm extremely pleased and proud to be among all the wonderful writers in this line!"

Why is JUST JESSIE special to you?

LB: "Apart from the characters, who captured my imagination and my heart, I love the setting–a remote farm in Maine. The setting is more than a family farm, a dying way of life. It's an exotic locale, a harsh, enduring place full of mystery, excitement, drama, backbreaking work, heartbreaking isolation and breathtaking beauty. And, of course, love, joy and rebirth. I plan to revisit this setting in future books."

Chapter One

Stone's End. The crooked sign hung from a sawed-off fence post. Ben Harding dug out the directions and checked again. This was it. Stone's End. He'd been around, but he'd seldom seen such dismal-looking countryside. Fitting, he thought with a grim smile. He'd run out of places to run to.

On the road in between jobs, he'd been hitting truck stops, camping out, living rough. Tonight, he wanted a bed. So much for freedom. He would trade it in a minute for a hot meal—anything as long as it didn't come with a side order of fries. With a mental shrug, Ben swung his motorcycle onto the narrow dirt road. Lined with a stone fence, it snaked up a hill, then was swallowed in shadows.

So far, he wasn't impressed with northern Maine—a cold, inhospitable place as far as he could tell. Miles of woods had given way to backcountry farms. A steady rain was falling, with encroaching dusk adding to the misery index. Fingers of fog rose from the ground and fat raindrops dripped from the trees. He went over a bump. That was another thing; the ad in the newspaper hadn't mentioned potholes and washed-out roads. "Just follow the split-rail fence," a gruff male voice had instructed over the phone.

Leaning into a curve, Ben spotted a hulking red barn attached to a silo. A canopy of leaves stole the last of the daylight and shielded him from the worst of the wet. And there, dead center in the road, a hunched figure trudged along.

Ben shouted, "Watch it, fella!" and swerved through a wide puddle. In his wake, mud splattered in all directions.

"Hey, you!" In baggy pants and a shirt, the lone figure shook a fist. The motorcycle's roar drowned out a volley of angry sputters.

Relieved he hadn't hit anyone, Ben almost missed the gray-shingled house—an odd assortment of shapes tacked onto a story and a half. He parked his bike and ducked under a roof overhang. A pale solitary light drew him toward the rear of the building. Ignoring the pull of weak muscles, he crossed the narrow, railed porch. His mood deteriorated further when he knocked on the door. A dog started to bark and the door cracked open.

Baring his teeth, an ungainly dog, a brown-and-tan mix with coon eyes, poked his head around the door and growled. The door swung wider.

"Damn sight about time you showed up," Ben's new employer barked, greeting him in a passable imitation of the dog. In the dim light, the white-haired old man looked as if he could use a haircut and a shave. "Ben? Ben Harding, is it?" He grabbed the dog's collar and hauled him back inside. "Any relation to that Harding over by Bethel way?"

"No, sir, I'm afraid not," Ben said, regretting his haste in accepting a job over the phone.

Ira Carlisle grunted, "Good thing." With a stiff-kneed limp, he moved back and motioned Ben inside with a curt wave of his hand. "Man's a thief, a chicken thief. Ain't nothing worse, 'cept maybe a fed."

Ben laughed, surprised at the rusty sound of it. Maybe he had been on the road a little too long.

Watch it, fella. The words lingered after the roar of the motorcycle died in the distance. Jessie Carlisle swallowed the last of her sputters. The silence closed in around her. It was a familiar silence. Sometimes she felt she was drowning in it. She remembered when Stone's End had been a place people came to; now it was only a place they left. The farm was deep in mud, debts, broken promises and broken dreams. Jessie had forgotten how to dream.

The biker's warning had come too late. A thick spray of mud covered her in slime. Her hand shook as she wiped her cheek and left a long smear from brow to chin.

"Fella," he'd called her. The ultimate insult.

Treated as one of the boys, Jessie had known little softness, less comfort and no luxury in an all-male household. With her father claiming new clothes were a waste of hard-earned money, she'd swallowed her objections and her pride, and had worn her brother's hand-me-downs. As a teenager, she'd fared no better—all her pleas for pretty things had gone unheeded. Finally she'd stopped asking. At the memory of childish taunts, she ran work-roughened hands along the harsh denim of her blue jeans. Clumps of mud clung to her fingers and restored her senses.

With a brisk impatient motion, Jessie pulled her wide-brimmed hat down on her head. Jamming her hands into the pockets of her sheepskin-lined denim jacket, she continued marching down the middle of the road. At the house, she went around to the back, where a shed served as a mud room. She let the door slam to vent her irritation. With a grimace of distaste, she sat on a dark pine bench to pull off her boots. Only her father's strict code of morality prevented her from stripping down to the skin and wrapping herself in the large towel kept handy.

Moments later, Jessie entered the country kitchen. The heat from the crackling fire in the fireplace reached out to enfold her. The dog raised its head with a glad bark.

"Hey, Bandit." She bent to scratch the dog's ears.

Catching a glimpse of movement to her left, she looked up to find flinty blue eyes staring at her. A stranger, in his mid-to-late thirties, sat at the oak table with her father. A day's growth of dark stubbly beard hid the man's features, all except his mouth, which had a sensuous twist. His dark hair was thick and slightly long. A motorcycle helmet and gloves sat on the table by his elbow. Jessie's lips tightened as she identified him as the biker who had nearly run her down earlier. Arms folded across his chest, long legs stretched under the table, he looked oddly at home. Despite his casual pose, she sensed a leashed strength, a restless energy. A faint flicker of curiosity narrowed his dark blue eyes as their glances collided across the room. Jessie reacted instinctively. Feeling unsettled, she decided she didn't like him.

Her father's brow beetled into a frown. "You're late."

"Sorry, I just checked the mailbox." Nothing from her brother—Jared hadn't written in weeks. "If you'll excuse me, I need to change."

"A little dirt never hurt." Her father waved her over. "Come, I want you to meet Ben Harding."

With rising color, she watched the stranger's lips twitch in amusement at her less-than-immaculate condition.

"Ben answered my ad in the paper," her father explained.

"What ad?" She threw the stranger a suspicious glance,

then wished she hadn't betrayed any emotion when his gaze hardened.

"I advertised for a farm manager."

This came as news to Jessie. But perhaps hiring someone would eliminate some of the pressure. Her father had been sick all winter. Despite her efforts to manage on her own, the debts continued to mount daily. She couldn't bear to think of failing, of losing Stone's End. It would break her father. Yes, they needed someone—but this man would never do.

"Ben, my daughter, Jess," Ira added, as an afterthought.

Ben stood. His voice was polite, a bit distant, as he stretched out a hand. "How do you do?"

Surprised by the gesture, she reached out, then stared at her small hand extended toward his larger one. His hand was hard and tanned, long fingered and well shaped. And clean. Clenching her hand, she withdrew. "Sorry, I have to wash up."

"Sorry about the mud." His smooth Southern drawl sounded foreign to her ears. One more thing to distrust. "I didn't expect someone out walking in this downpour."

"That's all right," she murmured. But it wasn't.

"Ben will be staying, Jess," Ira said. "We'll discuss the job over supper."

Jessie said nothing as Ben settled his tall, lanky frame back onto the ladder-back chair. Accustomed to people passing through on their way to someplace else, she assumed he would move on—after she fed him. He looked as if he could use a decent meal; several, in fact. With his gaze following her from the room, she felt a shiver of awareness, as if he'd touched her with more than his eyes.

Ben watched the girl leave and refused to admit she'd aroused his curiosity. Perhaps it was all that negative energy, he thought, recalling her barely contained animosity.

Ira's quizzing brought him back. "Where did you work last?"

"Down South."

"Seems you got itchy feet." Ira frowned at the list of references. "These go back two years. What did you do before?"

Ben felt his stomach muscles tense. Under Ira's keen gaze, he took a deep breath and forced himself to relax—the way the doctors had instructed. "I was in the military."

Ira met his eyes, then looked away. After fifteen minutes of questions, he appeared satisfied. Ben felt he'd been grilled by an expert. Then the daughter returned. Jess.

Her altered appearance caught Ben off guard.

To his surprise, she cleaned up to advantage. A little shorter than average height, she was slender. Young. Her hair was neither blond nor brown, but some soft silky caramel color in between. Drawn off her face, the practical hairdo revealed a wide brow and gray eyes. Her eyes held him for a long moment. Clear and candid, they shimmered from silver to pewter with suppressed emotion. Pink lips and a leftover winter-pale complexion made her appear vulnerable, yet she worked with brisk precision as she set the table.

Round, sturdy plates sparkled white against a red-and-white checkered cloth. The cutlery gleamed. Seeing no evidence of another woman, Ben could only assume this young girl was solely responsible for the mouthwatering smells from the kitchen. With her small chin and firmly set mouth, he had yet to see her smile.

Ira dominated the conversation over supper. "Jess pulls her weight around the place," he said, offhand about her position.

Ben made no comment.

Jessie rearranged meat and vegetables on her plate and colored to a rosy hue each time her father addressed her directly. Ben suspected that for all her boyish appearance and abrupt manner, Jess Carlisle was uncomfortable around men.

"I've had to depend on her since my son took off." Ira spoke as if his daughter wasn't present. Ben frowned, then dismissed the observation as none of his business. "Damn fool! Wants to see the world. We were getting along fine until I took sick." Ira pushed away from the table, putting an abrupt end to the meal. "We'll finish this discussion in the den."

Ben rose.

Ira stopped midway across the room. "Did you get those new feed bills entered, Jess?"

She nodded. "Yes, the books are all up-to-date." Sliding her chair back, she reached for a plate.

Ira walked out without a backward glance.

Ben looked at the array of empty plates and serving dishes. "Let me give you a hand with this."

Her startled gaze flew to his, soft encountering hard. The wariness was mutual, he assumed.

"Thank you," she said. "I can manage."

"If you insist." Ben slid his hands into his pockets. "Thanks for the meal. I enjoyed it." He meant it. He'd been embarrassed to go back for thirds. The stew had been thick and hearty, the bread homemade. He couldn't recall the last time he'd eaten freshly baked bread, not to mention apple cobbler—New England country-style; thick syrupy apple wedges covered with light-batter dumplings. Sweet.

"I'm glad." Her smile, though scant, softened the contours of her face to a youthful prettiness. "Dad's waiting for you."

When Ben entered the den, Ira's gaze was impatient. They discussed salary—a man wouldn't get wealthy working for the Carlisles, Ben concluded.

"The job's temporary, just until my son comes home," Ira said. "Think you can handle it?"

"Yes," Ben said firmly. Glad the interview was over, he stood. He shoved his hands into his pockets. "That suits me fine. I don't like to stay in one place too long." A military brat, he'd been on the move most of his life, apart from idyllic summers on his grandparents' farm.

"Humph! None of you young fellers want to plant roots. At your age, you should be thinking about the future, a wife…" Ira went silent, his frown suddenly fierce.

Ben shrugged. "Things tie you down." He knew all about duty. He'd had his fill and preferred to go through life unencumbered. At this stage, he wanted peace, solitude. When life got too complicated, he moved on.

"Get your gear. Jess will show you your room."

Dismissed, Ben left the den with mixed feelings about moving on. He followed sounds of activity coming from the pantry, a narrow utilitarian room off the kitchen. From the doorway, he silently observed Carlisle's daughter putting away the last of the dishes. There was little to appreciate about the bleak farm, the owner or his daughter. Ben felt a stab of discomfort. He supposed he shouldn't judge the girl too harshly. From all the signs, her life wasn't easy.

Hooking his thumbs into the belt loops at his waist, he leaned against the doorframe and waited for her to finish. His gaze wandered. A bare light bulb hung overhead. The wallpaper—green ivy climbing a white brick wall—was yellow with age. The linoleum was cracked. A hardy brilliant burst of lush purple, pink and white violets bloomed defiantly on the windowsill. His gaze lingered there for a long moment before turning back to the girl, slim and lithe in blue jeans. A thick navy sweater swallowed her breasts, if she had any. With little difficulty, Ben dismissed her figure as boyish and unappealing. His gaze drifted downward. The beaded fringed moccasins added a nice touch to her surprisingly dainty feet. Although he had to admit she had a certain coltish grace, he liked his women with a little more flesh, a few more years, and a lot more confidence.

There hadn't been many women lately. Ben knew the dangers in finding an ounce of appeal in this one. Luckily for him, she didn't appear to realize she had any.

Jessie dried the last pot. She switched off the overhead light, turned, then gasped at a looming shadow. Recognizing the biker, she pressed a hand to her waist. "What do you want?"

Though impatient, his voice was cultured, with a soft drawl to it. "Your father said you'd show me to my room."

"Your room!" Surely Dad hadn't hired this drifter. When he straightened, she stepped back and stared up at him.

"That's right," he responded to her challenge. "If you have any objections, discuss it with your father."

Jessie snapped her teeth shut. Dad hadn't given her feelings a moment's consideration in twenty-three years; he wasn't about to start now. But how could she share her home with this stranger who threatened her with his steely eyes?

They had three bedrooms—two up, one down. Her father slept in the downstairs bedroom. Ben Harding would have to sleep upstairs in the room opposite hers; they would have to share the bathroom. She started to object, then stopped. The man looked exhausted.

Earlier, she'd noticed a slight limp. Evidence of strain and fatigue lined his eyes and mouth, nevertheless, his pride remained unbent. She wondered at that. She didn't have to be told he needed this job. Yet instinct told her he would never bend, beg or break. Unable to condemn anyone without a fair trial, Jessie accepted the inevitable. He was staying.

"All right." Drawing a deep breath, she eased by him in the narrow doorway, anxious to remove herself from the small dark confines of the pantry. "I suppose you can stay."

"Thanks," he murmured dryly.

She ignored his sarcasm. "You can put your motorcycle in the garage out back." She kept her voice courteous and distant, and felt relieved when he left.

Ben wasn't gone long. When he returned, he found the girl stacking sheets, blankets and towels into a neat pile.

She placed a bar of soap on top and spared him a brisk glance. "This way."

Hugging the linens tightly to her chest, she led him up some dimly lit stairs. The fourth tread squeaked with age. The sixth, seventh and tenth joined in harmony. These ended in a small upstairs hall with three closed doors. Layers of wallpaper thickened the walls. Overhead, rain hit the tin roof with a staccato beat. Outside, the wind howled.

Ben knew he should be grateful for any sort of shelter from the storm. But he wasn't. Instead, he felt reluctant to accept the Carlisles' hospitality. All he wanted was a temporary job, not an ailing old man and a helpless young girl. It felt like a trap. Like a fool, he'd let his momentary irritation with this slip of a girl influence his decision to stay.

She opened the middle door to an outdated bathroom.

"Who sleeps there?" With a nod, he indicated the second door and wondered if he would get any privacy.

"I do." With that terse announcement, she entered the room opposite. "You should be comfortable here."

Looking around, he had his doubts. Though spotless, the room was bare—no curtains, just a window shade. A bed.

A desk. Some shelves. The room's stripped-naked look echoed his lack of welcome in this house.

The girl moved to the bed. With a smooth motion, she shook the sheet out over the exposed mattress. She hadn't stopped working since he'd met her. Her small face had appeared weary even then. Now she looked exhausted, with pale violet shadows under her eyes, her mouth a tight line. Her shoulders drooped. Apparently, sheer willpower alone kept her upright.

For some reason, that annoyed Ben. He reached for the sheet. "I'll do that." He just wanted her out. A woman, a bed—it was far too intimate for his peace of mind.

There was a slight tug-of-war until she released her grip on the crisp white cotton sheet. It fell to the bed.

"Thanks." She started to leave, then turned back. "If it turns colder, you'll find extra blankets in the closet. The mattress isn't new, but it's comfortable." She blushed at the personal turn in the conversation. His eyes never wavered from her face. She drew in her bottom lip, as her composure slipped another notch. "Give me five minutes," she finished in a rush, "then the bathroom's all yours." This time, she almost made it to the door. "If you need anything, just…"

He lifted an eyebrow; her voice wavered, then trailed off. In silence, she closed the door. Left alone, Ben stared at the solitary window at the far end of the narrow room, expecting to see bars. Well, he'd lived in a lot worse places. He tossed his backpack to the floor, where it landed with a thud.

When he picked up the sheet from the bed, he caught the clean, light scent—fresh air, apple blossoms and sunshine.

Spring.

Ben's features broke into a reluctant smile. Girls like Jess Carlisle were out of his experience. He'd never met anyone remotely like her. Boyish and uncommunicative, she was almost awkward in her manner. Yet, she was undeniably domesticated, feminine in a fresh, natural way. Womanly, despite her youth. Though belated, her kindness had surprised him. Ben shook his head—women were experts at tying a man in knots.

With the timely reminder, he made up the narrow single bed. It didn't take long to store his meager belongings. After giving her an extra five minutes, Ben headed for the bathroom.

He stopped short. On the landing outside the girl's bedroom door, the large misbegotten dog—a collie-shepherd mixed with something indefinable—sat night watch over his mistress. Hair on end, Bandit growled at Ben.

Ben was tempted to growl back.

Chapter Two

In the morning, Jessie added layer upon layer to her jeans and red-and-black buffalo-plaid shirt. She yawned. She'd slept poorly, disturbed by every real and imagined sound from the occupied room across the hall. Even now, with pale morning light peeking around her window shade, she felt Ben Harding's presence. And resented it.

His deliberate coldness spoke volumes, warning her to keep her distance. She shivered. Last, she pulled a green wool sweater over her head. It was one of her brother's castoffs, his Henderson High varsity football sweater. She smoothed the large sweater low over her hips, recalling happier times when she'd cheered Jared on to victory. Unlike her, Jared had always been popular, confident, sure of his place in life. Loved.

A bold letter H crossed her breasts. The sweater, like a protective cloak, kept her safe, just as Jared had. With only two years' difference between them, they'd always been close.

How could he have left?

Things hadn't been the same since. Her father had grown older. He'd let the farm go downhill. Lately, he'd grown testy, his moods erratic. With a troubled sigh, Jessie tidied her long hair into a thick braid. Her thoughts ran ahead to breakfast and the blueberry pancakes she planned to make—if her father hadn't eaten all the berries. Ailing and housebound most of the winter, Ira Carlisle had complained of boredom more than anything else.

Frowning, she reached for the door. She'd set her alarm early to avoid Ben. Ben. His name slipped easily off her tongue. But he wasn't easy, comfortable or gentle. As if she needed a reminder, Jessie walked out of her room and collided with a half-dressed, full-grown male coming out of the bathroom.

He'd shaved.

Astounded, she bit back a comment. In addition to the black stubble, he'd shaved several years off his appearance. He looked younger, yet somehow more formidable. His face looked carved out of stone—with a discerning artist's eye. A lean handsome face with a chiseled mouth and set jaw arrested her gaze. Only a slight bump from an apparent break marred the straight patrician nose. It was not a gentle face; there was too much evidence of living. Yet, experience was far more intriguing than perfection. A thin white scar slashed his left temple, giving it a sinister cast. In addition to the scar, there was too much intelligence, too much knowledge in his eyes. No, he was not an easy man.

"Good morning." Jessie absorbed the physical shock to her senses. His damp hair was slicked back, emphasizing his wide intelligent brow and dark-lashed, startling blue eyes. He was more muscular than she'd expected. His bare chest was bold, with thick, coarse black hairs.

He draped a white towel around his neck. "Is it?" He

looked vaguely amused, with good reason. It was a typical Maine spring morning, a dew-wet world shrouded in gray mist.

She felt a need to explain, "The fog will burn off later." Her curious gaze skittered down the line of black hair arrowing to his waist. She released her breath. He was wearing blue jeans, unbelted, and his stomach was hard and flat, without an ounce of spare flesh on his ribs.

Ben's voice drew her attention back to his face, where a faint smile teased his lips. "Is it always this cold and wet in April?" His eyes mocked her obvious reaction to him.

"Mmm," Jessie murmured. Cold? Her face on fire, she cleared her throat. "Usually things warm up a bit in May."

Her eyes strayed again, then widened with shock. One, two, three—three round white puckered scars laced his side just below his ribs. Bullet-size scars. Her gaze flew back to his. His mouth tightened, waiting for her to comment. A hundred questions crowded her mind and remained unspoken. He could be a cold-blooded criminal! Had he paid for his crime? From the look in his eyes, she guessed he had. The thought made her shudder, but not with repugnance....

"Excuse me." She bolted down the stairs, fleeing from her response to a man who should have frightened her, but somehow didn't. And that frightened her most of all. She skirted the parlor on her way to the kitchen and passed her father, who asked if she was sick, or ailing or something. Or something.

The dog raised its head and whined. Unable to explain her reaction, Jessie pulled open the door and let Bandit out. A welcome draft of cold air struck her heated face.

Her father's voice drifted over to her, "About Ben..." He explained the man's duties and ended with the warning,

"He's a hard man, Jess. Don't get any foolish ideas." As if she would!

"Why did you hire him?" she asked.

"I've had the ad in for a month. He's the first response."

She couldn't argue with his logic. Farm help was hard to get. Anyone qualified had his own operation. Even seasonal farmworkers were at a premium. Each year, local farmers seemed to depend on migrant workers more and more.

"I want you to stay away from him. Do you hear?" he added.

Jessie nodded. She didn't need a lecture, which usually started and ended with the litany, "Like mother, like daughter." She couldn't dispute his accusation. Her memories were vague, but she'd grown up with the small-town gossip, along with her father's disillusionment. Apparently, her mother had been a city girl. After seven years of marriage, Avis had gone back to the bright lights with the first man to sweet-talk her into going along for the ride. She'd left behind an embittered husband with two small children. After Avis, there was little softness left in Ira; she'd taken the heart out of him and left an empty shell.

Jessie understood that her father's warning about the hired hand was for her own good. In his clumsy way, he was only trying to protect her. She knew all that, but his lack of trust hurt.

By the time Ben came downstairs, Jessie had restored her sense of balance. Nevertheless, she looked up with a start to find him halfway across the kitchen. Instead of warning her off, her father's words made her more curious. Overnight, Ben Harding had lost the slight limp. He had an easy way of walking—tall and erect, and proud. He certainly looked fit. A night's rest had done wonders for him. Jessie wished she could say the same of herself.

She felt disoriented, as if her world had tilted.

His eyes were direct—too direct. They looked right through her. With a brief indifferent nod in her general direction, he addressed her father. "Morning."

Feeling deflated, Jessie joined the men at the claw-foot table where her father liked to conduct business dealings over a meal. A stickler for routine, Ira frowned at Ben. "Breakfast is at six sharp. Be here, or you'll miss it."

Raising a casual eyebrow to the verbal challenge, Ben helped himself to hotcakes and sausages.

Jessie poured coffee. "Sugar?"

"Yes, ma'am. Two." He drowned his hotcakes in sweet maple syrup, took a bite and released a sigh of pleasure.

She swallowed a smile. The man had a weakness. She caught her father's warning gaze. His dour mood put a damper on the meal. When conversation turned to the farm, she became aware of undercurrents. They needed a good season. They needed a strong hand to manage the large number of migrant workers they would be hiring shortly. Unfortunately, they needed Ben Harding.

At the end, her father said, "Jess will show you around. Anything you need, just ask her."

Aware of Ben's sardonic expression, Jessie couldn't imagine him taking her directions seriously. No one did, except perhaps Fred Cromie. Fred had worked at Stone's End for as long as she remembered. His wife, Hazel, had kept house until Jessie was old enough to take over. Among other things she'd taught Jessie—such as saving herself for the right man—she'd shown her how to cook. Somehow the two were inseparable in Hazel's mind. In an age of microwavable gourmet dinners, Jessie suspected Hazel's well-meant advice might be a little outdated. So far, she hadn't put it to the test.

After breakfast, Jessie hoped Ben would find his way around without her. When she ran out of indoor chores, she found him sitting on the porch railing. She shivered in the cold damp morning, grateful the fog had lifted. A pale sliver of sunlight penetrated the mass of black storm clouds.

A quick flick of his dark-browed gaze on the letter H stretched across her chest left her feeling scorched. Branded. With her heart racing, Jessie pretended she hadn't felt the unrestrained tightening of her breasts. She attempted a weak smile. "Ready to go?"

Arms folded, Ben frowned at her. "Where to?"

She slipped her arms into her barn jacket. "We could start with a tour of the property."

"Fine." He peeled himself from the rail.

Jessie climbed into the pickup and cranked the engine. It fired on the third try. The interior shrank when Ben climbed in beside her. As she backed the truck out of the driveway, the tires stuck and spun in a rut. She shifted gears. "The setup is standard. We've got nearly five hundred acres. Two hundred are tillable, fifty are set aside for grazing." She threw him a glance.

His gaze climbed the evergreen hills. "Any logging?"

"We've had offers, but Dad refused."

"Isn't logging profitable?" With a few more choice words on the subject, he took command of the conversation.

Jessie relaxed under his businesslike approach. She knew about farming. Her family had owned Stone's End for two hundred years. Generations came and went; the land remained. At times, it made her feel small. Who would provide future generations? Her brother was in no rush to settle down. And she didn't date.

At a break in the fence, they got out and walked. Jessie took a deep breath. The breeze stirred the tiny tendrils of hair escaping her braid. She stuck her hands in her pockets. So did he. In silence, they plodded through the field. Beyond the shelter of the thick tree line, the wind raced through like a funnel, whipping her clothes around her.

Ben felt the cold.

Aware of the girl's discomfort, he regretted their awkward start—not that he had any intention of putting her at ease. Encouraging her friendship would be a damn fool thing to do.

He bent to scoop up a clump of dirt, crumbling it through his fingers. The rich scent of earth and minerals teased his nostrils. If there was anything he cared for, this was it. When everything else in his life had gone haywire, he'd turned back to the land, to the lessons his grandfather had taught him.

"This is rich farmland," he murmured with pleasure. "What sorts of crops grow in this climate?"

"Potatoes..."

Ben's mouth twitched. With all his high living and wandering, he'd come to earth on a potato farm. If some of his old buddies could see him, he would never hear the end of it. He straightened as the memory drove deeper. All his old buddies were dead.

"And broccoli," she added. "There's also a large apple orchard. We rotate oats and corn for the cattle."

Ben stood on bare brown earth and thought of a green jungle where life was traded for the cost of white powder. Gradually, the girl's soft voice penetrated his dark thoughts. The sinking blackness receded. He focused on her, on her voice—a steady flow of humdrum details, everyday words. Like a lifeline, he clung to them. To her.

"We keep a herd of dairy cows," she was saying. "The surplus milk goes to a co-op." Her voice had a slight huskiness to it as she continued her stiff little lecture.

What a funny girl, he thought, unable to understand why she'd captured his attention so totally. Serious, practical, boyish in her sturdy clothes and work boots, she was the kind of girl a man might want for a pal—if he was young and unscarred. Ben was neither. He raised an eyebrow. "With your father sick, you're in charge of the entire operation?"

"Oh, no. Fred's retired, but he comes in every day." Her slight smile turned into a frown. "He can't do any lifting or heavy work. The dairy's well equipped. We manage just fine. And there's Cal Pierce, who helps out after school when we're rushed. He lives just down the road at the next farm."

Translate that to a minimum of five miles. Ben had been in New England long enough to know "just down the road" could mean anything. What was he going to do with a skinny young girl, a semiretired hand, and this Pierce kid, Cal-who-helps-out?

When he didn't say a word, she continued, "For the seasonal work, we hire extra help."

"From where?"

"Workers turn up every summer. They stay at the Pierce migrant camp down the road."

He digested the information. "I've worked on produce farms in the South. The setup must be the same."

She heaved a visible sigh of relief. "Fine. Then you won't need me." She broke off when he chuckled.

"No," he agreed. "I won't need you." That was the last thing he intended. He swung away before she could add a word.

When she hastened after him, taking two steps to his one, he added, "You can go back. I'll find my way back to the house."

"I didn't mean it that way. It's just..."

He turned back to her. "You're right. We've both got work to do."

"Mr. Harding, I'm sorry."

He felt a stab of conscience. He'd done precious little

to put her at ease. "Make that Ben, Jess." His tone wasn't exactly friendly, just less harsh and abrupt.

She smiled, correcting him. "Jessie."

Ben hesitated. Something long forgotten in him recognized the unspoiled sweetness of her youth, the gentle persuasion in her eyes. "All right, Jessie." He drew out the last syllable. What harm could it do? "See you at lunch."

Jessie watched him walk away. He'd left her standing in the middle of the field. Stunted trees bowed to the wind. Dried brush and dead leaves danced behind him. Under a pale sun, he cast a long, lonely shadow. She bit her lip at the urge to follow him. Shaking off the wayward notion, she went back to the truck and drove home.

Lunch was a rushed affair.

Ben had apparently put her out of his mind. Over chicken and gravy, he discussed the farm. "You said your son would be coming back," he said at one point. "When do you expect him?"

Ira's face closed. "Soon."

Jessie glanced up. Her father averted his eyes. Two years ago, Jared had left and hadn't been back since. She raised her cup. Her thoughts drifted to her absent brother while her father went into an explanation about some new equipment he intended to buy, come spring.

Jared had escaped, she thought enviously. After an argument with his father, he'd enlisted in the army the day he turned eighteen. That was eight years ago. The break had added tension to their relationship. For the next three years, his infrequent leaves home had usually ended in arguments. After the service, he'd come home for a time, but left again to work his way through veterinary school with the help of scholarships. He'd come home for summers and holidays—until two years ago when he and his father had clashed again. Jared hadn't been back since.

Despite some natural resentment, Jessie missed him. He added a spirit of fun and adventure to the household—a spark she didn't possess. She had no idea what had caused the argument between her father and Jared, or what it would take to end it. Perhaps something as simple as an apology, she thought ruefully. Jared had inherited her father's stubborn streak. For that matter, so had she.

Over lunch, it soon became clear that her father had no intention of airing the family squabbles. Jessie glanced across the table, surprised to encounter Ben's gaze. It was steady, unwavering, curious, as if he'd read her troubled thoughts. She returned the look with equal intensity, until she saw a gleam of humor light the depths of his eyes. She amused him. A hot tide of color filled her face. Looking away, she lowered her cup. It rattled against the saucer. Inwardly she groaned at her gaucheness, wishing she had more experience in handling men like Ben Harding. If only she could find him as entertaining as he appeared to find her! She didn't find him amusing at all. She found him scarred and brooding, dark and dangerous. And fascinating.

"When does the danger of frost end?" he asked, turning back to his conversation with her father.

"Sometime in late May. You'll want to have everything in place by then," Ira said, giving Ben a free hand with the spring planting.

Her father must be more ill than she'd thought. Jessie hardly had time to register that when her father excused himself. "I'm going to lie down awhile." She stared after him in concern.

Ben left the table with a brief, "Thanks, Jess."

Jess.

Her shoulders drooped. Her offer of friendship, barely acknowledged, withered and died. Whenever he ordered her to do something, her father called her Jess; when he asked, he softened it to Jessie. From earliest childhood, she'd understood the subtle difference. This would be the pattern, she thought, watching both men disappear. She shook her head at her foolishness. What had she expected from Ben? Friendship?

The afternoon was busy, yet the day seemed to drag, until supper—when she saw Ben again. He ignored her.

After supper, she went for a walk. Usually her solitary walk to the pond soothed her. This evening, she felt more than alone—she felt lonely. Spring tantalized her with its promise.

It was still early when she prepared for bed.

Unable to sleep, she read. Her eyes grew pensive as she heard Ben's footsteps mounting the stairs. Moments later, she heard sounds from his room. Doors opened and closed. A drawer stuck, wood grated. More footsteps. The dog growled. A muttered curse. The old pipes in the bathroom protested, then gushed. Ben was taking a shower. She wouldn't think of him shedding clothes from his sleek, muscled body. She wouldn't.

Her window was open. Soft night murmurs mingled with the sound of rushing water. A new moon played shadows on her ceiling. Jessie closed her eyes, willing herself to sleep. At this rate, she would be a hag by week's end. Drawing in even breaths, she groaned in defeat when she recalled her morning encounter with Ben. Even now, she felt a hot, piercing tide of embarrassment. And excitement. She reached for the clock and set it permanently for half an hour earlier.

Jessie drove to town the following morning. Wherever she looked, tender leaves grew on limbs of beech, oak and maple trees. Here and there, pale shades of lilac budded. Gradually the hills sloped to the town, nestled in a valley. Henderson wasn't a pretty place. It was a working town, with a sawmill at one end, a truck stop and a trading post at the other. And in between, a few official buildings and a row of businesses struggled to survive. Nevertheless, Jessie looked for beauty and found it. Beauty in the weathered faces of those whose ancestors had stubbornly carved out a town—a place to belong in the far reaches of a northern wilderness.

She stopped at the health clinic where the receptionist greeted her. "Hi, Jess, what can I do for you?"

"Dad's prescription expired. Is there a refill?"

"Let me check." She left and came back with the doctor, a crusty old Mainer who looked more at home herding his precious sheep than doctoring people.

Dr. Peterson didn't waste time on pleasantries. "I warned that ornery old fool to come in for a checkup." He waved a stern finger at her. "You tell Ira I want to see his hide in this office before the month is out."

"I will," Jessie agreed, adding, "his medicine ran out."

"And I suppose he waited till today to tell you?"

"Mmm." Shrugging, she slipped the tips of her fingers into her pockets. "He probably forgot." Her face turned pink at the blatant lie when the doctor grunted.

He scratched a few words on a prescription pad and tore a sheet off. "How's he feeling? Any chest pain?" He handed her the prescription.

Jessie slipped it into her pocket. "He won't tell me."

"Is he still working?"

"Actually, he just hired someone to manage the farm." She was aware of a small glow, probably relief, at the words.

"Well, that will take the load off your shoulders. You know where to reach me." The doctor's troubled glance met hers. "And Jessie, call if you get worried."

She smiled. "Thanks, I'll do that." Her smile slipped the minute she walked out the door.

Jessie drove to The Trading Post and pulled her truck into a narrow vacant space between two other pickup trucks. Hers was the most disreputable, she noted. The tailgate hung at an angle. More rust than paint clung to the battered green body. A layer of dried mud covered it all.

The store was crowded. People greeted her with native curiosity. "How's your dad?"

She pinned on a smile and replied, "Better," until her jaw ached. She couldn't bring herself to reveal a litany of complaints and concerns. Her fear for her father's health went too deep, to the heart of her.

With a bit of maneuvering, she managed to get her shopping cart up and down the aisles. She scanned the shelves with a practiced eye. She needed baking supplies. She hesitated over chocolate chips. They were on special—buy one, get one free. Ben had inhaled cookies hours earlier. At this rate, she could only hope he would earn his keep. She feared he was going to cost her more than the inflated price of a few groceries. With a resigned shrug, she tossed two bags into the cart. To that, she added a few more supplies, then two more bags of chocolate chips.

She squirmed at the checkout when the items totaled to a staggering amount. Digging into her pocket, she came up with several bills and the exact change.

Jessie left the store. A shadow fell over her as Drew Pierce fell into step beside her. His parents owned the neighboring farm. Cal, who worked at Stone's End, was his youngest brother.

"How's Ira?" Drew's gaze settled on her mouth. Classically handsome with curling dark hair and sinfully irreverent black eyes, he oozed confidence. He was also wealthy...and the local heartthrob. His bad-boy reputation only added to his appeal, but Jessie knew him too well. "Cal tells me your dad's been sick."

"He's doing better," Jessie murmured. The thought of

a scarred, dark-browed stranger crossed her mind. Not breaking her stride, she reached the truck. Shifting one grocery bag to her hip, she reached for the door handle.

Drew leaned a hand against the door and stopped her. "I saw your father's newspaper ad. Get any applicants?"

"As a matter of fact, we—"

He interrupted her in midsentence. "Tell Ira not to worry. I can spare some time until he gets back on his feet."

"Thanks, but we already hired someone." Jessie didn't trust Drew, or his motives. The Pierce property bordered Stone's End. In addition to importing migrants, Drew's family controlled extensive logging and banking interests where they employed half the locals—the half who weren't farming. Just a month ago, her father had refused Drew's offer to buy Stone's End.

"Who did he hire?" he asked curiously.

"You wouldn't know him. He's from out of town."

"Ira hired an outsider? What does he know about this guy?"

She shrugged. "Enough, I suppose."

"I hate to say it, but your dad's losing his touch. He should know better than to trust some drifter looking for a free ride."

"We're doing just fine."

"Are you?" He cast a disparaging glance at her pickup, then turned his appraisal on her. "When was the last time you had a day off?" His gaze slid down the front of her shirt tucked into her jeans. He chuckled when she reached for the edges of her open jacket and drew them together. "Call if you need anything."

"Thanks anyway," she snapped. "We can manage."

He merely grinned and walked away.

Jessie drove home, feeling harassed by Drew's offer of assistance. He made her uneasy; he always had. As a child, he'd taunted her with cruel nicknames. Jared had always risen to her defense. Who would protect her now?

She was ten miles out of town when Drew's flashy red car came up behind her on a curve marked with a No Passing sign. It would be just like him to ignore the law.

At a bend in the road, Jessie averted her eyes from a crude marker under the gnarled maple tree. Jared's dog, Sunny, was buried there. The memory still had the power to upset her. That fall, to please Jared, her father had posted the farm against deer hunters. That hadn't stopped Drew and his college friends from trespassing. Somehow, they mistook Jared's golden Labrador retriever for a deer. Jessie was with Jared when they heard the shots. They'd found Sunny, critically wounded. After wrestling a gun from Drew, tears streaming down his face, Jared sighted in his dog. One of Drew's friends laughed nervously. In growing horror, Jessie watched helplessly. The dog yelped with pain.

Jared's hands were shaking so bad...

In the end, she'd grabbed the gun, aimed and fired one clean shot. An awful silence followed. Jared had simply looked at her with gratitude. Now, Jessie blinked moisture from her eyes as she recalled his expression. In ways, the silence had never been broken. Drew had never apologized. From that day on, no one had discussed the incident. But Jessie knew how much Jared had loved his dog. Sunny was special, a last gift from his mother.

Her thoughts came back to the present when Drew's car tried to pass on a straightaway. He didn't have room. To the right, gray rock slabs had tumbled in a recent mud slide. All the way home, he tailed her. At her driveway his car turned, then veered away. Puzzled, she glanced at the house and saw the hired man walk out of the shadow of the porch and into the sun.

She drew a relieved breath. The rich scent of chocolate

filled the interior of the truck. She released her white-knuckled grip on the steering wheel. Fighting a wave of nausea, she sat still until it passed, then swallowed and gathered the tattered remnants of her composure.

Steeling her nerves for another encounter with Ben, she climbed down from the truck. He watched as she reached back for the groceries, then slammed the door with a metallic clang. His gaze remained fixed on her face and rigid mouth as she crossed the driveway and the yard.

He raised an eyebrow. "That the boyfriend?"

She released a shaky laugh. "No!"

His gaze sharpened. "Anything wrong?"

"No," she said, her breath a whisper of release as the tension drained. "That was just Drew Pierce, a neighbor." She looked into his sun-bronzed face and met his sober gaze; a response stirred inside her. For the first time since his arrival, she felt a strong emotion other than confusion or resentment. Perhaps irrationally, she no longer felt threatened by his scars, his silence, his dark brooding glance.

She felt safe.

Jessie stifled the thought at birth. Nevertheless, she must have communicated it to Ben. She caught a gleam of sharpened awareness before a shutter came down over his eyes. She might have imagined that look, but suddenly she felt like a rare endangered species—a virgin.

Chapter Three

Rounding a corner of the barn the following morning, Ben heard a warning shout, "Watch it, Jessie! Homer's on the warpath!" Too late. Jessie had just released the barn door.

Ben froze in his tracks as the ugliest bull he'd ever seen came charging out, straight at her. Holding back a hoarse shout, his breath suspended, he watched Jessie turn and spring for the nearest fence. She nimbly caught the highest rail, hauled herself up and straddled the top of the fence. The black sway-bellied bull rammed it—inches below her left boot. A thick, curled, ivory-colored horn scored the wood fence. The bull bellowed a roar of frustration.

"Whooeee, that-a-girl!" A young man—Cal Pierce?—cheered her on. "Homer's fast, but no match for you."

Ben watched in disbelief as Jessie grinned and hung on. Her perch shook as the bull again rammed his huge head into the fence before veering away with a disgruntled snort.

Jessie was still grinning when she felt two hard hands circle her waist and haul her down. She landed on her feet with a teeth-rattling thud.

Ben grabbed her shoulders and spun her around to face him. "Are you trying to get yourself killed!"

She gulped. "I..." His hands clenched, stopping her speech. She stared into the black depths of his eyes. His face contorted with a deep-felt emotion she couldn't identify.

He lashed out, biting off each word. "What kind of fool would pull a stunt like that? If I ever see you anywhere near that beast again, I'll have him sliced an inch thick and served up for dinner! You got that?" He shook her when she didn't respond at once.

She caught her breath and swallowed. "Yes." His fury drained, Ben looked as pale and shaken as she felt.

Beads of perspiration dotted his brow. He released her, leaving the marks of his fingers branded on her skin and in her memory. He shot a dark look at the two men staring in awe and snapped, "You! And you!"

Eighteen-year-old Cal rocked back on his heels and nearly fell. "Yes, sir." His voice cracked.

"I want that bull on a lead. Anytime you can't handle him, come and get me. Don't let her anywhere near him again." Ben walked off, eating up the ground with a long, furious stride.

Once he was out of sight, Fred Cromie spoke in an awed voice, "Hell's fire! Who in tarnation was that?"

Jessie released a long slow breath. Her heart steadied to a regular beat. Arms crossed against her chest, she rubbed her shoulders. The day was warm. She felt the heat of the sun beating down on her bare head. So why was she shivering?

"That's the new boss." Her eyes remained fixed on the corner of the barn where he'd disappeared.

Fred took off his hat, holding it between two fingers as he scratched his head, and mumbled, "Well, I'll be."

A faint smile touched Jessie's mouth. She angled her hands into the side pockets of her jeans and turned back to the men. "Let's get Homer's stall cleaned out and sweetened up."

Homer snorted.

Jessie decided she would rather tangle with her father's prizewinning Angus bull than Ben any day. Giving orders seemed to come naturally to him; he would be a hard man to cross. As if a finger had trailed down her spine, she recalled the chaotic feel of his hard hands, the turbulent, cold dark fury in his eyes.

And the anguish.

Ben rounded the corner and stopped cold. He leaned against the barn siding, welcoming its ridged hardness against the taut muscles of his back. He closed his eyes. The girl had almost gotten herself killed! And he'd stood there, frozen. Unable to save her, unable to distract the crazed bull. Fear had paralyzed his ability to act. He'd lost his nerve. Damn it! He'd been trained; conditioned to act first and think later. He'd lost it. One second's hesitation could have cost her life. If anything had happened to her...

An ache twisted in his gut. He couldn't bear to have more blood on his hands. A groan rose from the depths of his soul. He rammed his fist into the barn siding.

At lunch, Ben ignored Jessie's concern. When she saw the torn skin on his knuckles, she said softly, "That looks raw."

He buried his hand in his pocket. "It's nothing."

She set a pitcher of iced tea on the red-and-white check- ered tablecloth. "I'll just get some antiseptic, and—"

"I said, it's fine." Ben scraped his chair back and

shoved away from the table. "Excuse me, I have work to do."

Ben didn't want or expect her kindness. A woman's kindness always had strings. That sort of indebtedness was exactly what he'd sworn to avoid. That night, however, he wasn't surprised to find a tube of antiseptic, a box of gauze and a roll of tape on the bathroom counter. With a grim smile, he reached for them.

He cleaned the wound, wincing at the sharp antiseptic sting. Hell! When was her brother due home? Not soon enough to suit him. He wasn't going to stay here long. He knew it, and the sooner the Carlisles realized it, the better he would feel. The old man and the girl were getting to him; they were too needy. He'd learned to avoid emotional traps.

Later, before falling into a restless sleep, he thought the situation over and made up his mind to resign in the morning.

That had been his intention.

But Jessie came downstairs in a dress. It was simple, plain cotton, a bluish-greenish shade. Turquoise. While not overly flattering, it revealed what thick layers of sweatshirts and jeans had hidden. She had a waist and breasts. And she had legs—long, silky legs and delicate ankles.

Ben swallowed hard.

She hesitated on the third step. Her feet looked impossibly dainty in low white heels. Ben's gaze swept up again. Her hair was paler than he'd realized—silky, straight, and falling free around her shoulders. Her eyes were soft, rainwater gray. She looked young and fresh and totally unaware of her appeal to a hungry man. His mouth tightened. He watched her face close at his hard expression. "Going somewhere?"

"To church." She slipped around him. "It's Sunday."

Sunday. He'd forgotten there were still people who went to church on Sunday. When had his days started to flow together meaninglessly? And why did it matter now?

Ira called from the depths of the house, "Jess, come on. We'll be late." Without a backward glance, she walked away.

Ben gritted his teeth. When they got back, he would resign—immediately after lunch. But they got back late, and lunch was rushed. There were still chores to do, Sunday or not.

Later in the afternoon, she made cookies. Chocolate-chip cookies. When he walked into the house, the seductive aroma hit him like a brick wall. And he knew she was going to drive him crazy.

It took Ben ten days to realize there was no television in the house. Each evening after dinner, Ira invited him to play cribbage, at which the old man cheated. Tonight, it was Ben's move. He studied the small, strategically placed pegs on the board and wondered how he was going to get himself out of this fix.

In the background, music filled the growing silence. Proud of his Scots-Welsh ancestry, Ira favored Scottish bands—bagpipes and all. The music reminded Ben of ancient Celtic warriors—swirling, sighing, squeezing sounds of war that stirred the blood. Sounds that celebrated war and mourned the losses. Though hopelessly archaic and primitive, they struck too close to everything Ben had tried to forget.

"Your move," Ira grunted.

Ben's mouth tightened. "Right." It was his move, and he was sitting tight, seduced by a crafty, sly, cheating old man and a guileless young woman who knew how to cook.

The following day, Jessie attacked his laundry.

Ben had left a pile of dirty shirts and jeans on the bathroom floor with the intention of doing it himself. When he returned midmorning and found it missing, he went looking for Jessie. He found her in the laundry room, turning his pockets inside out before adding his jeans to the wash.

"Where do you think you're going?" he demanded, as if he couldn't see with his own eyes. Before he could object more strenuously, she added a second pair of jeans to the wash. After spinning the dial to Start, she turned to him with an irritated frown. Behind her, the washer hummed and spun into action.

She reached for his shirt. "You've got a button missing."

"I don't need a maid," he snapped as he took the shirt from her. He certainly didn't need her.

Jessie got the message. She stared at him in disbelief. Of all the stubborn, pigheaded, headstrong, obstinate men she'd known. Men! She lost her temper. "Do you intend to wear these filthy things again? Air them on the line, then recycle?"

Ben's face turned red. "I planned on locating the nearest Laundromat."

Tight-lipped, she yanked the washer open and delved into it. "Fine!" Her voice rose with pent-up anger. "You want your laundry, here it is." Let him discover there wasn't a Laundromat within a hundred miles! He could eat dirt for all she cared. She hoped he choked on it! She tossed his jeans at him.

Stunned, Ben caught an armful of wet denims. Gray, nonphosphorous suds ran down his front and puddled on the dull tiled floor. Dripping and furious, he opened his mouth, but all he caught was a flash of blue. And Jess was gone. As the moisture seeped into his clothes, a series of doors slammed somewhere in the house. Fred had arrived at the tail end of the argument.

Now he grinned, clearly enjoying Ben's predicament. Fred shook his head at the two of them. "Damn fools."

Ben lifted the soggy mess away from his chest. "Stay out of this." What was he supposed to do now?

"Seems to me an extra pair of jeans in the wash don't add up to all this fuss. Now you got Jessie all riled up. She just likes to help out when she sees a need."

That was what Ben wanted to avoid—needing Jessie.

Avoiding Fred's censuring gaze, Ben quit the room. His boots squelched as he climbed the stairs. Muttering a string of mild curses, he dumped the jeans in the upstairs bathtub before going to his room to change. Finding a dry, clean, respectable pair of jeans took some effort. Finally he dragged an old pair from the bottom of his backpack. He pulled them on, cursing fluently when he had to draw in breath to snap the waist shut. Now he was gaining weight! She was going to be his ruin.

For the rest of the day, Jessie avoided Ben. After dinner, she made an attempt to work off her anger. With the danger of frost gone by, she got a start on her vegetable garden.

Tilling the patch of ground as if her life depended on it, she was determined to finish by nightfall. It was hard work. With a clang, she struck a stone and dug it out, placing it with the growing pile destined to add another layer to the miles of stone fences marking the property. Each spring, after the heavy rains, stones worked their way to the surface—as much a part of spring as the greenery and wildflowers. Stones and flowers. Her father used to say they grew stones in New England instead of crops. That was before he lost his sense of humor.

Jessie sighed.

Certainly her sense of humor could use a lift. Why had she let Ben get beneath her defenses? Why did she find him so aggravating? He was like a stone—hard and impenetrable.

At length she hit a smooth patch of ground, where gradually the rhythm of her movements soothed her and she slowed. The sun dropped in the sky. A flock of long-necked geese flew overhead, gliding smoothly from cloud to cloud. Jessie stopped to rest. Leaning her chin on the long smooth wooden handle, she stared up at the sky.

Another sound broke the silence—a metal hoe striking hard earth with a crunch. Jessie looked down the row, her eyes widening at the sight of Ben working the opposite end. As if aware of her curious stare, he raised his head and stared back.

The tension drained from her shoulders. She didn't say a word; neither did he. Hiding a small smile, she bent to her work, her back to Ben.

The next morning, his laundry was piled atop the washer. With a small laugh, she added it to the wash.

Once it was under way, Jessie enjoyed spring planting. The farm took on a cultivated look—brown earth carved into long, even rows that stretched out to the sun. The prolonged dry spell ended. For three days straight, rain lashed the newly plowed fields without mercy, without any sign of letting up.

Ira stared out the window. "Looks like a lake out there."

Jessie couldn't hide her own concern. "The pond's close to overflowing." Each spring, a rambling offspring of the pond, a swift-flowing, rock-strewn stream, widened and threatened to flood. "Ben's keeping a close eye on it."

Ben came to collect his rain gear. "Call Cal and Fred. We need to sandbag the stream."

Jessie made the calls, threw some food together, and grabbed a waterproof poncho. "Wait for me." She was in time to hitch a ride in the truck. Fred was already seated in the pickup; he squeezed over to make room. Firmly ensconced in the driver's seat, Ben glared at her. Naturally, she thought. Where else would a man of action be?

"Where do you think you're going?" he demanded.

Fred made himself small. Cal vaulted into the truck bed behind them. With a small start, Jessie realized they'd grown accustomed to Ben's military tone of voice.

Ignoring his irritation, she lifted her chin. "I'm coming. You're going to need all the hands you can get." For once, Ben couldn't argue with her logic. The pickup rumbled off down the road. Visibly disgruntled, Ben hit every pothole. Jessie shot him a provoked look when they arrived downstream where a family of beavers had dammed the natural flow of water.

Ben glowered back, unsure why the mere sight of her in her bright yellow rain slicker irritated the hell out of him. "Let's get to work," he ordered, deliberately turning his back on that one ray of light.

As the dismal day progressed, the bright yellow slicker shone like a beacon. Jessie. She was small, lithe, graceful. And she worked as hard as the men, he noticed. He couldn't keep his eyes from straying to her time and time again. She pitched in to help, laughing at Fred's corny jokes, responding to Cal's teasing with a grimace and a roll of her eyes. Her voice was light and mixed with the wind, the gurgle of the stream and the patter of the rain. In her natural element, Jessie became part of it.

The other men accepted her presence with ease—somehow, Ben couldn't. Instead, he kept the wide stream between them.

Raised in upscale Southern military-school tradition, Ben had been conditioned to think of women as fragile flowers to be pampered, protected and spoiled. An indestructible belle, his mother had found the perfect niche when his father retired from the military and was assigned to a small obscure country whose name Ben couldn't even pronounce. There, she played the role of ambassador's wife to the hilt. Oh, he knew women weren't soft. He'd met women—career officers who competed for rank, not to mention available women who hung around military bases all over the world. He'd learned about those, as well. He'd never been able to take what they offered. Now there was Jessie. And in Maine, where women stood shoulder to shoulder with a man, she was as fragile as a flower, strong as a weed. He wasn't sure what to think about Jessie.

They stopped for lunch. The food hamper was on Ben's side of the stream. He watched as Jessie gingerly crossed a fallen log spanning the water. When she reached the grassy shore, she looked up as he offered her a hand. Her foot slipped.

Ben grabbed her and grunted as she fell hard against his chest. "Are you all right?"

"I'm fine." Her hands held him off. Her eyes widened, staring into his unsmiling face.

For the life of him he couldn't summon a smile. A drop of rain trickled down her face. Exertion had made her cheeks pink—or was that her reaction to him? Did she feel some of the things he felt? That faint but insistent stir of curiosity, desire? No. She was too young. Too innocent.

She blinked when he carefully set her aside.

"You're doing a good job," he muttered, his voice deliberately curt. "Keep it up."

She took a deep breath. "Yes, sir!"

"Don't be cute." He hid a smile, amazed she'd gotten up the nerve to get fresh with him. To avoid further temptation, he sat on a rock under an overhanging pine tree and ate his lunch.

Jessie found a distant rock.

In the afternoon, they continued to shore up the banks. Finally, when the stream ran straight and free, they piled into the pickup and headed for home. Jessie yawned and fell asleep before the first mile was up. When she slumped toward Ben, he felt her warmth seep into his bones. Her head came to rest on his shoulder, her small breast pressed into his side. His body hardened. He couldn't remember when he'd last held a woman.

His mouth grew grim as he acknowledged the fact that this stubborn, boyish, half-baked female could wring an unwelcome response out of him, despite his iron control. What control?

Fred looked across and gave him a knowing glance.

Ben clenched his hands on the steering wheel and stared straight ahead. When they arrived at the house, Fred chuckled and deserted him to his fate. Jessie. Ben took a deep breath. Her nearness generated more than heat. He groaned when she snuggled closer.

Looking at her sleeping face, he took in long silky lashes against petal-soft skin. Her complexion was rosy, healthy, unblemished. Her hair looked soft. He smoothed a strand from her cheek. At his touch, she stirred.

Slowly she opened her eyes, then blinked. She looked adorable, her eyes dusky gray with sweet confusion. As if drawn by an invisible thread, her gaze drifted to his mouth. Ben fought the urge to drag her against him. The dewy promise of her skin begged for his touch. He cupped her chin and ran his thumb along her jaw. Her lips trembled. He felt her delicate shudder.

The close confines of the truck grew steamy as moisture condensed and fogged the windshield, enclosing them in a private world. His head started to bend—

The dog started to bark. The porch light came on and Ira stepped out. Ben froze. Jessie's eyes clouded as she shrank away from him. She scrambled out of the pickup.

By the time he recovered, Ira was still there, standing in the open doorway, waiting. Ben felt like an adolescent as he filed past the older man.

Ira frowned, his gaze clearly warning Ben away from his daughter. Ben didn't have to be told. Actually, he owed Ira a debt of gratitude for preventing him from making a terrible mistake. What had he been thinking?

The way Jessie affected him, he would never be satisfied with just one kiss. He couldn't understand her irresistible appeal. She wasn't beautiful, sophisticated, witty or exciting. She was just Jessie. Jessie, like a summer sigh born on a spring breeze.

It rained the rest of the week.

Tempers were set at hair trigger, including Ben's. He waited for the rain to end, the sun to shine—something. And while he waited, Cal griped, Fred scowled, Ira bit heads off and Jessie made herself scarce, at least whenever Ben was around.

On Friday, Jessie disappeared after supper, as usual.

Ira retired early, complaining, "My arthritis is acting up. Must be this damp."

Left alone, Ben poured over books on pesticides and assorted plant diseases, attempting to brush up on his knowledge. After a couple of hours, he yawned and slammed the book shut. Enough was enough. He rose and went to the window where he stared out at the dismal night. Rain streamed down the glass. Though physically tired, he knew he wouldn't sleep—not until exhaustion claimed him. At night, Scottish bagpipes merged with bloodcurdling screams in his dreams. Choppers spun, crashing down. A green jungle. He closed his eyes, wiping the vivid memory from his thoughts, knowing it would return the moment he laid his head on a pillow and slept. He'd been running from the memory for two years. When would he forget?

Ben stared into the black depths of night. The house was silent. Jessie had left hours ago on her nightly solitary wandering; it was nearly nine now. Some part of him always registered the time she left, and the time she returned.

Tonight, he hadn't heard her come back. He didn't let himself think of her whereabouts. Perhaps she had a boy-friend, after all. Drew Pierce? He frowned at the thought.

Half an hour later, the back door opened. The dog barked.

Jessie entered the kitchen, her voice soft as she bent over and scratched the dog's ears. "Down, Bandit." Bandit panted in ecstasy, rolled over and made a pathetic display for her affection. She fussed over him for another moment or two.

Ben saw her stiffen when she became aware of his presence at the far end of the room. He leaned into the door-frame. "You're late," he said, immediately wishing he could bite back the words. He sounded like her father. And why not? She could use some looking after. It was obvious Ira had abdicated the position.

"Am I?" She shrugged off his concern. "I dropped in on Fred and his wife. Have you met Hazel?"

He felt ridiculous for overreacting. Her explanation was so simple. "I didn't know Fred had a wife."

She draped her raincoat over a chair. "Well, he does." The cuffed legs of her jeans were dark and wet.

"What's she like?" Ben felt an urge to prolong the con-versation. Jessie intrigued him—her long silences, her se-crets. There was no denying she got under his skin.

"She's just like Fred."

Ben winced—a female Fred. "How do you mean?"

"She's got this instinct about people." Jessie smiled ruefully. "At least, she seems to know what I'm going to do before I do. She's bossy and gossipy and kind and caring."

"That sounds like Fred."

Glancing down, she picked up his book. She read the title and lifted a delicate eyebrow. "Potatoes?"

He half smiled. "I never guessed it was such a delicate plant. If the grubs and beetles don't get it…"

"The ring rot will," she said with a soft laugh.

His smile filled out. He met her eyes briefly.

She glanced away. "Is that how you learned about farming? From books?"

"Partly," he admitted. At his abbreviated answer, the hint of disappointment in her eyes made him add, "When I was a kid, I spent summers on my grandparents' farm in Virginia."

"I see." She didn't push for more. Taking two steps toward the stairs, she said, "Well, good night."

"Ben." His voice stopped her. She glanced back at his harsh tone. "My name is Ben." Her eyes widened. "Say it."

She drew in a quick breath. "Ben," she whispered. A quicksilver smile changed her face, edging out the caution and insecurity. The soft glow of her warmth appealed to him more than he cared to admit. "Good night, Ben."

"Good night, Jessie."

Jessie.

Jessie nodded once, her step lightening as she climbed the stairs to her bedroom. Humming, she prepared for bed, unsure why he'd had a change of heart about her—if he had a heart, she thought with a rueful smile. Perhaps they could be friends.

Wrapped in her quilt, she sat in her rocker, pretending to read the mystery she'd started. The book fell to her lap. Lost in her thoughts, Jessie smoothed the palms of her hands over the chair's wooden arms and leaned her head back. The chair had belonged to her great-grandmother, part of a dowry. Jessie smiled— such an old-fashioned term. Her great-grandfather had traveled to Scotland for a bride. Had he loved her? He'd carved the chair by hand for their first child, her father's father. It was all part of the past, real yet mystical.

Once, Jessie had dreamed of being part of a loving family. She'd dreamed of studying land conservation, restoring Stone's End to its former glory, raising a family, rocking her own babies....

She closed her eyes to the empty room. What had happened to all her dreams? Ben, her mind whispered.

When his eyes touched her, he made her aware of things she'd never noticed before—the dark depths of his eyes, the shape of his hands. What would she do if he looked at her and saw a woman, not a girl? Faint hope. Her tension drained, she relaxed. Feeling drowsy, she went to bed. Since those first awkward days following his arrival, she'd lost most of her wariness and distrust. She wasn't sure when she'd started to sleep despite his presence, just that she had.

Downstairs, Ben reached for his book again.

By morning, the rain had stopped.

Ben went out to check if many plants had survived. He walked through field after cultivated field and caught up with Fred in the west end. "What do you think?"

Fred spread his mouth into a wide smile. "I think we got lucky. That's what I think."

Ben looked over an expanse of green plants. "So do I."

"Another day of rain would have done us in."

"It's well irrigated, aerated land." Ben walked between two straight rows that seemed endless.

Fred joined him. "The best. Ira knows his stuff."

"Mmm." Ben agreed with markedly less enthusiasm. He stopped to pull up a weed.

"Thought you were hitting it off with Ira. He trusts

you.'' When Ben shrugged off the comment without making a reply, Fred added, ''He's a hard man. But his heart's in the right place.''

Ben discarded the weed. ''If Ira Carlisle has a soft side, I haven't seen any evidence.''

''Now you're talking about Jessie.''

Ben shrugged. ''Yes, I guess I am.''

''Jessie reminds him of his wife.''

Ben had no intention of listening to gossip, yet he frowned and asked, ''When did his wife die?''

''Avis isn't dead. Least, far as anyone knows. She was a city girl. Young and pretty. Too young. Ira was forty—old enough to know better than to bring a girl like that home. Guess he fell hard.'' Fred shook his head. ''Jealous as all get-out. At first, she put up with his demands. In the end he drove her away. Heard tell there was another man. Anyhow, she just packed her bags and left.''

Ben released a long breath. ''I see.'' He started to walk again, his one desire not to hear any more.

Unfortunately, Fred didn't take the hint. ''Left Ira with two babies, a farm to run, and a pile of debts.'' Tagging along, he continued. ''Made a fool out of Ira, a laughing-stock in front of the whole town, Avis did. When she wanted to come home, he wouldn't let her see the kids. Sad business.''

''That's rough.'' Ben felt a pang of regret for Jessie's lost childhood. No one had tied bows in her hair, read her stories. He couldn't imagine Ira pretending to be the tooth fairy.

''Hazel and I never had kids, so we did what we could. Jared was a crackerjack kid. And Jessie... Well, Jessie was always special.... Kinda quiet, you know, but always thinking and feeling things.'' Fred sighed. ''Ira's crazy about his son. Thought his heart would break when Jared left home. All he's got is Jessie. Damn fool can't see she's just like him. Stone's End is in Jessie's blood. She's no quitter.''

Ben smiled in agreement. "That she isn't."

Fred nodded. "That's a fact."

They trudged back to the main house. Ben stopped abruptly. In the shade of a giant spreading oak, a flashy red sports car stood parked in the drive.

Chapter Four

The pungent odor of tomato plants rose from the garden. From her kneeling position, Jessie looked up at the sound of a masculine voice. "Hi, Jess." Drew Pierce stopped less than a foot away. She shaded her eyes against the sun's glare.

"Are you looking for my father?" she asked.

"I just saw him. He doesn't look too good."

Rising, Jessie brushed the dirt from her knees. "He's got an appointment next week. Dr. Peterson will fix him up."

"Doc isn't a miracle worker," Drew said bluntly. With a suggestive smile, he let his gaze run down her body. "You need a man to run this place. You're working yourself too hard. How about burying the hatchet? What if I invited you out to dinner?" Apparently he expected her to fall all over him with gratitude.

"Thanks, I don't need a free meal that badly."

His laughter sounded genuine. "You always had a sassy mouth. I like that. I could teach it to do something far more satisfying." Catching her off guard with his humor, he reached for her. His hands spanned her waist. "Maybe you need a sample."

"Don't!" Jessie turned her face when his mouth descended.

"Come on, sweetheart, don't be a prude. Give a little."

"Let me go." Aiming a kick at his ankle, she lost her footing and found herself squarely in his arms. Drew chuckled at her sputtered protest.

To her relief, she heard Ben's drawled, "Is there a problem here?" Drew released his grip.

Freed, Jessie took an involuntary step toward Ben, then stopped. Hands in his pockets, he appeared casual, yet she sensed an alertness ready to spring at the first sign of trouble.

His gaze held a weary cynicism. "Introduce us."

Her chin lifted at his frozen tone. His reluctance to interfere was evident. While Drew was all male ego, Ben's mature control and steely level gaze made more impact.

Her tone clipped, she said, "Ben's managing the farm."

Drew glanced from Ben to her. "That means you have to report to him personally, Jess?"

"Jessie's her own boss," Ben said to her surprise. "But anything concerning the farm, you can deal with me."

"Sure," Drew agreed, his smile set in his handsome face. "I guess I'll be going. I'll be seeing you, Jess." And with that he strolled back to his fancy car.

Slowly, almost reluctantly, Ben asked, "Are you all right?"

"Nothing happened."

He looked relieved. "In that case, I'll see you later."

Jessie watched him go. How easy it was for him to walk away. She stared down at the ground at the hills of crushed, broken plants. Drew had carelessly destroyed them.

That evening, she served coffee and apple crisp for dessert. Ben had seconds. Obviously, Drew hadn't put him off his food, she thought with a spurt of resentment.

Her father fixed her with a glance. "Drew came by today. Did you agree to go out with him? He's a good man, Jess. You could do a lot worse than hooking up with him."

"Hook up with Drew?" she returned in disbelief.

"What's wrong with him?"

"Everything!" Her voice shook. Drew was the second son, the black sheep of the Pierce family. He'd earned his womanizing reputation. At twenty, he'd gotten a girl pregnant, then refused to marry her. His father had paid to avoid a scandal.

Aware of Ben's appraisal, she felt her face burn with humiliation. She didn't care what Ben thought. Yes, she did. Perhaps he found the situation distasteful. She could feel him putting mental distance between them, rearranging the encounter in the garden to suit himself. Outwardly, it must have looked as if she'd encouraged Drew.

"Think, girl," her father argued. "You won't get a second chance if you pass up his offer."

An offer. A deal. This wasn't about her, Jessie realized. "Well, I did refuse, so that's that." She forced herself to walk, not run, from the room.

Ben found himself alone with a disgruntled Ira.

"Girl doesn't know what's good for her," Ira complained. "The Pierce operation is first-rate. What more does she want?"

Ben raised a cynical eyebrow. "How about love?"

Ira's snort refuted that remark.

Ben shifted restlessly. He was the outsider here and destined to remain that way.

Apparently tired of the discussion, Ira drew Ben into

their nightly game of cribbage. Ben lost the first and second games. After a third win, Ira complained, "You're making this too easy. Get your mind on the game, boy."

Ben grasped the excuse for a break. "How about coffee?"

He left Ira sputtering and found Jessie in the kitchen washing dishes. At her age, she should be spreading her wings, enjoying her youth before it declined. He cleared his throat.

"I was going to make coffee. Would you care for some?"

She ignored him.

"Jessie, your father means well," he said awkwardly. "He just wants the best for you." As far as reassurance went, the words sounded empty even to him.

Nothing.

All right, so she was annoyed with her father, probably with good reason, but she needn't take her hostility out on him.

"Look," he snapped, reaching for her shoulder and spinning her around with a firm grasp. Somehow, his hand got tangled up in her hair. Jessie blinked at him in obvious shocked reaction to his touch. At the same moment he noticed a wire wrapped around his thumb—a thin black wire connected to headphones and a portable radio. As the earpiece pulled away from her head, he could hear the staccato speech of a baseball announcer. She was listening to a baseball game! Well, it certainly beat bagpipes and highland flings, Ben thought, relaxing his grip.

He found the entire situation highly amusing. Was that how she retained her sanity and escaped her father's interference—along with his earsplitting bagpipes? She simply tuned them out. His mouth relaxed into a smile. Her hair felt like silk.

"Who's winning?" Ben asked.

"The Red Sox, four to one."

Standing this close, he felt the whisper of her voice, a breath against his lips. With the start of warm weather, she'd gotten some sun. Her winter pallor had faded; a healthy rose color kissed her cheeks. Her eyes looked larger, deeper.

"Are you a baseball fan?" he murmured.

"Jared taught me when we were kids."

He could imagine Jessie as a child—a sturdy little girl, a tomboy tagging after Jared, chasing balls, climbing trees. Somehow, his fingers had gotten tangled in her hair again. "I came in to make more coffee." His voice dropped to a husky tone.

"Did you want something to go with that?"

At the provocation, his gaze dropped to her mouth—those pale pink lips. Were they innocent? At the moment, he would give an arm and a leg to know. Living this close to Jessie was either heaven or hell; he hadn't decided which. At the oddest times, he thought about her. Now, he watched her awareness grow as her eyes darkened with some hidden emotion. He dropped his hand to her shoulder and felt her tremble. The cloth of her denim shirt was thin cotton, softened by countless washings, the color faded to match the incredible ash gray of her eyes.

"There's more apple crisp," she offered.

"No, thanks." His mouth twitched at her attempt to distract him. He'd met plenty of women who gave themselves for kicks or money, never for love. He'd never been able to take them, never been able to see past the hard emptiness in their eyes. When he looked at Jessie, he saw only his reflection. He filled her eyes...and knew he wanted more. Aware of their closeness, the silk of her hair, the scent of lemon soap, the tightening of his body in direct response, Ben released her.

Coming to his senses, he turned toward the stove.

"Don't go to any trouble. Just coffee will do." He reached for the pot. Only hours earlier, he'd caught her in the arms of another man.

He swore as he burned his hand on the pot.

A few days later, Jessie backed the truck out of the driveway. When Ben hailed her to stop, she rolled down the window. "Did you want something?"

"If you're going into town, can you give me a lift?"

She stumbled over some sort of response.

Ben climbed into the passenger side. He eased his long legs into the confined space. "Thanks, I appreciate it."

She was equally courteous. He was always scrupulously polite, but distant. Perhaps he was just a naturally cold man; a man like her father, she thought. To fill the awkward silence, she tuned in to a soft-country rock station on the radio. After a bit of static, Willie Nelson's crusty, lived-in voice sang about a man never being there for a woman. Jessie smiled ruefully at the timely reminder. Brushing a stray hair from her brow, she released a long breath and fixed her eyes on the road.

In direct contrast to her mood, the sun sparkled, dappling the winding tree-lined country lane. Sunbeams danced in and out of the thick shade.

"I've been meaning to ask..." His Southern drawl washed over her, making her aware of an inner heat that had nothing to do with the weather. He'd rolled up his shirtsleeves to reveal deeply tanned arms, lightly sprinkled with wiry black hairs. His hands were strong, lean, controlled—like him.

He was waiting for her attention. "About what?" she asked.

"About hiring extra help for the season," he continued. She wondered if he ever lost that formidable control.

"My father's probably made the usual arrangements. The migrant farmworkers work under contract for the Pierces."

"I see." Ben frowned, as if he had some doubts about the usual arrangements. More than likely, he would rather be giving orders than taking them from her father.

Impatient with her preoccupation with Ben, she found a convenient parking spot on Main Street. Before she could make a move, he came around and opened her door. Unaccustomed to the attention, she was surprised by his small act of consideration. He offered her a hand as she climbed down from the truck. Though fleeting, his touch was sure and firm, yet gentle. It hardly registered before his hand dropped. The memory remained.

A chance breeze cooled her hot face. He made her feel so silly, gauche…and young. Her great-grandmother would have said she was sickening. "Shall we meet back here?" she asked, aware of the need to escape him. "My errands will take about an hour."

"Suits me." He glanced up and down the short blacktop thoroughfare that made up downtown Henderson. "Where can I buy some jeans? I seem to be outgrowing mine."

His wry comment drew her gaze to the snug fit of his jeans. They looked just fine to her. Soft and faded with wear, they clung to his long, lean muscled legs and taut hips. She flushed when her gaze hastily swept up to encounter his.

His smile formed faint lines of humor in the tanned weathered skin around his eyes—faint because he rarely smiled. "Too many cookies, I guess."

"I could stop baking them."

"You needn't on my account," he said dryly.

Chuckling, she pointed to the sign. "It isn't fancy, but you'll find almost anything you need in The Trading Post."

His gaze took in the sight of six-foot-wide moose antlers

hanging over the door. "That's mighty impressive." He stepped back for a clearer look. "I've been hoping to spot a live one."

Jessie laughed. "Typical tourist." On that note, she left him to find his way inside the store. She found her smile lingering and felt foolish when someone threw her a curious look.

Sobering at the thought of being caught mooning over some man who generally treated her like one of the boys, she hastily selected three dozen healthy tomato plants to replace the ones Drew had destroyed. Her errand accomplished, she went back to find Ben at the front of the store.

She found him at the checkout counter, apparently waiting for change. Leaning casually against the counter, he watched her approach, his gaze narrowing. His eyes never wavered, making her aware of the unconscious sway of her hips, the inner rush of pleasure at his masculine appraisal.

"Have I kept you waiting?" he asked.

"Not at all." Jessie hoped she didn't sound as rattled as she felt. The place was crowded. Heads were turning.

Ben was aware of the wagging tongues.

Apparently, his appearance with Jessie in tow had set off the gossip. After completing his transaction, Ben took a firm hold of Jessie's elbow and steered her past several customers. When she stepped aside to allow someone to pass in the narrow aisle, she brushed against him. He felt her resistance to his touch. And her softness. Cursing himself, he let his hand fall. Hands-off was the best policy where she was concerned.

Outside, he stopped at a soft-drink machine. "How about a soda?" He flipped the tab and handed her one.

"Thanks." She hopped up on the truck's tailgate and sat. She looked like a mischievous little girl.

Smiling slightly, Ben helped himself to a soda. "Folks

aren't too friendly around here, are they?'' He glanced down the empty street. Henderson was a narrow, tree-lined strip of white-painted, tin-roofed buildings bordering a highway. He wondered where it went. Probably to another town exactly like this one.

"You're an outsider." The sun struck her face.

"Is that what you think I am?"

Her silky eyelashes fell. "I don't really know you, do I?"

"Does a man have to be born here to be accepted?"

"Not really." Her mouth tilted in a rueful smile. "But it helps if his great-grandfather was."

Shaking his head, Ben finished his drink, then loaded the tomato plants into the truck bed. He caught her wistful glance at a packaged rosebush, an exotic hybrid white tea rose edged in pink, and added it to the order. He insisted on paying for it.

Jessie hopped down. "Roses never survive the winter here."

Ben closed the tailgate with a firm thrust. "Then you can enjoy them for a season."

While Jessie stood there, slowly digesting that, wondering how to thank him, a truck camper—a dusty, tired-looking vehicle with Texas license plates—pulled to a stop. The driver got out.

"Good day." He looked middle-aged, dark-haired, dusky-skinned. "My name is Ramon Morales." He spoke in precise English with a touch of an accent. "This is my wife, Rita." The woman nodded shyly from inside the truck.

Jessie smiled. "Hello."

"This is my daughter, Serena," Ramon added with fatherly pride. The teenage girl was lovely. "And my son, Miguel." They were obviously one of the many migrant farmworker families who followed the harvests and came to Maine each summer.

Before anyone could stop him, the toddler tumbled out of the truck and ran off. "Miguel!" his mother called out.

Ben caught the squirming bundle in his arms. Miguel's little feet were still pumping. Ben grinned. "Hey, slow down."

Miguel stopped abruptly, his small plump hand touching the scar on Ben's face. "Does that hurt, mister?"

"Not anymore."

"I got one, too." The boy located a tiny white scar on his knee. "My mama kissed it better. Did yours?"

"I'm afraid not."

Bemused, Jessie wondered, had anyone comforted Ben? Her heart twisted at the reminder of the awful wounds in his side. Had anyone helped him recover from his injuries?

The boy's mother thanked Ben. Jessie noted his gentleness. Why did he hide behind a gruff exterior? To keep people away?

To keep *her* away?

"We are looking for the Pierce campground," Ramon said.

The Pierces operated the only camp for miles. Jessie explained, "It's another six miles up the road."

A moment later, as she watched the truck drive away in a cloud of dust, she felt a spurt of compassion. In her experience, a hard-luck story often accompanied the typical transient farm family. What about Ben? Like the migrant seasonal help, did Ben lead a nomadic existence? Did he choose it, or had it chosen him? Did he have a family? A wife? Children? It struck her that she knew very little about Ben Harding. Except that he was running from something.

When they got home, Jessie checked the mailbox. There were letters, bills, nothing from her brother. How long had it been since she'd heard from Jared—a month, two months?

What was going on with him?

Ben unloaded the tomato plants. Without warning, he put out a protective hand. "Don't move, he might be dangerous."

"Who?" She caught a movement in the shrubs. A young male moose ambled over. He was grayish brown, tall and gangly with humped shoulders. His wide set of antlers were still in velvet.

"I said, don't move." Ben dragged her back against him when she stepped forward. "Damn it, Jessie! Can't you just obey?"

She resisted the sensuous pleasure of being pressed against him. "I don't have to take orders."

"If you'd just listen." His hand pressed more urgently against her waist; his thumb grazed the soft underside of her breast, the most intimate invasion in her limited experience.

At her sharp inhalation her breast lifted, then gently came to rest against his hand. She felt him freeze. Then he moved—hastily, awkwardly, totally unlike himself. Ben shifted his hand lower to her waist, but somehow that only made the situation more intimate, her awareness more keen-edged. The bottom dropped out of her stomach. Aware of every living cell in her body, she supposed she should explain—about the moose—but she couldn't find the words to tell him it was safe, because suddenly she didn't feel safe at all. "Ben, it's only a moose," she managed.

"You can't predict what a young male animal in the wild will do." Rasped against her ear, the words set a gentle flame coursing through her. "He could lose control."

Were they discussing the same male animal?

"What are we going to do?" Jessie shifted uneasily.

Ben groaned. "Wait until he goes away." His voice sounded oddly constricted. Her move had been innocent; his physical response wasn't. She stiffened, then tried to wriggle away. He muttered something she didn't quite catch. Her face turned red when he finally snapped, "Will you stand still?"

At that point, she welcomed any interruption, even Fred, who had stopped to admire the tomato plants. "Well, now, I see you've been to town. These are mighty fine tomatoes."

Ben unleashed a volley of curses. Fred looked frankly shocked—then he started to laugh. Jessie sputtered. Ben glared at them. "What's wrong with all of you? Can't you see that moose? He might charge any minute."

Fred cackled. "That'll be the day!"

"Ben, it's only Beauregard," Jessie said. The stump-tailed moose just stared back with dark, long-lashed morose eyes that never seemed to blink. "He arrives about this time every year. He's a nuisance, but he's a family pet."

Fred slapped his knee in glee. "Jessie's right. Dumb moose comes a-courting one of the cows."

The joke was on Ben. Feeling guilty for leading him on, Jessie waited to see how he would take it.

A slow smile crept over his mouth. "Well, now, you don't say," he drawled, imitating Fred's Down-Easter accent.

"Gentle as a babe," Fred assured him with a chuckle.

Beauregard didn't move an ear. His upper lip hung three to four inches over his chin. The animal began to nibble some leaves from a shrub. Jessie walked around the moose and rubbed its nose.

"That has to be the ugliest animal in creation," Ben murmured with a wry shake of his head. When she agreed, his smile grew with a gleam of appreciation, perhaps even admiration.

Jessie dropped her hand, aware of undercurrents. No one had ever looked at her that way.

"You should smile more often," Ben said, then took a deep breath, as if he'd said too much.

Jessie felt a small pain in the region of her heart. Just a small one...

That evening, Ben watched Jessie carry the new tomato plants into the garden. Instead of helping, he headed for the barn, determined to keep his distance. Otherwise he might be tempted to test the limits of his willpower. Looking distinctly out of sorts, Homer wheezed a greeting and cast him a jaundiced eye. For once, Ben could sympathize with the penned-up animal.

Ben felt trapped. Jessie was growing more appealing by the day. After years of ignoring women, why did he have to develop a soft spot for this one? If he was going to get out of Stone's End with his heart and hide intact, he couldn't get involved.

Later, no amount of self-lecturing could ease his conscience when he viewed the results of her hard work. Her garden was planted in even rows, freshly tilled, not a weed in sight. He suspected he would never be able to eat a tomato without thinking of Jessie.

The following day, Ben planted her rosebush just outside the kitchen window where she could enjoy it.

Feeling like a condemned man waiting for parole, he marked off the middle of June on the calendar and asked Ira, "When did you say Jared was coming home?"

Ira looked away. "I didn't say."

Where was Jared? Whenever the topic of her brother came up, Jessie was just as closemouthed as Ira.

A few days ago, Ben had gotten some idea of her devotion to her conspicuously absent brother when he found her changing the spark plugs on the old truck. "That should give it some life," he'd teased her. "Who taught you to work on cars?"

"Jared." She wiped a greasy black streak on her cheek.

"I suppose he knows everything about cars."

She'd smiled at his wry observation. "And tractors."

"Of course."

The answer had amused Ben. He wanted to trace the mark on her cheek with his thumb, turn her mouth up for his kiss, make her forget all about cars, and motors, and her brother.

Jared.

The thought of Jessie's brother stopped Ben from reaching for her. Was there a mystery surrounding Jared? According to the terms of employment, Ben would be free at the end of summer; fall at the latest. He had to be free.

Chapter Five

In the morning, Ben pulled on a clean shirt. Rolling his sleeve to the elbow, he noticed the button had been replaced. A tear had been mended. The stitches were neat, almost invisible, but he knew they were there. He closed his eyes in pain. Jessie.

Not giving himself time to think, he went to find her in the milk barn. "I don't recall asking you to mend my shirt."

Fred was with her—cleaning out stalls.

Pitchfork in hand, she wrapped her slim fingers around the wooden handle and propped her chin against it. "Well, it needed mending, and I was doing some mending, so..."

At her innocent response, he released a furious breath. "I don't need your mending!" Mending, meddling, making him want things he knew he couldn't have.

"Then I'll stop," she said reasonably.

Ben didn't want her being reasonable. "Oh, no, you

don't." He reached into his hip pocket for his wallet. "If you're going to mend my clothes, I insist on paying you a fair price."

"Fair!" She tossed the pitchfork aside, barely missing his boot by a scant inch. "How about a dollar a shirt? Two dollars a meal?" She advanced on him and stood toe to toe. "Is that the going rate? Oh, and about those second helpings." She tilted her head. "What would be fair?"

Fred burst out laughing. "She's got you there."

Ignoring the urge to close the remaining space and kiss her outraged pride away, Ben frowned. "Tell her to cooperate."

The older man folded his arms. "I love a good clean fight."

Jessie continued. "If I put a price tag on the laundry, before long you won't be able to afford to live here."

Before long she would own him, body and soul!

Shocked out of his anger, Ben left before he got himself further entangled. How had he gotten himself into such a mess? He had to resurrect a barricade, put some distance between them. His mouth set, he left two dollars on the kitchen table.

As luck would have it, he was on hand later when she found it. Apparently determined to match his stubborn display, ounce for contrary ounce, she fetched an empty mason jar and set it on the sideboard. She dropped the money into it. Ben knew he should have been satisfied, yet somehow he wasn't.

The jar stood between them, like a glass wall. Thick, impenetrable as steel. Each time she looked at it, Jessie felt a dull nagging ache in the region of her heart. She could see Ben, hear him. But she couldn't break the barrier he'd erected; she couldn't touch his lonely soul. She stared at the jar and felt the urge to cry. It stood there—a harsh reminder and a bitter affront to her pride.

* * *

Over the next few weeks, she watched the jar fill with crisp dollar bills. One day, there was a five. With a tight smile, she wondered what she'd done to deserve it.

Ben didn't come home that evening. Jessie drew her own conclusions. He never missed a meal. This was his way of shutting her out. She was still angry with him, and he with her, apparently. But now the anger had acquired a sting. He didn't call; he simply didn't turn up. A loner, Ben clearly had no intention of answering to anyone, least of all her.

The weather was warm, almost sultry for June. At loose ends, she left her father napping in his recliner and strolled to the pond. Years ago, she'd discovered a secret cove. The forest grew around it, thick and wild with underbrush. Tall cathedral pines sealed it from prying eyes. A fallen log formed a natural bridge across the narrow gap of water.

Balancing, Jessie crossed the small inlet. Fed by a clear, cold mountain stream, sheltered by a virgin forest, the land gently curved around to form a freshwater cove. A soft breeze feathered the tall pines. With the stillness, her tension drained. Not a ripple stirred. Free from daily restrictions, she shed her inhibitions, stripped off her shorts and cotton shirt and waded into the water. The water cooled her bare skin.

She caught her reflection and felt something stir within. A yearning that was new. She wished she were more voluptuous. Would Ben think she was womanly if he saw her naked? Feeling hot and shocked and agitated, she dived into the depths. The cool water slid over her and she wondered what it would feel like to have a man's hands slide over her. The mere thought of Ben's touch aroused her. Would he be disappointed in her slight breasts and boyish figure? She recalled how he sometimes looked at her, and she felt a slow curl of sensuality deep within.

She swam until she was exhausted, until her emotions were spent. If anything, the recent episode over money had proved that Ben felt none of the things she felt. Why had she thought he might care? He wanted to pay her! Feeling older if not wiser, she waded out, got dressed and started the walk home. As night fell, the trees held shadows, and the road home stretched before her, long and empty.

Ben returned to a darkened house. His evening in town hadn't provided any notable distraction. Ira had turned in; there was no sign of Jessie. Heat lightning flashed in the distance. Feeling restless, Ben made a pot of coffee. While it brewed, he paced. Then he started to worry.

With a storm on the horizon, what if Jessie was out there somewhere—hurt, trapped? There were wild animals. His concern drove him upstairs to her room. Ben entered without knocking.

The sight of blue walls with ruffled sheer white curtains at the windows stopped him cold. On a bedside table, fresh wildflowers sat arranged in a milk-glass bowl. A well-thumbed paperback novel lay open, facedown, beside it. A thin white cotton nightie sprigged with delicate blue flowers drew his attention to the foot of the brass double bed. With an effort, he tore his eyes away from the lace-trimmed bodice.

Nevertheless, a seductive image of Jessie wearing it remained indelibly engraved in his head. The sticky heat of the day lingered in the light breeze coming through the open window. The room was Jessie. Where was she? Common sense told him she wasn't his responsibility. She knew how to take care of herself. She didn't need him. Ben left her room untouched.

Another half hour and two cups of coffee didn't help. She was innocent, untouched, out of bounds. He'd sworn to leave her that way. With a crash, he set his mug down.

He ran a furious, frustrated hand through his hair. Who was he kidding? He was worried about her. He cared! Hell! He went out and fired up his motorcycle.

Under a thin sickle of moon, the bike's single beam pierced the darkness. A couple of miles down the road, Ben saw her coming out of the woods. She swung from the footpath onto the narrow strip of road. Caught in his headlight, she walked toward him with that lithe, lyrical grace that marked all her movements.

He shifted the motorcycle into low gear and let it roll towards her. "Isn't it late to be out alone?"

"It was so hot. I went for a swim."

"A swim?" His gaze swept over her, not missing a thing.

Her legs were long, bare in cutoff denim shorts. She lifted her hand and ran her fingers through her damp hair. Her breasts lifted and fell with the movement. "The water was cool—I couldn't resist."

Did she have any idea what she was doing to him? Had it ever occurred to her that she might tempt a man? Her cotton T-shirt clung to damp breasts. Seeing no evidence of a swimsuit, he knew she'd been skinny-dipping. Inwardly, Ben groaned as his imagination filled in the rest. Naked, her body would be sleek—long legs, trim hips, narrow waist and small, high breasts, nipples that puckered when exposed to the cold water. Despite the temptation, Ben knew he could never take her innocence and walk away a free man.

Nevertheless, his relief in finding her safe broke down barriers. "I was worried," he confessed.

"You were?" A soft, incredulous look grew on her face.

Ben laughed. "Don't look so shocked."

"I'm not." Her low laughter spoiled her quick denial.

"Anyway, you shouldn't be out after dark." He stretched out a hand. "I'll give you a ride home."

Jessie held back. "It's perfectly safe out here."

He wouldn't accept that. "Climb on. It's late."

Jessie stared at him, while her heart dipped in her chest. All the emotions she'd felt at the pond came flooding back. Her nipples felt tight, her body felt fluid with the tug of desire. Deeply aware that she couldn't bear casual contact with this man, she held back. Could she trust Ben not to hurt her? What did she really know of him? He was a stranger, a drifter—a hard, embittered man who carried scars on his soul like some men carried college credentials.

At that moment, Ben looked like a black knight on a monster machine. A faint odor of oil and metal, mixed with pine trees and damp foliage, penetrated her senses. The bike downshifted to a mechanical purr that started a humming inside her. The night vibrated with supercharge. He waited for her to choose.

Jessie knew his patience wouldn't last forever. Feeling gauche and immature, she reached out and gingerly placed one hand at his waist as she swung a leg over the back of the bike. As if they were performing some natural dance, her legs aligned with his and her arms circled his waist. Her body strained with the effort not to melt against him. The bike took off. She clung tightly, her breasts crushed against him as the force of the takeoff threw him back. Could he feel her heart pounding? She hoped not. He would probably laugh if he knew how she reacted to him—like a pathetic, love-starved adolescent. Struggling to regain some space between them, she pressed back but couldn't find an inch as the road rose before them. The wind rushed at her. Perhaps some of her stiffness penetrated to him.

Ben called back over his shoulder, "Are you all right?"

The wind swallowed her reply. Leaning forward, she repeated the words directly against his ear, "Yes, I'm fine. This is wonderful." His hair curled slightly, brushing

softly against her cheek. They went over a bump and her
lips dragged against the side of his throat. Jessie felt a deep
shudder go through him and knew he wasn't totally immune to her.

The knowledge quivered inside her, humming; a soft
sensation of delight that threatened to overwhelm her.
Swallowing the urge to test her effect, she drew back and
felt his breath release. She smiled, wondering why she no
longer felt a sense of alarm. Perhaps it was her imagination, wishful thinking, moon madness. Yet, it felt right to
ride into the night with him.

On the way home, they crested a hill. Ben stopped at
the sound of her pleased sigh over the display of lights
below. Henderson lay snug in a valley between the surrounding hills.

"Seen enough?" he asked. When she nodded, he revved
the motor. "The road's rough in places." He placed her
hands more firmly around him. His foot rammed the gas
pedal; they took off, dirt flying. The night felt sticky with
a sultry heat.

Lightning chased from cloud to cloud. On an open bike
the air rushed by, cooling him, even as his body burned.
His body clenched as her breasts pressed against his back,
her soft breath brushing his neck. The feel of her sent a
pang of hunger shooting through him. He heard her laugh
and felt her tighten her hold on him. The sound of her
laughter rippled over him. She should laugh more often.
She sounded young, free, on the edge of womanhood, free
to give herself to a man.

When they reached the familiar markings of Stone's
End, the sky felt closer somehow. At the house, they
climbed the stairs in silence. When Bandit growled a low
warning, he ignored it.

At the top, Ben hesitated.

Jessie felt a rush of recklessness. She turned and leaned

her back against her closed door. His smile was wry as he flattened the palms of his hands on either side of her head.

"This isn't a good idea," Ben murmured, staring at her mouth.

Her mouth felt dry—he was going to kiss her! "No, it isn't," she said solemnly, agreeing but unable to stop what was happening between them. She had chosen him, back there on that long lonely road. He just didn't know it yet.

Whatever happened, now or never, she'd made the choice. Perhaps she could make it happen; perhaps she could make him love her. What did she have to lose?

Ben smiled. "Tell me you want this as much as I do."

Heaven help her, yes, she did. Jessie couldn't deny it, didn't even try. She wanted him to kiss her—more than she'd ever wanted anything in her life. Once, just once, she promised herself. Slowly he drew her into his arms. She'd waited for this moment; she wanted to hold on to the sensation.

Her silence drew him.

His hands moved from her shoulders to her waist, gathering her against him, and she went, like a new leaf toward the sun, seeking warmth, seeking life. Her body felt curiously light and boneless, inexplicably drawn toward his. New to physical displays of affection, she felt overwhelmed by the instant hunger at the slow slide of his hands. She tilted her head and watched his descend.

"Jessie," he rasped. He pressed his mouth against hers. His hands curved into her waist, urging her tight against him. Slowly she closed her eyes. A probe of his tongue opened her lips. She tasted him and felt the stamp of his possession—a gentle taking, and a giving. He did nothing to alarm her, perhaps sensing it was her first real kiss. Sensations filtered into her consciousness—the taste of his breath, the heat of his mouth, the hunger. Her hands awkwardly frozen at her sides, she could only feel, she couldn't respond.

When he slowly withdrew, she wanted to cling, but forced herself to rock back on her heels. "Good night, Jessie." A smile lingered on his lips.

"Night, Ben," she whispered, flushing because she could read the knowledge in his eyes. He knew he'd aroused her.

In the morning, Ben waited until Jessie came out of the bathroom after her shower. She smiled when she saw him, and he hated himself for what he was about to do. Surrounded in some lemon scent, she didn't speak but gazed at him in silence, a question in her smoky pale eyes. A flush rose up her cheeks and he knew she was recalling what had passed between them—in reality a pale imitation of a kiss.

However, he suspected it had been her first real kiss, and knowing that, he had to handle this carefully. "I don't know how to say it, Jessie, but we can't repeat last night." He smiled, hoping to soften his words. "I'm not saying I'm sorry, but let's forget it. All right?"

"All right," Jessie agreed, wrapping her robe tighter around her waist. She suddenly felt naked, her deepest feelings exposed. Who was she to argue with a man who had kissed her and insisted once was enough? Obviously, she didn't affect him the way he did her. Of course, he'd probably kissed more experienced women who actually kissed him back. The fact that he wasn't sorry was little consolation. Apparently, she was all too forgettable.

When her silence grew awkward, he said, "Well?"

She blinked, her lashes long and silky on her sunkissed cheeks. "Well what?" What did he expect her to say? That she'd hardly slept all night, that she'd anticipated seeing him this morning with a sense of longing that seemed foolish now?

A door slammed below. To her relief, her father's voice drifted up the stairs. "Jess, where's breakfast?"

Ben said grimly, "We'll finish this later." He hated the way his voice sounded threatening, but he was feeling desperate.

Later that morning, Fred didn't help. "How's Jessie?"

"Fine, I guess," Ben said absently, his gaze scouring a length of road for any sign of an overdue delivery truck. He had no intention of satisfying Fred's curiosity. The last thing he wanted was an inquisition.

Fred skirted a rut in the middle of the road. "Didn't see her this morning. She sick or something?"

"She overslept."

"She overslept?" Fred tilted his hat back. "That sure doesn't sound like Jessie."

"She stayed out late last night."

The older man raised an eyebrow. "Well, I'll be!"

"You're barking up the wrong tree."

"You and Jessie!" Fred grinned. "About time, too."

"Don't be an old fool!"

"Better than a young one. There's an old saying here in Maine. You can be old and dumb, or young and smart. It's the dumbness or smartness that counts."

Grinning, Ben shook his head. "All right, you win." He was in no position to argue the point. Fortunately for him, the delivery arrived to distract Fred.

The previous night had been a mistake. He shouldn't have kissed Jessie. He didn't know what he'd intended, how far he would have gone with her, although something along the lines of a bed had been very much part of the whole scenario. When he'd kissed her, her innocence had shocked him into sanity. He might be confused about a lot of things, but one thing was clear—he respected Jessie too much to lead her on.

At lunchtime, Ben went in search of Jessie.

He found her alone. She was chopping fresh vegetables and tossing them into a thick wooden salad bowl. She looked up when he entered. Before she could speak, he said, "Jessie, I don't know exactly how to say this, except straight. Don't get any ideas about last night." He continued with determination, "You're sweet and special, and I'd be a bastard to take advantage of you. We both know where this could lead." He waited for her to comment. When she didn't, he concluded, "I think we'd better stick to just being friends."

"I thought we settled that earlier. But, yes, of course." She bent back to her task—carving radishes, of all things. "If that's what you want."

Ben stared at the root vegetable in her hand as she deftly turned it into a delicate flower shape—a rose. "It's not what I want. But since it's all I'm likely to get, I guess I'll have to settle for it," he blurted out, feeling driven when she added nothing. For some reason, he needed to spell it out in black and white so there would be no further misunderstandings. "I may be a lot of things, but I haven't sunk low enough to go around seducing innocent virgins, then walking out on them. Besides..." He argued with himself, exasperated when she simply let him tie himself into knots and hang himself. "Jessie! Damn it! I'm too old for you!"

She didn't even flinch. "Yes, I know."

He felt like an absolute fool.

Ben was still standing there churning that over when Ira walked in. "Well, are we having lunch today?"

"Yes, coming right up." Jessie tossed the last radish into the bowl and followed her father out.

Later, when Ben had time to think, he found her simple

response a relief, but just then he'd wanted to wring her neck. While he stood there feeling like a crass pompous fool—an overage fool—she'd pricked his pride, then calmly returned to chopping radishes, turning them into works of art—roses.

Fred grabbed a seat at the table. "My, my, something smells mighty good, Jessie."

Jessie smiled with something resembling relief. "I made chili. There's fresh corn bread to go with it."

Cal joined them for lunch. Conversation was general. All four men made fast work of the spicy, meat-filled dish served over mounds of brown rice. Jessie ate little, Ben noted. Why should he feel guilty, when she hadn't bothered to argue the obvious fact—he *was* too old for her? She deserved someone young and strong who would fill her life with joy and laughter and her stomach with babies, not a battle-weary ex-soldier who jumped at loud noises and blanched at the sight of blood. But damn it—last night she'd made him feel again. He bit back a bitter smile. Well, she'd certainly put him in his place. He felt a spark of reluctant admiration.

Cal teased, "If I hadn't already promised my heart to Mary Ellen O'Connor, I'd marry you, Jessie." He blushed good-natured when everyone laughed...everyone but Ben.

Jessie, despite her forced smile, could find no humor in the subject of marriage, not with Ben staring at her with the same flinty look he'd worn the day he arrived. Back to square one.

After the men returned to their various chores, she sat there for a moment. Ben's on-again, off-again moods were a trial of nerves. He had kissed *her*,—or had he conveniently forgotten that small detail? Even if it was her first kiss, he needn't worry.

All right, so she'd underestimated the impact of two pairs of lips connecting. She might be young and she might be tempted to explore the sensations further, but she wasn't silly enough to chase Ben if he wasn't interested. She didn't need a man.

Thus far, her experience with the male species hadn't inspired her to go out and get one of her own.

As far as marriage went, the Carlisles didn't have a good track record. No, that wasn't accurate. She recalled her great-grandparents' wedding portrait—Grandma, plump and pretty in a blue velvet dress, and Grandpa, stern and stoic in a blue serge suit...except for his eyes, stealing a look at his bride. And Gran wore that secret smile. Olivia Carlisle had pressed a rose from her wedding bouquet into the family Bible.

Jessie wondered what advice Gran would have given her now.

Was this feeling for Ben love? This emptiness that needed filling? This craving, this wanting? And what, if anything, did Ben want from her? She was glad Ben had given her her first kiss. Nothing could ever take that away from her. For a brief moment, they'd exchanged taste for taste, breath for breath—a tantalizing sample that had felt strange and wonderful. And brief. Too brief.

A few days later, Ben caught Ira preening in the mirror. "I see the uniform still fits."

"Not bad." Ira sucked in, ignoring the strained seams. He polished a brass button with his sleeve. The army uniform recalled Ben's own pride in his West Point grays. Pride, duty, honor—he'd never questioned any of it.

Fred was impatient. "Come on, Ira. We're late."

Leaning a shoulder against the doorframe, Ben grinned at the pair of them in matching outdated uniforms. "What's the occasion, Halloween?"

"Independence Day." Fred bristled. "Let's get going."

He had a final word for Ben. "You'll have to bring Jessie."

His grin wiped away, Ben straightened abruptly. To his relief, Ira objected. "We can wait."

"Not if we're going to make the lineup." Fred grinned. "Parade starts at two sharp." He'd gotten the last laugh.

A man didn't stand a chance against the sneaky old codger. The door closed behind the pair. Ben turned at the sound of Jessie rushing down the stairs.

She stopped on the bottom step. "Did they leave?"

Ben slid his hands into his pockets, trying to ignore the way she affected him and failing badly. She was wearing her turquoise dress—the only dress she owned, apparently. The sun had streaked her hair to a paler shade. She was sleek and supple, graceful. If only he'd met her years ago, he could have swept her away and dressed her in silk and lace, even a diamond or two. But, no, he wouldn't have seen past her lack of glamour back then. And besides, silk and diamonds were all wrong for her. She was too real, too genuine.

The color of her dress did strange things to her eyes, stranger things to his heart—not to mention other parts of his anatomy. What was it about Jessie in a feminine dress that made him aware of all he was missing? A woman. That's all. Any woman would most likely do, as long as she had sun-streaked, flyaway hair and a smile that wreaked havoc with his hormones. She was gentle-hearted and sweet enough to tenderize the toughest hide, even his.

"They've gone ahead," Ben said huskily. "Looks like you'll have to come with me."

While she didn't look thrilled, he was practically salivating. A few moments later, he was telling her to hang on, as she climbed on the bike behind him.

As the motorcycle roared to life, Ben turned it onto the road in a widening curve that made her clutch him tighter.

At the added pressure, his heart knocked in his chest. He caught a tantalizing glimpse of tanned, rounded thigh before she pulled her skirt down and anchored it beneath her knees. Henderson was fifteen miles away, all downhill. By the time he got there, Ben felt as if he'd challenged Mount Everest.

With a feeling of release, he welcomed the sight of the first building. This was insanity. How could he remain immune when her warmth kindled a yearning he'd thought was long dead? "Where to?" he asked.

"The park is in the middle of town."

Flags were waving. For once, Ben welcomed a crowd, hoping to lose himself in it—after he delivered Jessie to her father. There was no room in his life for a woman—not even one as undemanding as Jessie. Main Street was roped off to through traffic and clogged with locals who had come out for the parade. A few outsiders, like him, stood apart.

For the first time in a long while, Ben felt the need to belong. He took Jessie's hand, unwilling to lose her in the crush. He didn't want to lose her. The silent words sent a shudder through him. A drumbeat started to pound.

Chapter Six

Slightly off-key, a band started to play. With the sun burning down on his head, Ben watched the small-town parade. It was standard fare—the floats, the band, the marching unit, the beauty queens. And then, a ragtag unit of army veterans marched into view. The crowd grew silent. Young and old marched in uniform to the drummer's beat—the crisp tan camouflage of Desert Storm, the motley jungle green of Vietnam, the faded blues, olives and browns of Korea and World War II.

Struck by an array of emotions too numerous to name, Ben tried to ignore a knee-jerk response. But it was too late. Once started, he couldn't stop the chain of memories. At twenty-one, he'd proudly graduated from West Point. Ten years later, he'd resigned his officer's commission, put his uniform in storage and his emotions on ice. Since coming to Maine, his feelings had started to thaw.

Ira marched by, head held high with pride. Fred saw

Jessie and winked; he gave a thumbs-up to Ben. The parade route wound up at the veteran's memorial. Ben tensed at the twenty-one gun salute; his body braced as the rifle shots cracked into the air. When the trumpet played taps, his eyes filled. Unbearably sweet and clear, the notes rose in the stillness.

Jessie shivered. The lone haunting trumpet sent chills down her spine. Her gaze strayed to Ben. His decision to attend the parade had surprised her, even more than his insistence on bringing her with him. As the sounds of the trumpet slowly faded and died, she watched his face contort with some sort of deep, hidden sentiment.

When he became aware of her, a shutter came down over his face. He stayed till the end, then turned and walked away. Filled with an unexpected urge to follow, she stared after him. He'd looked haunted. She'd seen that expression of grief on his face before, and had felt helpless then.

After all these weeks, she still knew so little about him. At first, she hadn't cared. Caring for Ben would only invite more hurt. She took a step, and then another. "Ben," she called softly, half hoping he wouldn't hear.

When she repeated it, he turned abruptly, his body rigid, his mouth set and impatient. "What is it?"

Not knowing quite what she was offering, she stifled the urge to snap back. "There's a picnic barbecue. I wondered if you'd care to join us."

His expression didn't soften. Without a flicker, he muttered, "No, thanks," and walked crossed the street.

Jessie stared at him in stunned disbelief. He'd cut her off without a hint of regret. She bit her lip. Had he caught the note of pity in her voice? All right, so she should have known pity was the last thing he would accept from her. It was all she had to offer. She should have known better than to tangle with a loner, a stray.

Moments later, she lost sight of Ben in the crowd.

The picnic barbecue tasted like sawdust. Her father and Fred ate the chicken and pasta salad and washed it down with lemonade while she pretended to eat. Her father threw her a worried frown but didn't comment on her preoccupation. The day passed in a flurry of speeches and demonstrations.

As the evening sky turned dark, Main Street was roped off for a street dance with a temporary stage at one end. Jessie looked on with interest. Not surprisingly, Henderson looked its best after dark. All lit up, it had a certain magic. Her foot started to tap when a local folk band took to the makeshift stage. The twangy soft music tugged at her heartstrings. The band soon warmed up the crowd.

"Say, Jessie, how about a dance?" Cal was extremely good-looking, and she was probably the envy of several girls there, but he was only eighteen.

Nevertheless she agreed, afraid to hurt his feelings.

They joined the dancers circling the clearing. Jessie caught a glimpse of Ben. He stood at a distance, leaning against a tree. Tall, dark-haired, aloof, he looked alien among the townspeople of the conservative community. Though obviously curious, people didn't venture close.

Cal twirled her away. She felt Ben's gaze following her. When the music ended, the band called for a break. Cal politely returned her to her father. "Thanks, Cal." She discovered he wasn't listening.

He was staring at the Morales girl. At sixteen, Serena stood out like a flower in a vegetable patch. Dressed in jeans and a red T-shirt, she was more than pretty. She was exotic—slightly built with delicate gold-tinted features, liquid brown eyes and long black hair that fell like black silk to her waist. Cal just stood there staring. She looked flustered at the attention. Ramon Morales didn't look pleased. But Cal didn't notice. He appeared poleaxed—

until redheaded Mary Ellen O'Connor, his steady girl, dragged him away.

Watching Serena get a stern lecture from her father a moment later, Jessie felt troubled. Typical of the migrants, Ramon Morales wouldn't approve of any kind of friendship between his daughter and Cal—the son of a wealthy local landowner. It was an unwritten code; the locals and migrants didn't mix socially. It was a barrier no one crossed.

After dancing with his wife, Fred turned to Jessie with a courtly bow, "How about it, Jessie?"

Perched on the end of a picnic bench, Jessie shook her head. "I think I'll just sit here."

"Pretty young thing like you shouldn't miss the fun."

Ira cleared his throat. "It's late," he grumbled and gathered himself to rise. "I want to get home."

"Well, you will," Fred said, frowning at his old friend, "soon as I get my dance."

"Well, go on, then." Settling back, Ira ordered, "Dance with him, Jess, and let's be done with it."

Hazel Cromie chuckled. "That's right, Jessie."

Hiding her amusement, Jessie moved into the crowd with Fred. After taking a turn or two around the perimeter in a fast two-step polka, he stopped. "Evening, Ben." One quick glance and Jessie wanted to shrink.

"Evening." Though heavily shadowed, Ben's frown was visible as he exchanged a reluctant word or two.

"Knee's acting up something awful." Fred's whine was pathetic. "I'm about done in." He rubbed his left knee. "You two go on and finish this dance."

Jessie said pointedly, "Fred, if you're tired, we can go home." She knew there was nothing wrong with his knee.

"Now, Jessie, you know you were itching to dance." Fred ignored her warning. "Well, aren't you going to ask her?"

Jessie squirmed with humiliation. Finally, when she thought he would never speak, Ben said evenly, "Well, shall we?"

Considering his lack of enthusiasm, she should refuse. Where was her pride? Rock bottom, apparently. Just once, she wanted to dance with someone besides Cal or Fred—someone who wasn't too old or too young. Who was she kidding?

Feeling helpless, she watched Fred limp off—favoring his *right* knee. The old fake. "Yes, I'd like that," she whispered, exhilarated despite the humiliation of being thrust at a man who plainly didn't want her. A man she barely knew. Was that true?

As strange as it might sound, sometimes she felt as if she knew Ben Harding intrinsically, from the inside out; as if her spirit recognized his. She felt hot and cold when he placed one hand at her waist and drew her closer.

"I'm not much of a dancer," Ben warned, guiding her between the other couples into a country reel.

Jessie smiled hesitantly. "Neither am I." Should she tell him she would rather sit this one out? Suddenly she knew she would be lying if she did. She wanted to dance with him.

"It's been a while," he confessed. "I'm rusty at this." A moment later, he stepped on her toe.

"You're doing fine," she murmured, amazed when his face darkened a shade. "Besides, it's dark. No one can see."

At her soft words, his rigid tension slowly eased.

"We won't win any prizes." When the tempo slowed to a waltz, he breathed an audible sigh of relief.

She expected him to release her and return her to Fred and her father; instead, he drew her closer. A twangy country tune pulled at her heartstrings. "Ben, you don't have to..."

"Shh." He smiled—a smile that actually reached his deep blue eyes. "I'm counting."

With a start, Jessie registered the change in him. He looked younger, his smile slightly rakish and teasing. When someone jostled her from behind, she landed against him. To regain her balance, she placed her hand against his chest and felt his heart jolt. She glanced up. His eyes darkened and tangled with hers. She felt him suck in a breath.

His hands dropped to her hips and tightened, as if he couldn't help himself. With the air rushing from her lungs, Jessie stood there locked against him. Around them, others danced. The song and music continued. Time stood still for her. She felt the sharp bite of physical desire. She never questioned why it should be with Ben.

What would it be like to link her hands behind his neck, to hold him close in her arms, to be held—to feel surrounded by his strength, to absorb it? She watched his face as he came closer. His scar seemed more pronounced. Her gaze fastened on his mouth. The memory of their first and only kiss burned bright in her mind. This time, she thought she was prepared.

But she wasn't. As his lips met hers, the humming burst in her ears; the lights, the music, the voices around her faded. She opened her mouth and he deepened the kiss.

Someone exploded a firecracker nearby.

Ben froze. With a muttered curse, he dragged her away, but not before she felt his response. Jessie's small moment of triumph died when Ben's eyes blazed down at her. Did he feel contempt?

"I'm sorry," he said, his eyes shuttered.

"So am I." Blushing a fiery red, she turned her face away from that searing look.

"I meant, we have an audience," he said dryly.

Suddenly she remembered where they were—in the

middle of downtown Henderson with every resident within miles probably watching. She looked around and encountered a few curious glances, a few frowns, a smile. Thankfully, they hadn't attracted too much attention. At least her father wasn't watching. She couldn't even see him. After a few more bars, the music came to an end.

Jessie felt awkward as Ben released her, her pleasure lost in that one moment of recognition. She might be innocent, but she wasn't ignorant about men and women. In theory, sex and reproduction had always seemed natural to her, but what she'd just experienced in response to Ben was frightening. For just the briefest moment, she'd forgotten who she was, who he was. While Ben might feel something for her, he would never acknowledge it.

A hard pulse ticked to life in his cheek. "Shall we find your father?"

Nodding, she snatched at the excuse for escape. She swallowed the urge to laugh. So much for wild attraction. It certainly wasn't mutual. "Dad's anxious to leave. I hope he hasn't overdone things today."

"Where is he?"

"Over there." But her father wasn't where she'd left him. Suddenly she felt guilty for forgetting his health. "I guess they've gone." She searched the crowd in vain.

Ben wasn't surprised. "I guess so," he muttered back, aware that Fred had engineered this entire fiasco right up to the end—leaving Jessie stranded with no choice but to accept his offer of a ride home. He was just about to suggest it when he noticed her wistful expression as she looked back at the dancers.

Instead of rushing her off, he glanced at his watch. "It's only ten. How about staying awhile before I take you home?" She looked surprised. Well, so was he. "We could both use a break from work. Let's enjoy it. How about a cotton candy before we check out the carnival?"

He added a smile to the invitation, hoping it was enough to convince her, because he wasn't at all convinced he was doing the right thing. Hadn't he vowed to avoid Jessie?

If that was the case, what was he doing offering to squire her around a country carnival and smiling like an adolescent at her acceptance? He bought her a cotton candy as they strolled. The lights, the noise, the music, the smells of roasting hot dogs and candied apples held a certain intriguing novelty for him.

"I've never lived in a small town or attended something like this," he confessed.

"And I've never been anywhere else." Her smile was edged in bright pink from the melted sugar.

It probably tasted as sweet as it looked, he thought wryly. If she was bored with small-town life, he had no intention of providing a distraction. She was twenty-three, Fred had told him. Twenty-three and ripe and ready for love. A dangerous young lady. As Fred would say, a man could find himself hog-tied in a hurry if he didn't watch out.

They strolled between rows of carnival stalls, taking in the sights and sounds. Jessie stopped to admire a display of Native American pottery. She ran a hand over a smooth vase.

The woman operating the stall greeted her with a warm smile. "Do you like that? It's handcrafted."

Jessie smiled. "It's beautiful."

Ben picked up a sterling-silver concha belt, inlaid with cool blue-green turquoise.

The woman turned to him. "Ah, you have excellent taste." Her dark eyes twinkling, she looked from Ben to Jessie. "The stones are turquoise. There is a legend, if you'd care to hear it...."

"Yes, please," Jessie said.

"After the rain, if you follow the rainbow to its end and

dig in the damp, fragrant earth, if you're lucky—and worthy—turquoise awaits.'' She took the belt and held it out to Jessie. ''Here the past comes alive, the future is full of possibilities. Everything is linked in time.''

If you are worthy.

Ben had heard enough. ''I'll take it.''

''I'm sure your lady will enjoy it.''

''I'm sure.''

Jessie objected. ''I can't let you buy me things.''

After exchanging payment for the belt, he held it out to Jessie. ''But I insist. Please, I'd like you to have it.''

She shook her head. ''I can't.''

Ben slipped his finger under her belt to release the buckle and the simple act of exchanging one belt for another became something else. He felt her suck in a breath.

She stared at his hand at her waist, then slowly raised her head to meet his gaze. Their eyes locked. Ben twisted the old cloth belt off, and felt an almost uncontrollable urge to reach for the top button of her dress. If they weren't in a public place, surrounded by lights and music, he knew his next act would be to undo each button with tantalizing slowness and just as thoroughly undress Jessie—

His breath caught at the thought of reaching inside her dress, touching her breasts, kissing them, holding her to him. And in some odd way, it felt so right, as if he'd done this before—which was insane. If their relationship continued, he would make love to Jessie. It was as inevitable as thunder following lightning, the sun following rain. He pulled off her old belt and replaced it with his gift, and somehow it became more—it became an act of possession.

The silver links slid around her small waist. He hooked it into place, then spanned her waist with both hands and pulled her against him. Tempted beyond hope of resisting, he bent his head and kissed her cotton-candy mouth because—

Oh, hell, he just had a yen for cotton candy. And just as he'd suspected, she tasted sugary sweet. Kissing Jessie was obviously habit-forming. With a murmur of enjoyment, she pressed back. She didn't look flustered when he released her. She looked all lit up.

With a rueful smile, he murmured, "Please forget I did that," and took her hand.

She choked out a laugh, and he felt oddly content, which was very odd indeed since he couldn't remember the last time he'd felt that way, if ever. He'd spent his life competing, developing his brain and his stamina, scrambling for position, training to kill and avoid being killed. But no amount of training could have prepared him to fail, to lie helpless and let people die. After all that, how odd to feel…content.

Ben subdued all the warning bells clamoring in his head. Perhaps he had reached the end of the rainbow. What had the old woman said—if he was lucky, and worthy?

Luck wasn't with him.

At a mock firing range, Drew Pierce called out, "If it isn't Jess and her fancy hired man."

"Drew, stop it," Jessie said, tight voiced.

Drew laughed at her small explosion. "What's the matter? Can't he speak for himself?"

"Let it go, Jessie," Ben said.

But Drew was determined to speak to Jessie. "I saw your dad leaving earlier. Are you here on your own?"

"Ben's taking me home," she said.

Drew reached out and pulled her toward him. "There's no need. I'll take you."

Ben had no intention of interfering. Nevertheless, the sight of Drew's thick hand on her narrow waist bothered him. The silver belt glittered and winked at him. Determined to remain immune, Ben slipped his hands into his pockets. His mouth tightened when Jessie sent him a troubled look.

She tried to object. "I don't—"

Drew plainly wasn't going to accept an excuse. Glancing over his shoulder at the bright marquee of lights setting off an array of prizes, he cut into her refusal. "How would you like one of those stuffed bears?"

She smiled rigidly. "No, thanks."

"Come on. Your friend here won't mind." Releasing her, Drew picked up a loaded rifle and threw Ben a challenging look. "Fact is, maybe we could have a round or two and see who can hit the target. Winner gets to take Jess home."

The winner got Jessie.

Gritting his teeth, Ben felt his stomach roil as Drew sighted in the target. Wincing as the rifle shots cracked into the air, he stood his ground.

After scoring a near-perfect round, Drew turned on a triumphant grin. "Beat that."

"I don't think so." Ben folded his arms.

"You mean you can't." Drew set the rifle aside.

"That's not what I said."

A small crowd had gathered around them. Playing up to their audience, Drew chuckled. "And you won't even try. Well, that's plain insulting to Jess, now, isn't it?"

A titter of laughter rose about them. At Jessie's painful flush, Ben grabbed the gun and aimed. One, two, three, four—the explosions went off in his head. Dead on target. He never missed. Sweat broke out on his brow. It was the first time he'd held a gun in years. He just held the rifle and kept pumping the trigger until the bullets ran out and it clicked empty. Empty. As if it were a live grenade, he dropped the gun to the counter where it landed with a dull thud. His hands were visibly shaking when he jammed them into his pockets.

There was silence, then the attendant laughed a little too heartily. "Hey, the little lady gets to pick a bear."

Ben needed a moment to collect himself as the crowd slowly dispersed. He was shaking. Once, he'd taken orders and given orders as naturally as breathing. He should have questioned his superiors. That was the hell of it. He should have refused to take his division into that drug-infested hellhole. If he had, they would all be alive.

Ben took long slow breaths, pulling himself back from the brink. Posttraumatic stress syndrome, the doctors called it. He knew the meaning all too well. It was like stepping into quicksand and being sucked under. Anything related could trigger his memory—a loud noise, a uniform, something as simple as a camera flash. For the most part, he'd learned to control it, but at times his subconscious took over, he relived horrific events again and again.

Thankfully, Jessie took her time selecting a large bright pink bear with a purple polka-dot bow.

Not a good loser, Drew muttered a disgruntled, "I'd still like to take you home, Jess."

Jessie hugged the bear to her chest.

Some choice, she thought. She could choose between a clearly annoyed Drew or a dark-browed, brooding Ben who seemed determined to ignore her existence—now that he'd kissed her senseless. Despite all that, the choice wasn't all that difficult. She chose Ben.

"I wouldn't want to take you out of your way, Drew."

"Guess you win this time, Harding." With a careless shrug that failed to hide his irritation, Drew accepted her decision and went off with his friends.

Jessie was left standing alone with Ben under the gaudy fluorescent lights of the marquee. "Are you all right?" she asked after a moment.

Instead of replying to her direct question, he said, "Are you sure you wouldn't rather go home with Drew?"

She struggled to find a smile. "Yes, I'm sure."

"Then, let's go."

This time, he didn't reach for her hand.

Shouldn't she have the sense to be wary? Moments later, despite her brief moment of bravado, she felt like laughing from pure nerves when she climbed on the back of his bike. In one hand she clutched her teddy bear; with the other she clung to Ben's hard waist.

Ben turned the bike onto the highway with a sense of impatience to be gone. The lights of town disappeared. After a few miles, the black night closed in as he drove through the dark countryside. He needed to put the entire evening behind him. Even Jessie's nearness didn't reach him. Filled with mental anguish brought on by the day's events, he couldn't shed his past, or the memories. For a brief time he'd hoped it was over; now he knew he was still on the edge.

When they reached the familiar markings of Stone's End, there were stars, pinpoints of light in a broad sky, the broadest he'd ever seen—from the ground. He looked into the velvet night and knew he would never fly again.

Perspiration beaded his brow as he recalled that last, spiraling free fall and the splintering crash that had followed.

He'd survived—the only one.

At the house, he parked the bike under the spread of the oak trees lining the driveway. Jessie hopped down and turned to him. She shifted the stuffed bear from one hand to the other, holding it against her like a shield.

He looked down at her bent head and realized she was afraid of his next move. What the hell was she afraid of—him? The realization galled him. "After you," he murmured, motioning her toward the house with a tight smile.

Jessie didn't move. She couldn't go inside; not yet. She needed to penetrate the wall around Ben. She knew one thing; he was no ordinary drifter. She'd seen men handle guns—hunting guns used for sport. Ben was an expert.

"You're not a farmer." She spoke with quiet conviction, demanding more than half-truths and evasions. "Who are you?"

A bitter edge of self-mockery cracked his voice. "I'm not a criminal, if that's what you're asking."

She swallowed hard. "Have you ever killed anyone?"

"Yes." His eyes glittered with deliberate provocation. "Satisfied?" he muttered when she failed to hide her shock.

She shook her head. "No, of course not."

He looked at her in silence for a long moment, as if deciding how much he wanted to reveal. Finally, he said simply, "I learned how to handle firearms in the army. You have nothing to fear from me."

Somehow she managed to tear herself away from the bleak reproach in his eyes and go inside the house. Alone in her room, she set the stuffed bear on the bed, then moved it to the rocker. Despite the traumatic ending to her day, she smiled at the sight of the plush toy, feeling a little foolish, yet comforted somehow. She'd never had a teddy bear. A waste of money, her father had long ago decreed. How odd that Ben should fulfill a long-forgotten childhood wish. She couldn't help feeling concern for him.

Something deeply disturbing had happened to him at the parade and later at the carnival. Something had happened and it didn't involve her. Jessie sighed, feeling weary. Why had he accepted Drew's challenge? He'd looked haunted after he'd emptied the gun. What awful memories had it revived?

Hours later, when she heard his stifled cry, she wasn't surprised. She closed her eyes. It wasn't the first time she'd heard him cry out, as if terror filled his sleeping hours. But tonight was different, somehow. Tonight, she lay awake long after he stopped.

Chapter Seven

"No." Ben tossed, unable to rouse himself from sleep. In the darkest hour, he was in a jungle. Bullets whined and hit his plane; smoke poured from the fuselage. A downward spiral ended in a crash, bodies hurling, then nothing. He ended it with a savage cry. "Oh, God, no!" He couldn't move.

Waking or sleeping, he relived it. Feverish, bullet wounds festering, one leg broken, he lay helpless while others slowly died. A week, it had lasted a week. Day after wretched day. His buddies, some children, two women— all had died, one by one. Their cries still haunted him.

Hours later, instead of gunshots and ragged cries, he woke to the blessed sound of silence.

The sun poured through the single window, nearly blinding him for a second. With a groan, he ran his hand over his eyes. Everyday morning sounds of the farmhouse filtered through the painful images burning in his brain—

an alarm clock, Jessie padding barefoot around her bedroom, humming some nameless tune, running water in the bathroom for her bath. Jessie. It was all so normal, so real—unlike the jumbled pieces of his life.

His last mission had ended his military career. Part of a drug-enforcement force, he had been assigned to rescue a drug informant's family from a vicious drug lord. He'd known the risks; he'd even argued with his commander. Nevertheless, he'd led his men into hell. He'd survived—the only one.

Guilt-ridden, he'd landed in Maine. And he'd found a measure of peace. Jessie was part of it, part of what held him bound when every instinct told him to run. He'd begun to think of a future with her; but not now, not after the carnival. Holding a gun in his hand again had shattered that cozy image. He'd given her the turquoise. And for a moment, maybe he'd thought their lives might be linked—if he was worthy. But his future lay buried in the past. How could he bring her into his nightmare? He had nothing to offer Jessie.

The following day, Drew stopped by to arrange for the seasonal workers. Jessie greeted him, glad that Ben was there to handle things. On second thought, maybe she wasn't. The two men were glaring at each other.

"Morning, Jess." Drew acted as if no hard feelings existed. She doubted his sincerity. "I brought some of my best men. You need any more, just let me know."

Jessie's mouth tightened with irritation. Drew treated the migrants like commodities. She supposed that was all they were to him—dollar signs, not men with pride and dignity. Each year, thousands of them followed the harvests north. They put up with poor living conditions to get work. Like Ramon, many traveled with spouses and children.

"Hello, Ramon." Jessie smiled. "Please, won't you introduce your friends?" After a brief glance at Drew, Ramon Morales introduced the men. They came from border towns in Texas or Mexico, and places like Guatemala and Ecuador. "Welcome." Jessie was aware of the friction, which wasn't surprising, considering Drew's lack of respect for the migrants. "Some of you have worked for my father. This year, he's ill."

She received blank stares from most of the men. "Ben Harding is managing the farm for us...."

Drew glanced at his watch. "Jess, can we get on with this? Half of them don't even speak English. Just show them to the fields and they'll know what to do."

Ramon's dark eyes glittered with resentment. "We may not all speak your language, but we are not stupid."

Until then, Ben had stayed out of the exchange. When he spoke to the men in Spanish, they responded with ready smiles.

Jessie found herself smiling as well, even though she couldn't understand a word he said. She was simply relieved he'd stepped in to ease the tension.

Catching her smile, Drew shook his head. "You're just too soft—not that I couldn't develop a taste for a soft woman," he murmured. "If you'd just cooperate."

"I wouldn't hold my breath."

"I need Ira's signature on the contract." Drew threw a parting shot at a silent, watchful Ben. "Hey, Harding, any of these guys give you any trouble, just let me know."

When Ben didn't counter the attack, Jessie swallowed her disappointment. She showed Drew inside to the den, then excused herself to make coffee, hoping he would be gone when she came back.

He wasn't.

Her father was speaking, "That looks fair and square, the usual percentage." He penned his name to a document.

Drew signed, as well. "I'm concerned about this guy, Harding. What do you actually know about him?"

Ira frowned across his desk. "Enough."

When Jessie offered coffee, Drew waved aside sugar and cream. "I doubt he can handle the summer crew."

Jessie frowned. "What makes you say that?"

"You saw what just happened. He handled them all wrong. They need to know who's boss."

Ira chuckled. "Ben's hard as nails." He leaned back in his chair. "As for handling men, he graduated from West Point, made the rank of major."

Drew looked skeptical. "So why did he quit?"

"Got himself shot up in some South American jungle—fighting them drug lords, or something."

Jessie couldn't hide her shock. "Did he tell you all that?" The information explained so much about Ben's past—the scars. But shouldn't he have recovered from those? There had to be something else eating at him.

"Didn't need to," Ira said. "I checked out his record through an old army buddy."

Drew's smile became strained. "You saying he's a hero?"

Ira shrugged. "I wouldn't know about that."

Jessie felt frustrated, wanting to know more about the root cause of Ben's nightmares. Of course, even if she did learn more, what would she do about it? She had no idea.

Ira insisted on showing Drew to the door. Jessie was still sitting there when Ben entered the den.

"How about a cup of coffee?" she offered impulsively, hoping to break the uneasy tension between them. "It's still warm."

Had she imagined the closeness when they'd danced? Kissed?

Ben raised an eyebrow. "I could use a cup." As she poured, he sat on the corner of the desk and folded his arms. "You might want to warn the boyfriend to back off."

The coffee spilled over. "He's not my boyfriend."

"He wants to be." Ben tried to sound disinterested, which was damn near impossible with the memory of Jessie returning his kisses last night. When she simply gazed at him in silence, he swallowed his exasperation. "All right, you tell me. Exactly what is there between you and Pierce?"

Jessie mopped the spill. "Not what you're thinking."

Smiling, Ben cocked an eyebrow. "How do you know what I'm thinking?" He was thinking he'd like to kiss the anger from her mouth, the wariness from her eyes.

"It's fairly obvious," she said stiffly.

"Then, tell me."

"Oh, for heaven's sake, Drew is just a neighbor."

"He wants you, and he thinks I'm competition." Ben watched her expression change. He'd shocked her. As far as he could tell, Drew wasn't accustomed to being denied, and he'd decided he wanted Jessie. Whether Drew had feelings for her was anyone's guess. "You can't deny your father handpicked him for you."

"Yes, well..." Her voice trailed off.

He stared at her mouth. She was just like Ira; proud, independent, prickly and stubborn. Unfortunately, she was also young and vulnerable. "All right, I'm sorry. I have no right to interfere. It's your life."

"Yes, it is my life." She stiffened her spine and turned to stare out the window.

Apparently, he wasn't going to get that coffee—unless he poured it himself. While he was at it, he poured one for Jessie. Ben added thick fresh cream to her coffee, just the way he knew she liked it...then stared at it. When had he noticed how she drank her coffee? He held it out to her.

"Jessie?" he murmured.

She looked at him in surprise. Then, lowering her gaze, she took the cup and saucer from him. "Thank you."

Ben took a sip. After sitting too long, it tasted bitter. He drank it anyway. Somehow, he didn't think her troublesome neighbor was going to go away. Despite his doubts about Jessie's ability to handle Drew, Ben buried his concern. She had a lot to learn about men. Unfortunately, he wasn't going to be around long enough to teach her. He felt angry at himself for caring, and angry at her for making him care.

A few days later, events temporarily interrupted Jessie's preoccupation with Ben. Cal Pierce needed her assistance to walk out of the health clinic. He limped, the result of twenty stitches. Homer had gone on a rampage and gored Cal's thigh. The injury was serious and messy, but not critical.

"Are you sure you want to go home?" One-handed, she managed to open the passenger door.

Cal climbed gingerly into the truck. "I'm not staying in that hospital. The food's rotten and the service is worse. My mother will look after me just fine."

Jessie hid a smile. Just then, Cal sounded exactly like the teenage boy he was. He was going off to college next year. She was going to miss him. "Well, if you're sure?"

He winced. "I'm sure."

Jessie hadn't witnessed the accident, but she'd heard the shouts. By the time she'd reached Cal, crumpled and bleeding on the ground, Ben had dragged the boy to safety and applied a makeshift tourniquet to the gaping wound.

Ben's outward composure hadn't fooled her. He'd shuddered at the sight of blood, his eyes haunted, his face pale. Shaken, she'd grabbed a pitchfork and prodded Homer into the barn. Ben had lost his temper and yelled at her.

"Can you tell me what happened?" she asked Cal now. "How did Homer get out of the pasture?"

"I don't know. It was all so fast. I turned my back, and he was on me. I hit the fence and blacked out."

"Thank God Ben was nearby."

"Yeah," Cal whispered, his voice sober. He closed his eyes and leaned his head back. "I owe him one."

Jessie drove slowly, trying not to jar Cal's injured leg.

The Pierce farm wasn't at all like Stone's End. It was profitable, for one thing. They were a large family. Several came running when Jessie pulled into the yard. Cal's mother turned white at the sight of her son.

"He's a little worse for wear," Jessie assured her, smiling at Cal. "Just a little less impertinent."

Cal grinned weakly. "I'll be fighting fit in no time."

His mother scolded, "I spoke with Dr. Peterson on the phone. You're to stay in bed. Cook has some broth simmering. The doctor said you lost some blood. My poor baby!"

Cal ducked his head. "Aw, Mom."

Jessie left them arguing and went home, to Stone's End.

The sound of masculine voices drew her to her father's den.

"I told you," Ben was saying in stiff tones, "Homer is dangerous and out of control. He has to go." The words stopped her in the open doorway where she stood unobserved. It wasn't as if she was eavesdropping; the two men were shouting.

Her father banged his fist on the desktop. "And I say no! Cal just got careless."

"Like hell!" Ben fired back, his body rigid. "He's not the only one at risk. Jessie was foolish to tackle him on her own. She almost got herself killed."

"Jessie knows her way around Homer."

"He was out of control, and she was in the middle of

it," Ben raged. Jessie caught her breath at the passion in his voice.

"Everything turned out all right," Ira insisted.

Ben exploded. "You are as bullheaded as that rogue bull!"

That brought Ira to his feet. "You're fired!"

Ben didn't flinch. "I quit." He turned toward the door and stopped. His eyes narrowed on Jessie's shocked face. Somehow, she knew he wasn't just turning his back on her father and Stone's End—he was running from her. He'd been different since the parade, more restless. She'd tried to stay out of his way.

His mouth tightened with determination. "I'm through, Jessie. Your father can get himself a new man." The words drilled her like bullets. A new man.

What about her? What if she didn't want a new man? What if she wanted Ben Harding—temper, scars and all? A man whose strength made her stand taller, a man whose gentleness made her weak? She pressed back against the wood frame as he brushed past her and slammed out the back door.

Turning to her father, she composed her features. "What was that about?" Her heart ached. Was that panic—the breath locked in her chest, the blackness filling her vision?

"You heard. I fired him."

She clenched her hands. "I just heard him quit."

"After I fired him," Ira blustered. "Homer's unruly at times, but he's staying." His mouth tightened with unspent emotion. It was all bottled up inside. Jessie knew the expression well. "Jared raised Homer from a calf."

Jessie placed her hand on her father's shoulder. "I know, Dad. I know." She took a deep breath, searching for something to salvage the situation. "Ben seems like a reasonable man. Maybe if you explained, apologized."

"Not hardly." Her father stood. "I'm not apologizing

to a hired hand. I'm giving the orders—and paying Ben Harding a pretty penny or two to obey. It's about time he remembered who's boss around here!''

"We need him, Dad.''

"No, we don't. Things were fine till he showed up.''

"No, they weren't,'' she insisted quietly.

"We'll manage.''

"With Cal out with an injury? For who knows how long?''

Ira ran a shaky hand down his face. "We'll run an ad.''

Worrying her lip, Jessie felt her spirits sink. How were they going to replace Ben? He'd fitted into their lives. He'd made a place for himself at Stone's End. A place in her heart. Now he was leaving. How could she bear it? Like he had everyone she cared for, her father had driven Ben away.

"We can manage,'' she said, trying to convince herself. "Jared will come home if he's needed.''

Her father sat down hard. "Jared isn't coming home. He called—he's got a job at a ranch in California.''

"When did he call?''

"A couple hours ago.''

Jessie wrapped her arms around her waist. "What else did Jared say?''

Ira looked away. "Not much.''

"You argued again.''

Ira shrugged. "It's between Jared and me.''

Between him and Jared. Ben clearly didn't want her. Where did she fit?

Ben was packing his gear when Fred approached.

"Heard you're leaving.'' Fred made no attempt to hide his disapproval. "Seems I was wrong about you after all.''

Ben scowled. "I'm heading out first thing in the morning.''

Fred scowled back. "Well, good for you. Can't change a mule when he's bound on the wrong track. Wouldn't even try. Just thought you might want to see something."

"I don't have time."

"You got time for this," Fred insisted. "It's only going to take a minute of your fool time."

"One minute," Ben agreed.

"Wouldn't want to keep you from nothing important. Lord knows, the road will be waiting on you tomorrow. You'll be at the state border by lunch and out of New England by nightfall. A few minutes of your time won't hurt."

Muttering to himself, Fred walked Ben out to the fenced pasture where the cows had broken loose, Homer among them, and trampled scores of healthy plants.

Fred lifted a broken gate. "Thought you might want a look." He handed the metal hinge to Ben. Several screws had been removed, the rest loosened. "Looks like someone went to a mighty lot of trouble to cause mischief."

"Isn't that a bit extreme, even for Drew?"

"Probably didn't mean no harm, just a bit of mischief. I don't suppose Drew had any way of knowing we were moving Homer today, or that his own brother would get hurt."

Ben's face tightened. "What's his motive?"

"It's no secret Ira's finances are in bad shape," Fred said shrewdly. "Looks like Drew wants to get his hands on Stone's End by fair means or foul."

"Meaning?" Ben said impatiently.

"Them cows did some heavy crop damage here today. Ira's hurting for cash. Last I heard, the Pierces still want logging rights. Maybe Drew figures he can force the issue and make a deal with Ira. Maybe he wants to buy Stone's End, since Jessie's not interested in a wedding—leastways, not yet."

Not yet.

The words sounded ominous to Ben. For a man who didn't want involvement, he'd landed himself in it when he came to Stone's End. It was high time he took himself off, away from the temptation to stay and fix things. Hadn't he proved he was no good at looking out for anyone but himself?

"Look, I just quit." Ben handed the broken hinge back. "You'll have to warn my replacement to watch out for Drew Pierce. Ramon would be a good choice. He's a good man. He's reliable and seems to know his way around a farm."

Fred glowered at him. "You're actually quitting? Leaving Jessie high and dry? Well, ain't that just fine!"

"I don't owe the Carlisles a damn thing."

"Course not," Fred said sarcastically.

"I earned my pay. I don't owe them."

"Who you trying to convince?"

Ben didn't respond. He was leaving. Absolutely nothing was going to stop him from shaking the dust from Stone's End.

That evening, Jessie served tomatoes at supper.

Ben stared at them. Damned if she didn't know how to turn the screws and make him feel guilty! She'd even started his laundry. The clothes dryer hummed in the background. Ben felt like a kid going off to summer camp— instead of a man running out on a woman. He felt guilty about leaving her. But he wasn't leaving her; he was leaving Stone's End. At the moment, he just couldn't distinguish between the two. Jessie was part of it—part of what had kept him here against his better judgment far longer than he'd intended; part of what was driving him away.

Ben looked around. "Where's Ira?"

"He insisted on a tray in his room." Jessie's eyes looked troubled. "I hope he's feeling all right."

Ben felt guilty. Nevertheless, he was relieved not to have to face the old man again. He didn't want another argument; he just wanted to be free. "How's Cal doing?" He latched on to the neutral topic.

"Fine. His mother was more upset then he was."

"I can imagine."

Jessie smiled slightly. "Cal will just have to put up with some pampering." Her polite conversation was served up along with Ben's favorite chicken and dumplings.

When she served blueberry tarts for dessert, he began to suspect she had a decidedly sadistic streak. "Sounds like he'll make it." He stared at the dessert dish, unable to take a bite. The tomatoes had given him heartburn.

"Yes, he will." Her voice trailed off.

The buzzer in the laundry room rang. Looking as relieved as he felt at the interruption, Jessie jumped up to take his shirts from the dryer. When she set up the ironing board, he exploded. "Leave the damn things!"

She threw him a wounded look. "All right." She dropped his shirt into the wicker laundry basket. She took a deep breath and blurted out, "Must you go?"

"Yes." The answer erupted. He stood just as abruptly. "I spoke to Fred about Ramon taking over my job. I think he'll work out just fine."

"So, you'll be leaving with a clear conscience?"

"Is there any reason why I shouldn't?"

"You tell me," she challenged softly, yet challenged nevertheless. There was nothing spineless or evasive about Jessie; she demanded honesty from him, even if it hurt.

Respecting that about her, he didn't cushion his words. "If we're talking about what's been going on between the two of us, Jessie, my leaving is for the best. You know I'm right. I'm not the man for you. We'd only wind up hurting each other."

Sliding her hands into her jeans pockets, she threw him a disbelieving look. "Could I hurt you?"

"Yes, I believe you could."

"I suppose I should thank you for that." Jessie smiled

slightly—a little cynically, he thought, which was something new for her. He hoped he hadn't taught her that.

"Our relationship was a mistake from the beginning. It can't go anywhere," he said. "I'm sorry if you thought it meant something."

She tilted her head to the side. "It didn't?"

"No."

"I see." Her voice sounded brittle. "I didn't realize you were playing games."

"I wasn't— That's not how it was!" For one wild, insane moment, he considered asking her to come with him. But no, he couldn't ask her to choose between him and Ira. Besides, what was he thinking? Marriage? He wasn't ready for that. And Jessie wasn't the sort to play around. She was a keeper. He couldn't offer permanence, a home, children. How could he while his past haunted him?

He took a deep breath and released it. "Look, Jessie. Maybe I did feel something," he admitted, then hastened to add, "but it's not enough. In time, you'll agree. It's easy to confuse loneliness for something else, especially love. I could also make a clear-cut case of proximity."

"Please don't." She folded the ironing board. "I think I've gotten the point. Since I won't see you again, I just wanted to thank you for all you've done."

What had he done? What sort of garbage had he spouted? He didn't believe a word of his own trumped-up excuses. How could she?

But apparently she did. Ben ached to reach for her and erase her closed expression. Instead, he clamped his hands by his sides. "I never wanted it to be like this. A clean break will be best. I never wanted to hurt you. Can you believe that?"

"I know you never wanted to get involved." She stored the ironing board in the laundry room, then returned. "Well, you're perfectly free to leave. No one's stopping you."

With that, Jessie walked out.

Ben felt about as free as a tiger in a cage.

He ran a weary hand over his face, then around the back of his neck, where he could feel a knifelike tension. How had she guessed he planned to leave at dawn?

Hours later, Ben prepared to spend his final night under the Carlisle roof. The mourning sound of a bagpipe was the last sound he heard before a restless sleep claimed him.

Jessie heard Ben tossing and turning. Another restless night. She groaned and rolled over. Only tonight, there was another element. When he called out, a chill swept over her.

She heard the terror in his voice, sharper than ever before. She closed her eyes tight but couldn't close out the memory of his reaction to Cal's injuries that afternoon. Ben had been shaking, his face whiter than Cal's. What devil drove him?

She bit her lip. She couldn't care; she wouldn't. Every instinct cried out for her to go to him. Yet, her common sense warned her to stay away. When he called out again, she buried her head in the pillow to drown out his tortured cry.

Her heart ached for him. His voice sounded muffled, then went silent. After a long moment, she lifted her head. Somehow, his silence only made it worse. What hell was he reliving? She'd seen it in his eyes. Suddenly she couldn't bear the thought of Ben's loneliness on this, his last night. Her motives for going to him were confused. He needed someone. Perhaps if he opened up and talked to her, he might stay. The thought was barely formed, but it was there. She shoved it to the back of her mind. Heart pounding, she tossed the covers aside.

Chapter Eight

The jungle was all around. At night the blackness was thick. Ben could feel the sweat on his face. He waited for death. Why did it take so long? Shadows moved at his bedside. Was he awake? Or dreaming? He ran a hand over his eyes. He'd never understood why he survived. For what? His soul was destroyed.

He demanded, "Who's there?" The enemy—they crept up on you...took potshots. In a dreamlike state, his mind could absorb only distant memories, people and places existing only in his nightmares. What would it take to drive the demons away? He rubbed his eyes, pressing his thumbs to his temple, easing the pain there. When he searched the dimness, again he distinguished shadows near his bed. One took shape. A breeze came through the open window—something long and white fluttered. He flung out an arm and encountered something soft and warm.

"Ben!" a soft voice cried in shock.

"Go away." His voice came out sharp, staccato and loud in the night. Like a gunshot. He lowered it to a rasp. "Get out."

Jessie whispered, "You're having a nightmare." She felt his hard fingers fasten on her arm, like manacles of steel.

"Who is it?" With a swift jerk, he pulled her into bed.

Landing on him, she felt winded. She placed a hand in the middle of his chest and pushed. It was like pushing a stone wall. Rigid with fear, she whispered urgently, "Let me go." His lips grazed the side of her throat. She tossed her head, seeking escape. Letting out a breath, she expelled it in a shocked gasp when he jerked her bodily against him. His hard naked length pushed against her. His hold was hurting, crushing, as if he wanted to absorb her. He was out of his head. She'd never felt so terrifyingly helpless. She couldn't tell where his breath ended and hers began. Each one hurt. Shallow, rapid bursts kept pace with her heart. She shook her head, unable to believe she'd been foolish enough to get caught in his nightmare.

Ben felt the brush of silken hair against his chest, like phantom fingers teasing him. He seized a fistful and held fast, urging her head down to meet his mouth. Pressing her mouth against his, he drank deeply. She opened when his tongue penetrated her lips and drove deep, exploring her mouth. When he released her on a long, drawn-out breath, his lips stroked down against the velvety smoothness of her throat. She tasted like honey, smooth and sweet, rolling smooth against his tongue.

"Isn't this what you came for?" he rasped against her skin.

"Ben," she pleaded, pushing ineffectually against his chest, denying him. Her body felt boneless, soft...

His teeth grazed her racing pulse. Releasing her arm, he swept his hand down her back, arching her to fit tightly against him. He eased her soft cry with another drugging kiss.

"Ben, it's me," she whispered. "It's me, Jessie."

He laughed softly, his laugh turning into a groan when her knee slipped between his. Her hip pressed against him, her thigh burned against his naked thigh. "I know very well it's you, Jessie." She fit him to perfection.

"You do?" Her voice trembled.

"Did you think I didn't?" he taunted, suspecting she was pretending confusion. She was Ira's daughter, all right—that sneaky, conniving cheat. If Jessie thought sacrificing herself was going to keep him here, she needed to be taught a lesson.

"You were dreaming. I thought you were asleep."

"Jessie, I'd have to be drunk out of my head not to know you." In the moonlight she glowed like a soft beacon, fixating his senses. His lips traced the narrow band of lace edging her gown and outlining the sweet, tantalizing curve of her breasts. Her skin felt dewy. Her cotton nightgown, not crisp but soft, was sprigged with blue flowers. How could he tell her how many times he'd imagined her like this, exactly like this? All he had to do was take her. Once and for all he would know her.

"You woke me," she whispered, drawing in a long breath that had her pressing her breasts against his chest.

Why on earth was she whispering?

Ira.

Ben groaned. Her father was under the same roof. That was all he needed—Ira hearing a commotion and running to the rescue.

"How did I wake you?" he asked suspiciously.

"You were calling out, shouting."

Ben closed his eyes. The nightmare.

"What's wrong?" She brushed a hand against his brow, all sweet concern for him now. "Are you ill?"

Ben came back to the present with an unpleasant thud. Her gentleness was oddly comforting. He could feel the uneven beat of her heart against his. The weight of her burned through him, exploding any hope of denial that he was aroused. And they said women were the weaker sex, he thought ironically, cursing his masculine enslavement to the senses. Through the soft fabric of her nightgown, he could feel every curve and hollow of her woman's body. He rolled onto his side and stared down at her moon-shadowed slimness within the curve of his arm. With her light-colored hair spread across his pillow and her eyes dark with unwilling arousal, she tempted him. His imagination had him losing himself in the depths of her kiss, the hollow of her throat, the swell of her breast, the damp heat of her femininity. She was the perfect panacea for the pain in his head. Clutching at some sense of control, he latched on to his conscience. He couldn't use this girl. His hold on her slackened by degrees.

He closed his eyes in agony. "If Ira catches you in here, there'll be hell to pay." Before he could change his mind, he released her. "Go, while you still can."

Ben bit back a bitter laugh when she left.

In the morning, he was awake when he heard a knock on his bedroom door. He wrenched it open and stared down at Jessie's ravaged face. He couldn't believe she would swallow her pride to face him again. Why? "Jessie," he said impatiently. "I don't have time for this now. I have to finish packing." He drew in a harsh breath when her lips trembled. "Don't do this."

He had to leave. For years, he'd been running from his past; now he was running from Jessie, from what she made him feel. If he stayed, he would have to face his demons, and he wasn't ready for that. He didn't know if he ever would be. Yet, he didn't want to hurt her. Jessie's eyes were shadowed with tension and fatigue.

"Let's make this a clean break," he said. "Last night, things got out of hand. Let's not beat it into the ground."

"But I..."

His mouth tightened. "Contrary to my behavior, I'm not interested in one-night stands or a quick easy lay!"

Already pale and drawn, she gasped, "Neither am I."

"That's all it could be for us. Jessie, I'm leaving!"

Recoiling as if he'd struck her, she shuddered. Then, as if fortifying herself for another blow, she said in a rush, "It's my father. He's had some sort of spell. It could be his heart. Please, will you help?" She turned, clearly expecting him to follow. For a moment, he couldn't move. Ben stood as if he'd been mortally shot. If only he could take the words back...

When Ben got downstairs, he found Ira in an irascible mood. Apparently, he'd fallen when he tried to get out of bed. He'd knocked over a bedside stand. Ben righted it and replaced a lamp and two books—a worn Bible and a *Farmer's Almanac.*

"I won't go to the hospital!" Clad in his striped blue-and-white pajamas, Ira shook off Jessie's hand.

"I called an ambulance. Dr. Peterson will be waiting."

"That old fool! What does he know? I'm feeling fine!"

"Then seeing him won't do any harm." Jessie slipped her arm around his shoulders. "You're overdue for a checkup anyway. Let's just get you back to bed." Ben moved to help.

"I just had a dizzy spell, that's all. Can't a man have a moment's peace?" Ira raged as Ben lifted him back into bed.

"Thank you," Jessie said, not meeting Ben's eyes.

"You can just go and cancel the ambulance," her father snarled.

Ben shook his head. "I don't think so."

"You're fired!"

Ben bit back a smile. "I already quit."

Jessie fluffed the pillows. "Dad, please. You're getting all riled up."

"Man's got a right to get riled." Ira leaned back wearily, closed his eyes and groped against the bed linens for Jessie's hand, clutching it until her fingers turned numb. "All this fuss over nothing!" His white hair stood in angry tufts.

Blinking back tears, Jessie smoothed it down. His hair had always been thick, curling naturally. When had it gone so thin? His pink scalp showed through, making him look frail. He'd always been so vain about his hair. "I love you, Dad."

He squeezed her hand tighter. "Don't go all weepy, Jessie, and tell Doc I'm not paying for his trip to Bermuda, neither."

"He's not going to Bermuda."

"That's what I just said."

By the time the ambulance arrived, he'd tired himself and didn't object too strongly when the medics lifted him inside.

"I'm going with him," she insisted.

"Jessie." Ben's voice made her turn back before she climbed into the waiting ambulance. He touched the side of her face, his eyes filled with remorse. "Jessie, I…"

Jessie tilted her chin away from his touch. His hand fell to his side. She turned away, her composure a brittle shell.

Everything that could be said had been said; whatever had briefly flared between them was over. What could he add but goodbye? A word she couldn't bear to hear. As the doors closed, she caught her last glimpse of Ben.

He would be gone before this day was out. Some part of her was glad—glad she needn't face him again. For the last time, he'd ground her pride to fragments. Instinctively she'd gone to him that morning, only to be rejected. Coolly detached, he hadn't given her a chance before pouring out his contempt. Even in her concern for her father, some long-buried part of her registered a deep hurt, a sense of loss. Instead of a fond farewell, their final words had been filled with hostility. Ben had rejected her without a sign of regret.

The ambulance siren wailed as they drove off.

Above the harsh, penetrating sound, her father's voice sounded weak to her ears. "Jess." They still had a long ride ahead of them. The nearest hospital was thirty miles away.

She reached for his hand. "Yes, Dad?"

"Jessie, about the farm…"

About the farm. Even now, her father's concern was the farm. "Don't worry, we'll manage." She didn't know how, but she would. Before Ben, she'd dealt with responsibility by not looking ahead too far. Just day to day.

Her father's sharp cry drew her attention. "Dad!"

Helpless, she watched his face turn gray with contortion. "Oh, please, please, help him."

A medic moved in to administer oxygen. Time stopped, seconds drew into minutes, stretched out in agonizing slowness. As her father struggled for air, Jessie held her breath until her ears rang.

At the hospital at last, the staff wheeled his stretcher into the emergency room. Shut out, she stared at the doors blindly. What if he didn't make it? She'd never felt so alone. If only Jared were here. If only…

With a hollow feeling, she rubbed her arms, looked around the waiting room, then found a seat. How had things gone so wrong? She thought of Jared again. According to her father, he'd just moved and changed jobs. Contacting him would be a nightmare.

Word of her father's illness traveled through the small community hospital. Someone brought coffee. Time passed.

Dr. Peterson came out. "Your dad's stable. We're keeping him sedated for now. He'll be more awake tomorrow."

She blinked back tears of gratitude. "Can I see him?"

"For a few minutes." His eyes offered understanding. "He's a tough old bird. He'll make it."

Jessie clung to those words. For the first time in her memory, her father didn't look tough at all. Surrounded by tubes and equipment, he'd shrunk. Her time was over so quickly. Feeling numb, she returned to the waiting room. She felt Ben's presence before she saw him or heard him speak.

He came forward out of the shadows of the long, dimly lit room, his voice a soothing rumble, "Jessie, how's Ira?"

She stared at him numbly. "You're still here."

"Did you really think I'd leave you to cope alone?"

"Yes." The word stood stark and alone. She had nothing to add to it. Yes, she'd thought he would leave her. How could she have thought anything else?

He stared at her for a long moment. "Well, you were wrong."

With his betrayal still fresh in her mind, she couldn't respond. Perhaps later when she'd had time to think about it.

But for now, Dr. Peterson had waited to speak to her. "There's nothing you can do tonight. Go home, get some rest." He nodded at Ben. "You be sure and look after her."

Jessie didn't stay to hear Ben's response. Suddenly she needed to escape. When she stepped out of the hospital, she was surprised to discover it was dark. Ben had parked the truck in the hospital parking lot.

He caught up to her. "Have you had anything to eat?"

She walked briskly. "I had something earlier."

"How much earlier?"

"This morning," she admitted, too weary to make any attempt at conversation.

"I would have come earlier, but I..."

She shook her head. "It doesn't matter."

"It does matter." He grabbed her arm and pulled her around to face him. "I didn't realize your father had had a heart attack until I called the hospital around midday for news. I thought you would call if it was anything serious. Why didn't you call me?"

She blinked in confusion. "I thought you were gone."

He winced with visible regret. "I guess I deserve that. I called for reports every hour after that."

"Did you?" She couldn't bear his pity.

He gritted his teeth. "Yes." Slowly, he released her. "I wasn't sure you wanted me to come."

She felt cold, alone. "I'd like to go home."

His face closed. "After we grab something to eat."

She didn't argue. If feeding her soothed his conscience, that was fine. She simply didn't care. When had caring gotten her what she wanted? They stopped at a diner. She had no idea what she ate but lingered over coffee. She dreaded going home.

After the third refill, Ben took over. "You've had enough." He took her cup away and signaled the waitress for the check.

Unaccustomed to being looked after, Jessie bit back a sharp retort. She stared out the window, wondering why her life couldn't be simpler. If it weren't for her father's illness, Ben would be gone, miles away by now, out of her life. A clean break, he'd said. This was a tangled mess. Enduring more of his presence when it was only temporary seemed a cruel twist of fate.

"Time to go home," he said, standing.

Jessie stood. She had no idea how she would manage to keep up some sort of mental or emotional distance until Ben left.

The long drive was accomplished in silence.

At the house, Jessie walked into the familiar country kitchen and felt as if she'd landed on the moon. Without her father's solid presence, it was just a room, four walls. She adjusted his wooden armchair at the head of the table. "He's going to need his things." Needing something solid to cling to, she smoothed her hands over the wood. "He has some fairly new pajamas and slippers, but he could use a new bathrobe. He's never owned one." Ben's compassionate expression made her rush on. "He's going to hate hospital food." She turned toward the pantry instead of rushing into his arms. "I could make him something light and special. Some maple custard, or..."

"Jessie, he's going to make it. Your dad's a fighter."

At Ben's gentleness, she blinked back tears. "Is he? But what if he's too worn-out to fight?" Everyone kept saying Ira Carlisle was a fighter, but she'd seen beneath her father's hardness years ago; she'd seen a lost and lonely man.

Ben crossed the room. "Ira's too mean and ornery to let Doc Peterson get the best of him."

She gulped. It was all too much. He reached for her. She struggled, then fell against him, letting her emotion pour out. Ben held her and let her cry, his voice soothing, his hands tender yet firm as he smoothed her hair off her face. Jessie couldn't recall the last time someone had simply held her and let her cry. When she felt the brush of his lips against her temple, she wanted to stay in his arms forever. Trembling, she forced herself to pull away.

Ben felt her stiffen and draw back, withholding her feelings with an inner strength he might have admired at any other time. Now it left him feeling helpless. And alone, as he'd never felt before. When she looked at him unseeingly, he felt as if a knife had pierced his heart. He'd lost the fragile gift of Jessie's trust—something he hadn't known he valued until it was gone.

He'd hurt her, instead of protecting her from more hurt by leaving before their relationship developed into something more. Well, he didn't have to worry about that any longer.

She hated him.

She would probably hate him more by the time he left.

Pale, her eyes red-rimmed, she said, "I'm going to bed."

"Good night, Jessie." With a bleak smile, he realized how cold it felt to be shut out of her thoughts. After she'd gone upstairs, Ben took his time, turning off lights and locking doors, before he climbed the stairs. He hoped to avoid another encounter, but she was just coming out of the bathroom.

Dressed in a terry-cloth robe and slippers, with her face scrubbed, she looked so innocent and young. But not naive. From her taut expression, he knew she was aware of their isolation. Their situation was undeniably intimate. No matter what he said or did, the previous night and its stolen intimacies stood between them. He'd gotten past her defenses. He'd come close to making love to her. If only he could rearrange recent events, undo the harm. He shouldn't have dragged her into his bed.

Why had he looked past the sweet innocence of her eyes and her delicate curves? He'd seen a woman, and he'd kissed her. Now that he knew the taste of her, he wouldn't be happy until he'd tasted her again. And yet, he was bound by honor to protect her from himself. "If you need anything..." His hand lifted, then fell.

"Thanks," she whispered. "There's nothing you can do."

Anything he said would be meaningless. She wouldn't ask for his help now. Jessie wasn't the clinging type. He should have felt relieved. Somehow, he didn't. Instead, he felt trapped in a silken web. She needed him. Between Cal's accident, Ira's heart attack and Jared's absence, Jessie needed him.

Somehow, that didn't feel so bad. It felt right—which scared the hell out of him.

That night Ben lay in his bed and traced the cracks in the ceiling until sleep came. And with it, the nightmare. Now Jessie was part of it—a pale shadow drawing near; then drifting away; pulling him back from the brink....

Jessie felt better in the morning, more herself. Ben was making coffee. His greeting, "Morning, Jess," didn't sting. She was back to being plain old Jess. Determined not to rely on his charity, she braced herself. He looked as if he hadn't slept.

All she needed was a moody male before her morning cup of coffee. "I called the hospital. Dad's condition is improved."

"That's good news."

"Yes, it is." She reached past him for the loaf of bread on the counter. "I'll make toast."

"Sit," he ordered, taking the loaf out of her hands.

Now he had her confused with the dog! While she sat and watched, he made toast and served up his version of scrambled eggs. His kindness didn't surprise her. She was grateful. That was all. After swallowing a bite of rubbery eggs with a gulp of coffee, she spoke the words aloud. "Thanks for staying an extra day." She watched his gaze harden. His eyes were blue and fathomless. "I know you want to get an early start."

He carefully set down his coffee mug. "Do I?"

His look made her hasten to add, "If you're wondering

how we'll manage without you, then don't. We'll be fine. We got along fine before, before…'' She couldn't bring herself to say before he came, but went on with her little farewell speech. ''Anyway, Fred can put in extra hours. You mentioned Ramon, and Jared will turn up eventually. Besides, Cal will be back on his feet before too long.''

''That's enough, Jessie.'' Cutting her off, he rose to his feet. ''I get the message,'' he rasped gently. The soft words grated against her nerves.

She wanted him to shout—so she could shout back. Why was he being so reasonable? Why was she being so polite? ''I know your bags are all packed.''

''But I'm not going anywhere.'' He turned and strode out, tossing the words over his shoulder. ''I'll be around if you need me for anything.'' He'd be around. For how long?

Jessie sat there and watched his retreating back. It would be a cold day in hell before she needed him! Ben had taught her a hard but necessary lesson. She'd be a fool to depend on him for anything. At the moment, she had enough to handle without adding a case of heartache.

She wanted to run from her feelings, from Ben, but couldn't. She had responsibilities. If she needed reminding, a glance at the Mason jar filled with crisp dollar bills was surely enough to firm her resolve. It was just one of the obstacles Ben had placed between them. If their relationship remained strained and distant, so much the better.

Later that morning, Jessie drove to the hospital for a short visit with her father—all she was allowed. A look of relief flashed in his eyes when she told him Ben was staying on.

''Least he could do,'' he groused, then closed his eyes. At this display of weakness, she felt a rush of concern.

Dr. Peterson walked into the room. ''Ah, Jessie, just who I wanted to see. Let's step outside.''

Jessie prepared herself for more bad news. "How is he?"

"He's going to recover, but not overnight. The next few days are crucial. We're doing more tests." That sounded less than reassuring to Jessie. "He might need surgery. We'll see."

Driving home, she mulled over her mounting problems. The list was growing. She hadn't had much luck reaching her brother. He was out of town, his landlady would try to send him a message through friends. It struck Jessie that she knew practically nothing about her brother's life. At one time, they'd been close. That was how relationships went, she reminded herself hardily. People in her life came and went—sometimes with the speed of a quick-change artist. Like Ben.

Admittedly, he was high on her list of problems.

When she reached the turnoff to Stone's End, a large flock of black crows suddenly lifted off a cornfield and flew directly in the path of her truck. Jessie hit the brakes. Like a dark shadow blotting the sun, they filled her vision. More than a hundred beating wings drowned out all sound, everything but the thud of her own heartbeat. Her hands gripped the steering wheel until her knuckles turned white. Though not superstitious, she couldn't shake a feeling of dread, a premonition of death or disaster. She tried to dismiss the irrational thought, blaming her unease on nerves and fatigue since her father's illness.

As the large flock of black crows flew in widening circles and the sky turned blue again, she breathed a sigh of relief, feeling a little foolish. Nevertheless, she drove the rest of the way home at a slower speed.

Somehow the day passed. Jessie couldn't settle to any one chore. That evening, she applied lip gloss to her mouth and frowned at her reflection in the mirror. She was getting a permanent frown line. She'd just showered and changed to visit her father. She looked tired and strained. Perhaps a brighter lipstick and some blush...

She'd missed not having a mother's guidance through the awkward teenage years. Now she worried about makeup at an age when most women felt confident about such things. With a shrug, she decided that wearing none was better than wearing too much. Was this preoccupation with her appearance connected to Ben? The mirror reflected an average appearance. Nothing unsightly, but nothing special, either. Certainly, nothing for a man to get excited about. What did she hope to see? A woman Ben wouldn't toss out of his bed?

With an impatient shake of her head, she went downstairs and came to a stop. Ben was waiting for her. His gaze slid up and down, making her conscious of her not-so-new denim wraparound skirt and plain tailored shirt.

He spoke firmly. "I have to discuss a couple things with Ira. We might as well visit him together, then eat out. You could use a break, Jessie. And frankly, so could I."

Relieved of her options, she glared at him. The only break she needed was from him. "I could fix something here."

"Just this once, how about humoring me? I'm tired of watching you wear yourself out trying to be some kind of a super woman."

"I don't know what you mean," Jessie said frigidly.

"If this cool little act is intended as a guilt trip for my bad timing in quitting my job the day Ira took sick, think again. Or is it because I had the nerve to drag you into my bed? Was I the first to try?" When she gasped, his voice hardened. "I didn't get very far, did I? Is that it? Are you angry because I *didn't* make love to you? Did you want me to?"

"You, you..." She'd buried her anger under layers of

reserve. Yes, he'd hurt her when he'd wanted to leave. His dragging it out grew more unbearable by the hour.

"Bastard?" Ben said helpfully. "Don't stop now. Don't you think I've called myself every name in the book?"

"I'm sure I could add one or two." Her only defense was to strike back. Unfortunately, she couldn't actually think of a name—one that would describe how she felt, not without revealing herself. Try "faithless lover" for one. He'd never been her lover, but he'd touched her heart, he'd touched her intimately; he'd made her his in every way but physically.

"I imagine you could." He ran a frustrated hand through his hair. "Don't you think I regret that night? And the following morning? I said some things I didn't mean. I let you down."

"Yes, well…" She swallowed painfully.

"I won't let you down again, Jessie."

That brought her gaze flying back to his. She searched his eyes in confusion. Could she believe him? Could she risk laying herself open for more heartbreak?

"Well, Jessie?" he prompted when her silence dragged.

"All right," she said simply.

His laugh was harsh. "What does that mean?"

"It means," she said in a stiff little voice, "that I accept your apology and your invitation to eat out."

At her deliberately evasive answer, his eyes darkened as he snapped, "Right. Now, can we go?"

She walked past him and out the front door. Standing on the porch, a feeling of impotence washed over her. Only Ben could make her feel this way, as if she was fighting herself. Her anger burned out, she closed her eyes. What was she doing? He'd worked hard all day. He'd apologized—even if he'd goaded her into a reaction first. He'd stayed.

Clouds swept by. A breeze cooled the heat of her face.

Suddenly she didn't care about their differences. She couldn't endure another second of this constant tension between them.

"I'm sorry," she whispered, swallowing her pride.

For her sins, she'd inherited the Carlisle pride. What good was pride when he would soon be gone? When he didn't say anything, she turned around. He wasn't there. He hadn't heard.

Chapter Nine

Jessie heard the back door close with a bang. A moment later, the truck started with a crash of gears. The motor revved—Ben was waiting for her, despite their argument. She breathed a sigh of relief. He was angry, for which she was partly to blame. He'd tried to smooth things over; he'd even let her vent all her resentment. She'd finally worked herself up to an apology, and he hadn't stayed around to listen.

At the hospital, Jessie found her father asleep, his face a battle-weary gray. His years showed in the deep, troubled lines, the frown he wore in sleep. She'd never seen him this low. She swayed, suddenly fearful for his recovery. Ben entered the room directly behind her. When he placed a comforting hand on her shoulder, she felt a ripple of shock to her senses, followed by an unfamiliar sense of comfort that was more than mere solace.

Instinctively, she leaned back, seeking his strength.

Ben's hand tightened when Ira's eyes opened. He saw the old man's reaction—the slow blink of surprise, followed by fatherly disapproval. "Hello, Ira. How are you feeling?"

Fully alert now, Ira raked his daughter and Ben with a look of suspicion. "I've been better."

Admiring Ira's undaunted spirit, Ben let his hand fall and stepped back. He wasn't about to tangle with Ira Carlisle over possession of his daughter. Ira's expression eased.

Conversation was stilted after that. Keeping his input to a minimum, Ben realized father and daughter had never shared a real conversation in all the time he'd been with them.

The nurse popped her head around the door. "Time's up."

Looking exhausted, Ira suffered Jessie kissing him on the cheek with a gruff, "Don't get all mushy, girl." He glanced over her head at Ben. "Don't go writing me off just yet."

"I won't." Ben accepted the challenge. Escorting Jessie from the room, he felt angry for her sake. What would it hurt Ira to be kind to his daughter?

When they reached the hospital exit, Ben held the door open and followed her out. "How about grabbing a bite at the diner?"

"You look as if you're planning to take a bite out of me," she said. "Are you still annoyed with me?"

"I'm not annoyed," he snapped. She raised a disbelieving eyebrow. "It's not you." Ben stared down the nearly deserted street, then met her gaze. "Let's not argue about your father."

"All right." Jessie felt his tension. Had her father picked up on it? It wouldn't be long before he realized things weren't running smoothly at Stone's End.

In silent agreement, they walked to the nearby diner. Though medium height, she felt small next to Ben. At a crosswalk, he took her elbow. When his hand slipped down to hers, she felt aware, as if he'd claimed her. Claimed a piece of her, a piece of her heart.

The waitress greeted them. "Back again, I see." She chuckled. "I've got your table."

Jessie felt a bubble of laughter rise within her chest. Next, they'd be playing "their" song. They took their seats.

Ben picked up the menu. "The stuffed flounder looks good. What do you think?"

His mundane comment brought her down with bump. "That sounds good." Clenching her hands, she dropped them into her lap when Ben caught the small movement. "Ben, I..."

She stopped when the waitress returned to take their order.

That accomplished, Ben asked, "You were saying?" His expression wasn't inviting. The moment for an apology was lost.

She shrugged. "Nothing. It's not important."

The stuffed flounder was delicious. Jessie refused dessert, but had coffee while Ben devoured a wedge of chocolate-cream pie. Sweets were his one weakness. It made him seem human, and vulnerable. Suddenly she blurted, "I'd like to apologize."

He looked wary. "For what?"

"For making things awkward when they don't have to be."

"Don't they?" he asked quietly.

She sighed. "You're not making this very easy."

"I'm not sure what you're driving at."

So, he wanted it in black and white. "I appreciate all you're doing. If I've made things harder, I'm sorry."

His eyes flickered over her, making her feel small and weak—with longing. "You have nothing to apologize for. Truce?"

He extended his hand in a symbolic handshake. His fingers curled around hers. Unable to deny her response to him, she felt like a moth drawn to a flame. She wanted to love him. It was that simple, and that complex. With an indication of mutual involvement and encouragement, she would give herself without shame or regret. If only he wanted her for the same reasons. But he didn't. The knowledge froze her heart.

"We were friends," he said. "Shall we try again?"

It was such a pale imitation of what she wanted. Could a man and a woman be just friends? Could she and Ben? Not by her definition. A friend wouldn't make her mouth go dry and her pulse quicken at a glance. A friend wouldn't have her mind at war with her body. And her heart? She could only hope Ben would leave soon, before he broke her heart.

"Jessie?" he murmured.

Despite all the sound mental advice, when his thumb ran over the back of her hand in a soft fleeting caress, her will to resist started to crumble. "Yes," she whispered.

They got home before eight. Even for country hours, it was too early to go to bed. Jessie made some excuse and disappeared inside. Ben stayed outside on the porch.

The languid day's heat had cooled; the hills were dusk-shadowed and sleepy looking. He felt tense. At a movement by the door, he looked up and knew exactly what—correction, *who*—was troubling him. It wasn't the weather.

"I just wanted to thank you for dinner," Jessie said softly from the screen door. The lamplit room behind clearly outlined her delicate curves. Her softness was so inviting.

"You're welcome," he said. It seemed they'd used up

all their polite conversation at the restaurant. What could he say to put her at ease that wouldn't add heat to another sort of tension? He was relieved when Fred's old pickup turned into the driveway. Fred and his wife, Hazel, got out.

Fred called out a cheerful, "Thought we'd just stop by for a neighborly visit."

Ben smiled wryly when Jessie turned to them with an obvious sense of deliverance. "I was going to make coffee."

Hazel climbed the porch stairs. She was a solid woman, as solid as the earth. Her eyes were kind, and Ben was glad that she was there for Jessie. "We're praying for Ira." She squeezed Jessie's hand. "And for you, dear. I know it's hard."

Grateful for Hazel's concern, Jessie worried that things were going to get harder. She had no idea what she would do when Ben actually left. While the men played chess, the women chatted. At one point, Jessie glanced across the parlor at Ben. He caught her looking at him. He smiled wryly. They were being chaperoned. The small private exchange made her feel connected to Ben. The realization filled her with dismay.

She was so unbearably aware of him—every gesture, every spoken word, every lift of his brow. Cradling a carved chess piece, he looked outwardly relaxed—like a lone wolf lying low, waiting to spring an attack. His thumb lazily smoothed over the marble piece, a queen, as he appeared to contemplate his next move. Jessie could imagine the cold marble warming to his touch, just as she had. His hands were lean, long-fingered and tanned; strong, yet gentle when he'd stroked her. He'd awakened strange new sensations that somehow seemed familiar.

It was odd, but at times she could read his thoughts, as if he'd awakened some dormant instinct in her, some feminine impulse that somehow linked her to him. She couldn't control it; she might as well stop the tide or shout at the full moon to stop shining.

Jessie flushed when his gaze snagged hers, suddenly wondering if he could read her thoughts. She sprang to her feet. When everyone looked at her in surprise, she said, "How about coffee? There's cake."

She took her time performing the mundane act to restore her composure. When she returned with a coffee-and-dessert tray, she found Drew had stopped by. "Just being neighborly," he said.

My, my, so much attention, Jessie thought, feeling a sense of unreality. Since when had events at Stone's End become such a center of interest? She could see the speculation in Drew's eyes as he looked from her to Ben.

"I'm sorry about Ira." Drew took her hand before she could object. "If there's anything I can do, just ask."

"Thank you. I appreciate the offer." She pulled her hand away. Obviously, she'd become a challenge to Drew. Her resistance only added interest to his pursuit. "How's Cal?"

Drew smiled. "Bored out of his mind." He left soon after, having extracted a promise to call if she needed anything.

At her words, Ben's expression darkened. After Drew drove off, he observed dryly, "If you didn't encourage him to drop in whenever he pleases, he'd give up."

Jessie flushed. "I do not encourage him."

His eyes glinted with irritation. "Don't we have enough problems without Drew having free run of the place?"

"What are you saying?"

"I don't trust him," Ben said flatly. "Who do you think is responsible for all the 'accidents' around the place?"

"Do you have any actual proof he's done anything?"

"Are you defending him?"

"No." She sighed. Was she avoiding the issue?

Ben looked away without giving her a chance to explain. Fred and Hazel said nothing. They left about ten. Jessie walked out to their car to see them off. Hazel climbed in.

Fred shook his head. "Heck, I don't know why you're mad at Ben, or Drew, for that matter. Seems to me there's only one reason a man interferes between a woman and another man."

Jessie fell for it. "What's that?"

"'Cause he's cutting her out of the herd."

She laughed. "Thanks a lot."

"Well, you asked." He took a moment to contemplate her with a wizened expression. His face bore more laugh lines than frown lines. "It's male instinct. You ever watch old Homer when he sets his heart on a fresh young heifer...?"

"Fred!"

He tried to look innocent. "Well, it's only nature taking its course. Homer, well, he's pretty good at doing what comes naturally. On the other hand, Beauregard doesn't appear to have a clue. Now, Ben here..."

"Stop." Red-faced, she placed both hands over her ears. She couldn't prevent a smile at his comparing Drew and Ben to the moose and the bull—only which was which?

"Well, you sleep on it. Sooner or later, you're going to have to choose." Fred climbed in and drove off.

How could she choose what wasn't offered?

Jessie strolled back to the house, in no hurry to go inside just yet. She felt keyed up, as if waiting for the eye of a storm to pass over. At a movement in the shrubbery, she caught her breath in alarm, but it was only Beauregard.

The large, ungainly moose delicately nibbled at her hydrangea bush. She warned him, "Scat," and chuckled when he actually did. She shook her head, amused when he made it only as far as the next bush. Still smiling, she approached the porch.

Ben was there. A shiver ran over her as she realized he'd been watching her. She felt exposed, as if each raw nerve lay bare. In the moonlight, he could most likely see her expression as clearly as she could read his. The moon was bright, and the night was soft and slow. It reached out to her.

With his back against a porch column, Ben sat on the rail. "Care to share the joke?"

She sat on one of the steps, then realized she'd practically planted herself at his feet. "Nothing, really—just Beauregard up to his usual late-night snacking." Her gaze fell on the rosebush he'd planted for her. It seemed so long ago. Although she'd neglected to water and nourish it lately, it flourished—its thick leaves and pale delicate rosebuds just ready to open.

Ben smiled down at her. "Fred tells me Beau's been mooning after a shy young heifer all week."

"That sounds like Fred." She laughed, then stopped when she felt his eyes heavy on her. "I could make more coffee."

Ben hesitated. "Jessie, this is not a good idea." He kept the harshness out of his voice. Did she have any idea what she was doing to him?

"I just wanted to..."

"I know." His gaze took in the trembling mouth. "Don't make this difficult."

Fire sparked in her eyes. She lifted her chin. "I wasn't offering more than coffee."

"Weren't you?" The words vibrated between them.

"No," she whispered across the dividing space.

"And what if I asked? Would you let me into your bed?"

She threw him a fathomless look that had him wanting

to grab her and drag her to bed, or turn tail and run. He drew in a breath and did neither. She spoke softly. "But you won't ask."

Her voice drifted over him, tempting him to forget all his reasons for not taking what the fates so generously offered. A night of love—something he hadn't had in so long it didn't bear thinking about. But there was still Ira. And honor.

Somehow he found the strength to resist. "No, I won't." When she started to withdraw, he should have left it at that. "It would be a mistake. I might be tempted to take advantage of Ira's absence tonight, but I like you too much to hurt you."

"Are you so sure I'd let you?"

Smiling wryly, he shook his head. "I refuse to answer that. Let's just say you bother me and leave it at that."

"I bother you?" Her words held skepticism.

He watched her smile start in her eyes. He'd noticed that before; now it meant more. Her smiles meant more—he counted each one, storing memories for when he was gone. In his life, no woman had ever made a lasting impression. Jessie Carlisle would.

He observed as her eyes rounded in amazement. Hadn't anyone ever told her she was perfectly delightful and unspoiled? Strong and independent, gentle and vulnerable, she was a special lady. He envied the man who would someday convince her. He envied the man who would teach Jessie how to love.

"You deserve someone who will love you like crazy," he found the strength to say. "Don't settle for less."

She stood abruptly. "But not you?"

His mouth tightened. "Not me."

Jessie absorbed the words. How many times could he hurt her? Once again, he'd warned her off effectively. He'd once accused her of attempting to keep him here. If her life depended on it, she would never give him the ammunition to level that accusation again. When it was time, she would let him go. He'd never been hers, after all.

"I know, just friends." She had to get away from him, away from temptation. "Well, I'm going to—"

"There's only one problem," he said huskily. Without warning, he drew her up to his lounging position on the rail. She was helpless against him. Their shoulders knit together. He bent his head and took her mouth, kissing her deeply until she opened to his invasion. With the tips of his fingers, he stroked her shoulders and throat. Easing undone the buttons on her shirt, his thumb slipped inside and grazed her breast.

The results were devastating, carving inroads into her self-control. How could she resist the sweet rush of desire? His groan revealed he was having difficulty reining in his own hunger for her. Silently she let her mouth speak, kissing him back with an eager response that must have betrayed her deep longing.

"Ben," she whispered. When she clutched his shirt and collapsed weakly against him, he released her.

The abruptness shocked her, as did his hard expression when he raised his head and drew in a ragged breath to speak. "I still want you, Jessie. That hasn't changed."

"I thought we'd agreed—"

"I never agreed to a damn thing. I'd be a liar if I did." The scar on his face looked stark white against the dark tan of his brow. "Just so there won't be any more misunderstandings, let's agree to stay out of each other's way, or else. At least, until your brother comes home."

Silenced, she simply stared back. How could she have forgotten for even a minute? He was itching to leave. Forget her dreams—she would cling to sanity. How could she depend on a man who kept his possessions in a saddlebag, and his motorcycle tanked up and aimed for the open road?

* * *

Ben wasn't at breakfast.

Jessie was relieved. She wasn't prepared to face him after his ultimatum—she was to stay out of his way, or else... Or else what? The thought tantalized her.

Fred came looking for Ben. "The work crew never turned up. With rain coming, we need to start that corner field."

"I'll look into it." Jessie reached for the phone.

Drew answered on the second ring. "Jessie, hello."

At the smug smile in his voice, she took a breath. "I think there's been a mistake. We're expecting a crew."

"No mistake," he said. "Why don't we talk about it? I'm at the camp store. I'll be expecting you." The line went dead.

Jessie stared at the receiver. He'd hung up!

Without taking a moment to consider, she drove to the Pierces'. Their farm boasted new barns and a gracious brick farmhouse. A mile farther, the migrants' camp was another world. Gray buildings with tin roofs and small windows. Some windows were broken, she noted with concern. Although it was August, nights turned cold. Several children played on an old swing set. There was no grass, just dirt—dirt everywhere. Jessie recognized Ramon's son, Miguel. When he waved, she waved back.

A small grocery store and gas station serviced the tenants. When she pulled into the parking lot, Drew opened her car door. "That was fast," he said. "My mother's expecting us for lunch."

"This isn't a social call. We can talk right here."

He shook his head, his smile amused yet determined. "Jess, Jess, why make this more difficult? I'm beginning to think I missed something all these years. You're a lot more entertaining than I expected. But the game's up."

"This isn't a game," she snapped, infuriated at his baiting.

"All right, let's talk about us."

"There is no us," she said. "If you think withholding the workers will change things, you're out of your mind."

"Now, Jess." He reached for her hand. When she tried to shake him off, his fingers cut into her wrist. "You're just playing hard to get. You know we both want the same thing."

"And what's that?"

His face hardened. "Stone's End," he said bluntly.

"Is that all? Then why not just make an offer to buy it?"

"Your father refused, remember? If you'll just stop fighting me, we can work things out. Why don't we start with the summer help? Maybe I'll cooperate, if you ask me nice."

She gritted her teeth. "Will you send the crew back?"

His smile widened. "No."

The heat of anger burned her face. "What do you want?"

"Must I spell it out? Stone's End was all I wanted at first. Now I want you, along with your farm." When she sputtered one of Fred's favorite barnyard words, he chuckled. "We'll date, all proper and respectable-like. That should please the parents."

"Surely you wouldn't marry me just to satisfy your father!"

"Why not? My father wants me to toe the line. And marriage is very much on his agenda. If it doesn't work out, so what? What have we got to lose? You're not holding out for some idiotic idea of falling in love, are you? And who knows, maybe we can arrange for that, too."

Fall in love with Drew Pierce? Never! Too furious to speak, she climbed into the truck and started the motor.

When he held on to the door, she simply put the truck in Reverse and hit the gas.

"You damn little fool!" Drew yelled. He didn't look amused when he had to let go or risk being dragged. He was still swearing when she drove away.

By the entry, a group of men had gathered. They parted to let her pass through. When Jessie saw Ramon among them, she pulled the truck over. He separated himself from the group and walked toward her. "What's wrong?" she asked.

He clenched his fists. "Drew wouldn't let us work. We're losing a day's pay."

"I'm sorry." Jessie hated feeling so helpless.

"One day, the Pierces will go too far," Ramon said, his resentment of the system evident.

Jessie glanced around the run-down camp, the children playing in the dirt where there was no green grass, no hope. In addition to her own problems, she couldn't run from the plight of the migrants. "I'll do what I can," she promised.

Debating her choices, Jessie drove home. The road bordered rich, cultivated fields. Long, neat rows of deep green plants stretched as far as she could see; they represented time and money invested. Without a high return this year, her father would go bankrupt. She knew it would kill him. They needed the workers; the workers needed them. Only Drew stood in the way.

Three black crows sat on the fence as she got home. Two flew away when she turned into the driveway. But one remained. It cocked its sleek black head and peered at her with soulless, glassy eyes. Jessie controlled a shudder and went inside. No one was home. Ben hadn't come back from town. How could he solve her problems? He wasn't even there. Apparently he'd taken his own warning—to stay out of her way—seriously. For how long? Would he come back? Had she driven him away?

Resisting the urge to check if his gear was still in his room, she waited on the porch for half an hour. Slowly, her anger drained. Ben wasn't there. How could she believe in a man who had no intention of sticking around? Before she could change her mind, she went inside and dialed Drew's phone number. He answered on the fourth ring. "Drew, about that date—"

"I'll pick you up at seven," he said, just as abruptly.

At six-forty-five that evening, there was a knock at Jessie's bedroom door. "Yes," she called out. "What is it?" To her horror, the doorknob turned. The door opened and Ben walked in. With a stifled gasp, she reached for her dress. Wearing only a half-slip, she clutched the thin fabric to her front, which still left far too much bare flesh exposed for her peace of mind. For Ben's as well, apparently. He looked as shocked as she felt.

Her mouth went dry. "You shouldn't be in here."

His eyes darkened at her seminudity. She felt a blush steal up from her breasts. As his gaze roamed over her bare shoulders, she felt her nipples peak in response, as if his eyes could penetrate the cloth barrier.

When he spoke, she shivered at the lack of warmth in his voice. "You got a phone call. Your date will be late. Is this a mystery date? Or can I have a few details?"

She gulped. "Like what?"

"Like, who are you going out with?"

"You're not my father!"

He braced his hand against the door. "What's going on?"

"If you'll excuse me, I have to get ready." She took a step forward to show him the door, then realized she was in a more precarious position and one step closer to Ben. "Drew will be here in a few minutes."

"Drew? You're actually going out with him?"

"Yes, I am. He'll be here any moment."

His mouth tightened. "I thought you had better taste."

She set her chin at an angle. "I know you don't like him."

"I don't have to like him. It might help if you did. But then, perhaps I missed something." His eyes flickered over her. "As a matter of curiosity, tell me—are you going to close your eyes and think of Stone's End when he crawls into your bed?"

Tears of shame welled in her eyes. While she struggled for words, he said, "Of course, I'm assuming you intend to populate Henderson with lots of little Drews—or should I say 'pollute'?"

"Why should it matter to you?" she asked, too shocked at the moment to feel insulted by his deliberate crudeness. She hated hard words, especially between her and Ben. She wanted...she wanted to love him. But he didn't want that.

What *did* he want?

He took a step, then stopped just as abruptly when she retreated. Out of the corner of her eye, she caught her reflection in the mirror over the dresser. She closed her eyes, as if she could blank out the entire scene. He had had a full view of her naked back—from the moment he'd walked into her room.

Opening her eyes wide to find him still there, still large and male and dominating her bedroom, she pressed her back against the nearest wall. "Please, just get out."

To her dismay, he didn't leave. "Jessie, I hate to see anything wasted. You're intelligent, independent. And let's face it, only a silly little fool would tie herself to the likes

of Drew Pierce. I know you're ambitious for Stone's
End...."

She couldn't bear his harsh judgment. In self-defense,
she objected, "It's easy for you to judge, but I have to
continue living here after you're gone." Feeling torn by
divided loyalties, she raised her hand and swept her tumbled hair from her face. "No matter how I wish things
were different..."

Ben fastened his gaze on her inner wrist, then crossed
the room and reached for her hand, turning it to expose
the dark bruise marring her smooth wrist. He sucked in a
harsh breath as he inhaled the scent of her lemon shampoo.
At his suppressed oath, she looked down at their joined
hands.

Ben knew the moment he touched her he'd committed
a tactical error, but he couldn't seem to stop. Instead, he
compounded it by cupping the side of her cheek and turning her face up to him. The fabric of her dress caught
between them slipped. He captured an enticing glimpse of
shadowed cleft between delicately rounded breasts and
knew one tug would remove the frail barrier; one seductive
press of his lips against the vulnerable curve of her throat
where it joined her shoulder would turn her into his arms.

Trying to control his response, he demanded, "Did
Drew do this?" His voice was husky with restraint.

Her hand shook as she tried to pull away; he refused to
release her. "Yes, but it's nothing."

Ben stared into her eyes and vowed, "He won't touch
you again." Shocked at his own anger, he gently smoothed
his thumb over the dark blemish marring the delicate
veined smoothness of her inner wrist and felt her shudder.

"Please," she pleaded with drowned eyes. "Will you
leave?"

He went.

Chapter Ten

Ben closed her bedroom door and leaned back against it. He should have walked out at the first sight of Jessie's partial undress. But he hadn't. Looking feminine and vulnerable with her back bared—a long, smooth, unblemished, tanned expanse unbroken by swimsuit marks—she'd captivated him. She'd felt something; he'd seen it in her eyes. She was vulnerable.

If he took advantage, he would be no better than Drew Pierce. Walking out and leaving her untouched had to be one of the most difficult things he'd ever done. He was honor-bound to protect Jessie. How else could he face Ira? The man was practically on his deathbed! Despite everything, Ben felt a reluctant affection for Jessie's difficult father. What a damnable situation!

Ben headed downstairs and made coffee. With his hands occupied and his temper cooled, he tried to think logically. He tried. But one fact kept getting in the way—Jessie had agreed to date Drew. Drew Pierce, of all people! Just the thought of it burned a hole in his gut. For the first time, he felt possessive about a woman. He had no right to feel that way about Jessie; he knew that. Against every intelligent reason, he'd let her creep under his skin.

Under his skin? He slammed a mug on the counter. Hell! With her shy come-hither smiles and rainwater eyes, she'd undermined his common sense and crept into a small corner of his heart. And what about Jessie's heart? Did she have one? Had Ira's Scottish tightfistedness affected her, too?

Ben knew the farm was in debt. Aligning herself with Drew Pierce would put an end to all Jessie's financial woes. She alone could save Stone's End, or so she obviously thought. In addition, Ben knew how much earning Ira's love meant to Jessie. How much would Jessie sacrifice? Herself? Somehow he couldn't believe she was mercenary and cold-blooded enough to marry Drew.

But he couldn't be sure—not about Jessie. With all that stoic Yankee pride, she kept joy, sorrow and pain to herself. Maybe she preferred a cold bargain. And maybe he should get the hell out of Stone's End while three-quarters of his heart still remained intact.

Fifteen minutes later, she joined him.

Ben glowered at the thin peach-colored fabric of her sundress. Her shoulders were bare, tanned to a golden color. She looked young, healthy, vibrant, ripe for the picking.

"All this for Drew Pierce?" He failed to keep an edge out of his voice.

She clenched her hands. "It's just a date."

"One date leads to two, then what? Do you think Drew will act the gentleman and drop you off at the door with a friendly peck? More than likely, he'll be all over you like a rash."

She swallowed a hard laugh. "That's not funny."

"He's not going to keep his hands off you."

"Unlike you," she blurted, then flushed.

He laughed shortly. "Am I supposed to feel jealous?"

"At least I know Drew's intentions are honorable."

"Is that what all this is about?" Ben filled his words with accusation. "Are you holding out for a marriage proposal? Does the first man to come up with a gold ring win the prize?"

"No, no!" She closed her eyes. "I just..."

"Jessie." He reached for her, his hands closing on her upper arms. She wrenched away from him, her eyes drowning in unshed tears. Shocked at the hunted expression in her eyes, he rasped, "Jessie, honey, I'm sorry. Look, I..." He reached for her hand and found it fisted. Outside, a car door slammed.

Drew had arrived.

"Let me go," she whispered.

"Not yet." He drew her closer. "Not until you tell me what's wrong. And don't give me some lame manufactured story about a harmless little dinner date."

"It has nothing to do with you."

"I think it does." His eyes narrowed as she trembled at the sound of Drew's footsteps on the wooden porch. "Has he threatened you? Tell me."

She closed her eyes and took a deep breath. When she looked at him again, he could feel her tension. He felt it dissolve when she broke down and told him of Drew's threats to ruin them if she didn't go along with his plans to court her. "Dad wouldn't survive losing Stone's End," she concluded.

"And that means everything?" he demanded in a hard tone. At the moment, he didn't feel very sympathetic toward either of the Carlisles. He felt curiously let down.

More than let down. The thought of her going with Drew for any reason made him see red. She stared at him mutely.

When a knock came at the door, Ben caught the flicker of distress in her eyes before she blanked it out. He gently set her aside. "I'll take care of this. Will you trust me to handle him?"

"I can handle him," she insisted.

He smiled tightly. "The way you always handle him, Jessie? The last time, he crushed a few plants. This time he used blackmail and left some bruises. What's next?"

"What choice is there?" she retorted heatedly. "Dad can't lose the farm."

His mouth went taut. "Will you trust me to handle things?"

"How?"

His eyes darkened.

"Will you?"

She couldn't look away. Jessie wondered, could she place her trust in Ben? It was asking a great deal. Men had never proved terribly reliable in her experience—Ben included. She might respect his discipline, the logical working of his brain, but she wondered about his heart. Unsure, she stared at him until he stirred impatiently.

"Jessie?"

She nodded after a long moment and went to answer the door.

Drew greeted her with confidence. "Are you ready?"

"She's not going," Ben said quietly.

"Stay out of it, Harding. This is between Jess and me."

Ben smiled—a hard smile without a trace of humor. "But you chose to mix business with pleasure when you involved the farm in your negotiations with Jessie."

"So, she told you." Drew sent Jessie a furious look. "Jess knows I have the interests of the farm at heart. Besides, I intend to make it up to her. There's nothing you can do about it." He grabbed her hand. "Let's go."

"Not so fast." Ben folded his arms and leaned back against the edge of the table. "Aren't you forgetting the little matter of a contract? You agreed to provide all the workers we needed to get a crop to market."

"A contract!" Jessie looked at Drew, who flushed red.

"It's just a piece of paper," he insisted.

"A piece of paper?" In the stress of her father's illness, how could she have forgotten the contract? She glared at Drew until he released her hand. He'd been playing with her, using lies to make her fall in with his ambitions. In reality, he had no power over her, she realized with relief. "You lied to me."

"Now, Jess, sweetheart."

"Don't 'sweetheart' me!" she raged. "I don't want to hear it. I just want you off my property."

"All right," Drew said. "But I'll be back. I know this looks bad, and I'm sorry. When you've had a chance to cool down, we'll talk. You'll see I'm right." He threw a resentful glance in Ben's direction. "Harding's on hand now. Where will he be in six months when the snow flies? You planning to go with him and run out on Ira?" She shook her head, unable to deny Drew's words. At her silence, he looked pleased. "In the end, I think you'll see your future is with me, right here at Stone's End."

Drew was right about Ben, but wrong about her! She put ice in her voice. "I want you off my property."

Ben inserted dryly, "By the way, that piece of paper will hold up in any legal courtroom."

Drew ignored Ben. "That doesn't change anything, Jess. My offer will be open after Harding's gone. You'll need someone."

"I think that's *my* problem," Jessie said, pulling the fragments of her dignity together. Why was she always making a fool of herself? And why was Ben always on hand to witness her humiliation? She was relieved when Drew gave up the argument and left.

After he'd gone, Jessie didn't know what to say to Ben. Once again, he'd saved her from making a serious mistake. Evidently Drew was more unscrupulous than she'd realized. She should have listened to Ben's warnings. She met his steady gaze.

"Thank you," she said simply.

"You're welcome," he said just as solemnly. His eyes said even more. She felt grateful, but confused about his motives.

Jessie recalled the intimate scene in her bedroom. She'd clung to her anger and ordered him out—not that he frightened her. He wanted her. The intensity with which she wanted him back scared her witless.

"This doesn't change anything," she said, feeling threatened.

He lifted an eyebrow. "Of course not."

Why didn't she believe him?

The following day, Jessie felt awkward at the thought of facing Ben, so she simply avoided him. Their relationship had taken on a new edge. Unsure if he felt more than a sense of responsibility, she didn't know how to react when she faced him before going to visit her father that evening.

Ben surprised her with the words, "I have something for you. A peace offering." Ben held out a plain square box.

It wasn't gift-wrapped.

"For me?" Jessie peered inside. Ben lifted out a dazzling blue motorcycle helmet; she blinked at it.

"You don't like it," he said at her lengthening silence.

She stared at him, then ran her fingertips over the smooth surface. She loved it; how could she tell him? A motorcycle helmet! It symbolized so many things—permission to be carefree, young; an invitation to share another wild ride. She swallowed an emotional lump in her throat. "Thank you. It's just a surprise." She placed the helmet on her head and fumbled with the chin strap.

Ben stepped closer and took it from her. She drew in a breath at his nearness and felt his tense response. He fastened the strap, then ran a long finger down her cheek. Unable to contain her shock, she looked up and encountered a wry gleam of humor in his dark blue eyes.

"Ready?" he asked, amused. No, she wanted to shout; she wasn't ready for this. Since his arrival, he'd put distance between them; now she wanted to maintain that distance.

An impossible task, she realized a few moments later. She sat perched on the back of his bike. Aware of the astonished glances in town, she had even more difficulty clinging to her dignity. Oh, well. She relaxed and enjoyed an unexpected sense of freedom. Heads turned as they drove through town, but she didn't worry about the gossip. Not then.

The hospital gift shop offered a small selection. Jessie looked at the cut flowers. "What do you think?"

Ben reached for a ceramic pot. "How about a cactus?"

The saleslady chuckled. "Shall I wrap it up?"

Ben's eyes glinted with amusement when Jessie agreed, "Yes, please." She was still smiling when she entered her father's room. Ben's hand rested lightly on her shoulder as he ushered her through the door ahead of him.

"Take your hands off my daughter," Ira warned ominously.

Jessie felt Ben's hand dig into her before he loosened his hold on her. She felt cold and abandoned when he did.

"Sure, Ira." Ben stepped back, hands up, like a fighter indicating he wanted a clean fight.

Ira glared at her. "What's this about you and Ben?"

Cactus in hand, Jessie came to a stop at the foot of his bed. "What do you mean?"

"I may be old and breathing through a tube, but you can't fool me, girl. Drew came by to warn me. He had some interesting things to say about you and Ben. Seems like everyone's talking." Ira directed his next comment at Ben, who stood rooted by the door. "I trusted you to take care of Jessie and the farm. You took my money, slept in my house, ate my food. Then dragged my daughter's reputation through the mud."

"Dad!" Jessie's instinctive defense infuriated her father even more. "I've done nothing," she whispered.

Her father collapsed back on the pillows. "You've done enough to get yourself talked about."

Ben said quietly, "Ira, it's not the way you think."

"You have no idea what I'm thinking!" her father shouted, sitting up. For a sick man, his voice contained a powerful rage. "Your sort only knows how to use a woman."

"Stop right there." Ben's voice grew taut.

A staff nurse rushed in. "What's going on in here? Now let's relax," she urged Ira. "I've paged Dr. Peterson."

Ira shrugged her off. "You relax. I've got business to tend to before I die."

"Mr. Carlisle! Ira," she said more gently. "Don't do this to yourself. You're upsetting the heart monitor."

He swore hardily. "I've got things to say, and no space-age machine's going to stop me!" He glared at Ben. "What will it take to make you do the honorable thing?"

Jessie choked on a dry sob. Years of large and small disappointments paled to insignificance. "Dad, please don't."

"Tell me one thing, Jess. Have you ever been in his bed?"

Her face flushed at the searing memory of that one night when Ben deliriously dragged her into his bed. Ira's eyes sank at her sign of guilt. "Nothing happened!" she insisted too late.

Catching the nurse's warning look, she didn't argue with her father—a futile exercise in any case. Somehow, he always won.

Ben's look of pity made her feel ill.

Her father demanded, "What are you going to do about it?"

"What are you suggesting?" Ben asked warily.

His lips turning blue with effort, Ira laid his cards on the table. "I don't know where you come from, but around here, it takes a wedding to repair a woman's reputation. If you need more of a motive to do the right thing, Jessie stands to inherit half the farm. It's yours...if you marry her."

At this wholesale auction of her future, Jessie cried out in shock. The clay pot fell from her nerveless hands and shattered. "Dad, you can't mean it," she whispered.

His eyes met hers. "You going to shame me, just like your ma?" At the accusation, Jessie drew in a sharp breath.

"Jessie." Ben's low voice reached her. Through her blurred senses, he looked like a fractured painting, like a portrait someone had cut up and pieced back together. He grasped her shoulders. "Jessie, honey." He swallowed visibly. "Let's get married."

Marry this stranger? "No." The word squeezed past the lump in her throat.

"Why not? We discussed marriage, remember?"

She felt a sense of unreality. Yes, they'd discussed marriage—between her and Drew. Not Ben. Without an ounce of sentiment, she could never agree to his proposal. She would never know if Ben married her for herself or for the

farm. All her dreams dissolved in that one moment of realization.

Ben continued, his voice soothing and persuasive. "It
will make your father happy. We could make a go of it."
When she remained mute, he turned back to a silent,
watchful gathering. "We'll be married as soon as it can
be arranged."

Ira's eyes lifted in relief. "When?"

Ben looked at her. "A week."

Jessie opened her mouth to argue, then saw her father's
face ease and knew she couldn't risk his fury just now.
When he felt better, she could explain. She would explain.
Ben nodded at her in approval; she couldn't recall agreeing
to his proposal.

The nurse hurried them out.

Riding home on the bike made conversation impossible.
At the house she hopped off and removed her helmet.

"We have to talk," Ben insisted. Nothing was settled.

"Not now," Jessie pleaded, feeling a headache coming
on. Clearly, her father wanted her married at all costs. If
she had to choose, Ben was the more obvious choice. It
was so tempting to say yes.

"The problem won't magically go away." Ben spoke
in an exasperated tone. "I'd like an answer."

Couldn't he see she was trying to save him from himself? "Then my answer is no," Jessie's voice trembled.
She left the helmet dangling from a handlebar.

Ben came around the bike. "Jessie, we are going to
talk."

His tone stopped her. "Why, why are you doing this?"

"Do I have a choice?" he asked dryly.

"Is it the farm?"

"No." His gaze was direct, hard and cynical. "Although I do understand the farm means everything to
you."

Not quite, she wanted to say, but couldn't. "Should I be grateful for your generosity?"

"Don't make me the villain. On second thought, maybe you *should* be grateful," he said, brutally frank, as if she'd driven him to it. "Maybe I just saved your father's life."

Jessie closed her eyes. "Dear God."

Fred, who hadn't gone home yet, approached at the sound of their raised voices. "What's wrong? Is it Ira?" He looked apprehensively from one to the other.

With a muttered exclamation at the interruption, Ben said, "Nothing's wrong." His gaze clashed with hers, daring her to deny him. "In fact, there's going to be a wedding."

"No, there isn't," Jessie insisted.

Ben laughed harshly. "Drew overplayed his hand." A hint of satisfaction crept into his voice. Astounded, Jessie realized he was jealous of Drew. A small hope sprang to life. Ben's next words crushed it. "Ira's determined to have a wedding. It's purely chance that I wound up playing the groom. If Drew hadn't fed Ira a pack of lies, he'd be engaged to Jessie, not me."

Fred shot back. "Well, what do you expect? The doctors aren't guaranteeing Ira much of a future. He's looking out for Jessie. He can't leave her alone with this farm to run."

Ben didn't sound convinced. "As usual, Ira's prime concern is Stone's End, not his daughter."

Hurt and bewildered, Jessie fumed. They were discussing her as if she didn't exist! Fred shrugged. "Maybe so, but a bride like Jessie tossed in with Stone's End is a mighty fair bargain. If you ask me, maybe you just got lucky."

Ben's laugh sounded hollow. Unwilling to hear more, Jessie broke in. Her voice shook with suppressed anger. "In any case, there's not going to be a wedding."

At her interruption, Fred managed to look shame-faced. "Aw, Jessie," he groaned. "That didn't come out right."

Ben remained cool and remote as he stared at her, his expression unreadable. She lifted her chin, her eyes fixed on her closemouthed fiancé. "It's just as well I heard. As soon as Dad's stronger, we'll explain."

Ben's eyes darkened. "I gave my word."

"Your word?" she repeated in disbelief. "And that's more important than what I want?"

"At the moment, yes," he snapped.

His admission cut through her, bringing instant rage to her response. "I won't marry you!"

He smiled without a shred of pity. "I think you will."

"You're wrong." She clenched her hands and unclenched them. Men and their misguided code of honor were a complete mystery to her. She wanted to be calm, matter-of-fact and distant. Like Ben. But her attempt fell flat. "Arguing with you is like talking to a stone wall!"

In a temper, she left the two men standing there. Or at least, she tried. Unfortunately, Ben wasn't about to grant her the last word. Hearing his footsteps crunch on the gravel drive behind her, she speeded up—her one aim to escape another confrontation.

She'd almost reached the barn before he caught her.

Ben grabbed her arm and spun her around. "Jessie, I'm sorry you had to hear what I said to Fred."

She brushed his hand away. "At least I know how you feel." At his determined expression, she took a step back.

"You have no idea how I feel." Ben took a step toward her.

"Then tell me." She wanted to shout it. *Tell me!*

"Look, I know you're frightened." There was that bone-melting look in his eye.

"I'm not." Jessie drew back, recalling the other times

he'd looked at her that way. Suddenly she felt a new threat.
More than his feelings or hers were at stake. He would
want a complete marriage in every sense. A few days ago,
she would have jumped at the chance. She'd wanted him
that badly—and she'd dared to hope he wanted her. Now
she couldn't imagine letting him sleep in her bed. And by
the wolfish expression on his face, she knew neither of
them would be getting much sleep.

"I won't rush you," he said, as if he'd read her
thoughts. "That night in my room, I overreacted. Making
love doesn't have to be like that. It could be good."

She stared at him in amazement. Even now he was looking at her with a gleam of admiration. Even while struggling to come to terms with her own emotions, she
couldn't fight the attraction she felt for this enigmatic man.
In fact, she wanted him with frightening urgency. There,
she'd admitted it. And he thought she was afraid of him.
How could he be so blind? All she feared was his leaving.

Jessie grasped at any defense. "I won't sleep with you."
She despised the cowardly desperation in her voice.

"Won't you?" Ben's expression didn't change.

He was simply stating his intentions. The fact that they
were honorable left her speechless. Somehow, he'd backed
her through the open barn doors. Her heart beat madly.
Humiliated, hurt, disappointed, she'd never considered the
possibility of a marriage proposal from Ben, much less a
coerced one. She reached for the nearest defense—a pitchfork—and aimed it at him.

"Don't you dare," he warned, his eyes gleaming.

Undaunted, Jessie whipped her anger into a fury to keep
Ben from touching her, because if he touched her...

"I won't marry you." Her voice started evenly, then
gradually rose. "You lying, leaving, low-down polecat.
You, you..." She searched for the right word, something

lower than low, and came up with one. She threw the final insult at him with venom. "You...Southerner!"

His gaze narrowed, as if he couldn't believe what he'd heard. His eyes were nearly black—with fury or arousal? Jessie wasn't about to risk finding out. "What did you call me?" he said.

She leaned the pitchfork against the wall, then backed away, repeating the litany in a cracked voice, "You lying, leaving, low-down..."

He shook his head. "Not that."

"Southerner," she spat.

Ben laughed and caught her before she could run. "That's what I thought you said." Dragging her against him, he gazed into her eyes, his own gleaming, as he bent his head to kiss her. She struggled briefly but he held her close, until all the fight went out of her. "Yankee witch," he rasped with evident satisfaction against her lips and kissed her until she was breathless and clinging to him. Pleasure curled her insides, turning her bones to putty and her objections to empty denials.

When he ended the kiss, she kept her eyes closed, afraid to look at him, afraid of what she would see—triumph. "Let me go," she whispered, wincing at the desperate sound of her own voice.

This time, he let her go with no objection.

He'd made his point, she realized. She felt a moment's weakening, but, avoiding his gaze, she walked away before she gave in to it. Ben didn't love her. Nothing he'd said reassured her about their relationship. This time, he didn't follow.

Jessie let herself into the house and flipped on a light to ward off the emptiness. She rubbed her eyes, weary of all the emotional strain. What if she simply gave in and married Ben? Did she dare take the risk? Stone's End needed a strong hand to manage things, at least temporarily, until her brother returned. What if Jared never returned? She still hadn't heard from him.

Of course, there was always Drew. Given a choice between the two, she would choose Ben any day. Her gaze fell on the mason jar filled with cash. She picked it up. It was a bitter affront to her pride. For weeks, Ben had deliberately kept her at a distance, treating her like a servant instead of a friend, paying for her services. Now, in some misbegotten notion of honor, he was going to concede to her father's demands and marry her. In a wild moment, Jessie wondered if he planned to pay her for sex as well as for everything else.

Her anger restored, she wanted to smash the glass jar, but she didn't. The money would salvage some of her pride. It was her money—she'd earned it. She twisted the lid off and took out a wad of dollar bills. She stared at it. Her determination almost failed, but then she hardened her heart.

She was through with being manipulated by the men around her. She had a clear choice. If Ben left—Drew, or someone like him—would attempt to get his hands on her property. Stone's End needed a strong man. At least, Ben was fair and evenhanded—except when it came to her, she thought with some bitterness.

However, from a purely practical standpoint, her decision was easy. The only sensible choice, really, was to marry Ben. She ignored all the impractical reasons why she wanted to marry him. Those she could control. All she had to keep in mind was the knowledge that sooner or later he would leave. Their marriage was only temporary, a last-ditch effort to hang on to Stone's End.

A week later, the ceremony was performed at Ira's bedside. The only festive note was Jessie—in her white bridal finery. Ben wondered where she'd gotten a new dress. In any case, no bride could be purer on her wedding day. She'd made sure of that by making Ben sleep in the barn—"to stem the gossip." No amount of argument could convince her it was too late.

Now, Ben's eyes took their fill of Jessie. The delicate white eyelet embroidery of her dress flattered her slim grace with a pretty round neckline, full sleeves and a skirt adorned with a flounce or two. He wanted to smile when he saw it. The dress suited Jessie—cool and crisp, and feminine.

She'd arrived on Fred's arm. Fred was beaming ear to ear. Jessie's eyes sparkled—with resentment. She barely looked at Ben before turning away. For the hundredth time since he'd proposed, he wondered why he'd done it. To save her? To save himself?

In time, he might even open his heart—the part she didn't already own—and fall in love with her. There was also the matter of beds to negotiate. Ah, well, she could be stubborn. But then, so could he. And he was tired of sleeping with Homer. In the meantime, he was just glad he'd bought a new suit.

Ben's wry gaze fell on Ira sitting erect in the bed. Unable to add to an overburdened conscience, Ben hadn't been able to break a deathbed promise to Jessie's father. Thus, he'd insisted on going through with the wedding—over Jessie's objections. Of course, once Ira had gotten his way, he'd improved daily. He'd survived. In a few minutes, Ira Carlisle was going to be his father-in-law.

Hell, Ben hadn't thought of that until now. *Till death do us part.* With the fire of self-righteous indignation burning in his eyes, Ira looked as if he was going to outlive them all.

The reverend, a jovial little man clearly determined to ignore the sour faces all around him, placed a worn Bible, a Carlisle family heirloom, on the table—a firm reminder

to the participants that this was indeed a sacred moment
not to be taken lightly. Nevertheless, Ben thought the ster-
ile atmosphere bore a gloomy foreboding for the bride and
groom. Jessie looked miserable. She looked alone, although she stood only a foot from his side—a very sig-
nificant foot. They should be holding hands, shouldn't
they? The irony of his situation carried Ben through the
brief sermon, the vows.

Reverend Bissette intoned the words from a worn mis-
sal, "Do you, Jessica Carlisle, take this man..."

Aware of Jessie to the depths of his soul, Ben felt her
stiffen, then whisper a thready, "I do."

"Do you, Benjamin Harding, take this woman..."

Ben had the sudden urge to run. He'd been running for
two years. He searched the room for a way out. Several
nurses barred the door. A bedside table stood directly in
his path. Then there was Ira—the biggest obstacle of all.

Trapped well and tight, Ben stated firmly, "I do." After
he'd said it, he heaved a sigh of relief, until he realized
everyone was looking at him expectantly. Now what?

Frowning, Reverend Bissette mouthed, "The ring?"

Chapter Eleven

The ring.

Ben stared blankly. He'd forgotten to buy Jessie a ring. How could he have forgotten? He looked into her face and watched a humiliated flush creep over her pale cheeks. Like little flags of defiance, she'd applied lipstick, blush and eyeliner. In her ears, tiny pearl earrings gleamed like tears and matched the unshed moisture swimming in her eyes.

She was going to hate him for the rest of their lives. Ring or no ring, they were man and wife. With a battery of eyes looking on with varying degrees of condemnation, disbelief and censure, Ben hid his guilty conscience with a small shrug. Unable to look at the contingent of guests witnessing his wedding—a few nurses, doctors, and Hazel and Fred Cromie—he stared straight ahead at a huge arrangement of flowers. A basket of tall, wilting, pink, white and red gladioli filled his vision. Attached to it, a greeting card read, Get Well, Ira.

Inwardly, Ben groaned. Flowers. Another lapse. He hadn't ordered a bridal bouquet, not even a posy. How could he have overlooked a ring and flowers? In their male contest of pride, he and Ira had cheated Jessie out of a decent wedding.

Ben took a good hard look at himself. He didn't like his conclusions. He was just as guilty of negligence as Ira. And poor Jessie had probably just become the most un-celebrated bride in Aroostook County history. The gossips would have a field day over it. The remaining ceremony seemed anticlimactic.

Jessie was aware of the lack of frills. But then, no amount of props would change what was happening. "Will you take this man?" the reverend had intoned while her mind screamed in silent protest.

With a heavy heart, she had whispered, "I do." She didn't want to take; didn't want to be taken. She didn't want to commit herself to this strange, silent man. Dear Lord, for the rest of her life. A life sentence—if it lasted that long. Men took without giving anything in return. She wanted to be free, free.

He hadn't even bought her a ring.

After the sham formality of a marriage ceremony, Ben's mouth lightly touched hers. Jessie felt nothing. If she al-lowed herself to feel an emotion, it would be hatred, and she knew how that could corrode the soul. She didn't want to hate Ben, she wanted to love him. And there lay her dilemma. This should be a day to celebrate; instead it was like any other day of her life—loveless. Colorful bits of confetti rained on her head. There were gifts, a bottle of champagne, a set of lovely crystal glasses, a hand-painted ceramic lamp. A camera went off in her face. She blinked rapidly, stemming back tears.

Hazel presented a gift-wrapped box and whispered,

"This is just for you." With Fred looking on with a watery smile, she hugged Jessie fiercely. "Be happy."

Be happy.

It sounded like a long shot. All the way home, Jessie kept thinking, now what? At the house, they entered through the front door. If Ben dared to sweep her over the threshold...

She never gave him a chance. She swept past him before he could say a word to add to her humiliation. Clutching Hazel's gift to her heart, hoping to contain the pounding rhythm inside, she climbed the stairs to her room. She couldn't wait to shed her wedding dress. She'd purchased it with Ben's money. Her money. What was his was now hers, and vice versa, she thought with a growing sense of panic. In her bedroom, she tossed the box on the bed and slipped off her shoes.

Curiosity drew her back to Hazel's gift. The gorgeous wrapping came off to reveal a labeled box from a pricey dress shop in Caribou—the same shop where Hazel had taken her to select a wedding dress. Lifting the cover, Jessie parted the thin pink tissue paper to expose a sheer white confection of silk and lace, an exquisite bridal set. How extravagantly foolish and wasteful, Jessie thought with a rueful smile. Letting it sift through her hands, she sat down heavily on the edge of the bed and stared at the white negligee. It was the most beautiful thing she had ever seen. Hazel must have spent a fortune for it. How could she ever thank her? It was lavish, sheer and sexy, white and virginal. How could she ever wear it? It was such a waste. She absolutely loved it.

In her rush, she'd left the door ajar. Ben stood in the opening. "Jessie," he started to say and broke off when he saw her sitting on her bed surrounded by yards and yards of delicate fabric spread on her lap.

When she rose hastily, the negligee drifted to the floor.

Mesmerized, Ben watched it float down. For a long moment, he could do nothing but stare at the transparent froth of white lace and silk pooled at her feet. He wanted to rescue it, wrap it around her, then slowly peel the layers away. What had he forsaken in this marriage, besides love?

"What do you want?" Jessie asked, her voice cool and remote. She clutched her hands at her waist.

What did he want?

He would be damned if he knew. All day, he'd expected her to crack under the pressure. She hadn't. He'd waited for tears and recrimination, a last-ditch effort to back out. He'd waited for some sign of emotion, passion, even hatred. There was none. Did she feel nothing at all? It struck him that he knew precious little about his stoic Yankee bride. "We have guests," he said.

Revealing the first sign of weakness since his proposal a week ago, Jessie rubbed her forehead. "I can't go down there."

"We'll do our piece, then get rid of them." He smiled when she glared at him. Not letting her lack of welcome deter him from entering her room, he stepped inside. It wasn't a large room—only slightly larger than his, with dormered extra windows. With widening eyes, she stepped back when he came close, until she came to an abrupt stop against the bed. When he raised a hand to her hair, she tilted her head, then flushed when he held out a flake of confetti. His eyes gently mocked her.

Embarrassed by her overreaction and confused by the tender gleam in his eye, Jessie straightened her spine. "Shall we go?"

Ben nodded. "After you," he said with that slow ease that made her want to throw something at him. Herself?

The sound of Fred's reedy harmonica drew her outside, where friends had gathered in a clearing by the apple orchard. Several tables were loaded down with food, drinks, and a three-tiered wedding cake complete with a ceramic bride and groom on top. There were fresh flowers—not the hothouse kind, but wild natural flowers.

Fred broke into a rendition of "Here Comes the Bride."

Jessie faltered. She looked at the sea of smiling expectant faces and wanted to run and hide. As if sensing her panic, Ben reached for her trembling hand. A tight feeling filled her chest. Then someone greeted her and someone else reached to shake Ben's hand. From some reserve, Jessie found the presence to greet their guests.

At some point, Ben drew her against his side. She felt as if she'd come home. But then she saw Drew watching them with a cynical expression and wondered if Ben had done it to present a solid front. Some guests were openly curious, but too polite to voice any disapproval.

The dancing started. With everyone watching, she went into Ben's arms. Her smile felt false, yet it felt so right to be with Ben; to dance with him. A hard pulse beat in his jaw. He drew her closer as the dance came to a swirling end.

He released her with obvious reluctance. It was time to cut the wedding cake. Ben held her gaze for a long moment. She had so few options left. Cutting the cake was only part of a ritual. It didn't have to mean anything. Just because his eyes were burning into hers and her body was melting at the core didn't mean anything. Jessie picked up the knife and placed it on the cake next to a pair of white confectionery doves.

Ben's hand slid over hers. He bore down firmly. Together, they cut the first slice of cake. He broke off a piece and held it to her lips. His eyes compelled her to accept his offering. She opened her mouth and felt his hard fingers against her lips for just a moment before his hand dropped. They were standing close, closer than they'd been in days.

Jessie wanted to deny the wild beating of her heart, the fear, the expectation.

Ben couldn't shake the feeling of possession. It was his wedding night; she was his bride. His. Suddenly, it was all too real. And not real enough. There would be no wedding night. This was the hollow bargain he'd made—one more sleepless night to add to his long list. The sweet cake icing reminded him of the time he'd kissed Jessie's cotton-candy mouth at the carnival.

It had all seemed so simple then—just a man and a woman. Now, there was this farce of a wedding, Ira and the farm, and heaven only knew what other complications. Ben saw the wariness in her soft gray eyes and realized he'd handled the situation—meaning Jessie—all wrong. A man couldn't compel, coax, or command a woman like Jessie. She was too proud. This wedding had wounded her.

He had to give her back her pride. Those bare silken lips drew his gaze. His head bent toward her, his lips landed to the left of her mouth. He heard her shaky breath and felt a small sense of satisfaction. She wasn't totally immune to him.

Someone toasted the bride and groom, and the celebration continued. Cal got into the wrong punch and asked Serena Morales to dance. His father glared and her father opened his mouth to object when Ben stepped in between the young couple.

"Come on, Cal, cool it." Ben grabbed the boy's arm and hauled him off for a walk and a private chat.

When they reached a fence, Cal shrugged Ben off. "What was all that about? I just asked Serena to dance."

"Is that all?" Ben said dryly. "Look, you're going off to college soon. Are you going to just drop her? Are you going to invite her to your fraternity parties?"

On the defensive, Cal retorted, "Why not?"

"She's only sixteen, Cal," Ben reminded him. "Give her a chance to grow up."

"Oh, I thought you meant—"

"That you'd feel ashamed of her because her parents are migrants. No, I didn't think that. But you did, Cal."

"Oh, hell!" Cal looked shaken.

"If you're not serious about the girl, maybe you should reconsider before you go playing with her feelings, hmm?"

Cal turned the tables. "Are you in love with Jessie?"

The question nearly stumped Ben, until he turned it around with a question of his own. "Would I have married her if I didn't?" Good question. He wished he knew the answer. Loving meant taking responsibility for someone's life and happiness. He wasn't sure if he could do that.

Cal frowned, then his face cleared. He grinned. "Yeah, right." He wandered off.

Ben returned to the party. Before leaving, Drew shook his hand. Ben was surprised at how much the thought of Jessie ending up in her neighbor's careless hands had bothered him. Face it. He wanted her for himself. He knew she didn't love him, but he would see that she didn't lose out in their arrangement. As Fred had said, Stone's End was in her blood. Ben intended to save it for her. Content with his bargain, he relaxed.

Drew appeared subdued. "I won't say the best man won, but congratulations."

While Ben absorbed that, Fred gave him a hearty cuff that almost dislocated his shoulder. "You be good to that girl, you hear me?"

"Yes, sir." Ben rubbed his arm.

As if cued, everyone left. When the last car disappeared in a cloud of dust, Jessie turned toward the house. Ben stopped her with a few words: "As long as Drew can make trouble, he will. The best way to handle him is to pretend this marriage is real.''

"It isn't real. Anyone can see our marriage is fake.''

Ben drew her against him and placed his open mouth on hers. His tongue teased her lips apart, stroking until she clung to him. He tasted champagne and wedding cake—a heady mixture. They were both gasping for air when he lifted his mouth. As the full moon broke through the clouds, he saw her expression. Her eyes looked dark and stormy, with passion alight in their depths. Jessie was staring at his mouth as if she were starved. Despite her objections, she looked lit up from inside.

With a groan, he bent his head and kissed her again, slowly this time, giving her time to adjust and respond. His reward came when her tongue returned his exploration with small licks that felt like fire.

He dragged her closer, letting her experience the full potency of his arousal. "Does this feel real to you?''

Turning her head, she whispered. "I'm sorry, I can't.''

Ben drew in a deep breath, then released her. "If you change your mind, you know where to find me.''

"I won't,'' she said, and marched into the house.

Despite his physical discomfort, he grinned. A man had to admire a woman with determination and the will to keep her brand-new bridegroom out of her bed. His eyes drifted over Jessie's ramrod spine; a man would be a fool to overlook the obvious—a trim waist and hips, long silky legs. She slammed the screen door. Ben winced. Cut off from their brief but tantalizing romantic idyll, he waited a moment or two before he entered the house.

To his surprise, Jessie was still downstairs.

He called out softly, "Jessie, whatever today lacked in the way of frills, I was proud of you. No man could have asked for a more beautiful bride." She had looked beautiful—her youthful features serious, pure, delicate; her hair streaked with gold, and her soft gray eyes filled with secrets. Graceful and feminine, she'd held herself erect, with touching dignity.

At his words, Jessie looked startled, as if compliments were the last thing she expected. Her eyes lowered, shielding her thoughts. With a murmured word, she drifted away, her skirts gently rustling. A moment later, Ben heard the sound of her bedroom door closing and felt a deep visceral pain.

Champagne bottle in hand, he went looking for a glass, resigned to toasting his bride alone. There was a certain irony in that. On top of the oak sideboard stood the glass mason jar.

The jar was empty. Ben smiled, glancing toward the stairs where Jessie had disappeared. She'd spent his money on a wedding dress. Perhaps their wedding day had meant something to her after all. His smile faded. On the other hand, she'd left the jar sitting there in plain sight.

The morning after was business as usual.

Ben hadn't realized how the situation would appear when he and Jessie, newly married, showed up for work just as the sun was rising. The workers were visibly taken aback. Cal wore a puzzled frown on his face.

"Let's not disillusion the kid," Ben said, appreciative of the sight of Jessie in a blue shirt and tight jeans. Her narrow feet were bare in strappy sandals. "He thinks we're in love."

"How could he think that?"

"Ah, well." Her pursed lips drew his gaze to her mouth. "I told him," Ben admitted. When she turned bright red and her mouth thinned with indignation, he added, "Well, what did you expect me to say?" Before she could raise an objection, he took her mouth in a satisfying kiss. He was satisfied, sort of....

Chuckling, the men walked off. Cal was grinning.

Jessie was furious, sputtering, "How dare you!"

"Then get even." He bent over her again. "Kiss me back."

Of course she didn't, but it was worth a try. She was even more furious when he released her. "What was that for?" Her eyes sparkled with banked fire.

"That was for me." When her cheeks flushed to a rosy hue, Ben walked off the porch. "See you later, honey." He winked.

Honey!

Jessie didn't feel like anyone's "honey" and certainly not like a blushing bride. She hadn't fooled Fred. As she walked toward the barn, he fell into step with her, muttering something about, "Damn stubborn fools. Never seen a pair make such a mess of things." He shook his head. "Bet all that fine silk and lace went to waste, too."

Jessie felt her face getting hotter.

"I knew it," Fred groused. "Damn shame. That lace was imported all the way from France." He looked thoroughly disgusted. Homer's bellowed greeting didn't help.

Watching Fred stomp off, Jessie decided he seemed more put out by her lack of a wedding night than she did. She'd been relieved—hadn't she? Did that explain the gnawing emptiness?

The day was hot. By noon, Jessie felt exhausted; she hadn't slept well. Fred sent her back to the house. She was dismayed to find Ben there.

"The men insisted I'm on my honeymoon," he said wryly. "I couldn't very well argue." A honeymoon.

This was an unforeseen complication. "It's so hot." She needed to escape. "I think I'll go for a swim."

"I think I'll join you." He issued the challenge.

She hesitated. Coward, an inner voice mocked. Was she going to let Ben curtail her single enjoyment? How could she stop him? Her father had given Ben rights to Stone's End, and to her. She trembled at the thought. "What about lunch?"

Ben smiled tightly. "I can wait."

Last night he'd discovered sleeping under one roof with Jessie was one thing—sleeping under one roof with a wife was another. In addition, he'd developed a nagging ache that only Jessie could ease. Along with that, he'd discovered some pretty archaic, traditional sentiments on the subject of marriage. Yes, he was feeling possessive. It wasn't just a matter of vows, it was a gut feeling. Jessie was his.

"I could fix sandwiches," she offered.

"Jessie," he said in a driven tone. "If you don't want to go for a swim, then just say so."

She sighed. "Why are you doing this?"

"Do I need a reason?"

She shrugged. "I suppose not. Well, let's go."

"What a contrary female." He shook his head. "Now I'm beginning to sound like Fred."

She laughed. It was a pleasant sound, a release, and he felt it to his bones. Jessie didn't laugh much, but when she did, it was rich and musical, like a finely tuned instrument. Jessie. She made him want to weep and laugh and hold her close to his heart where nothing would ever hurt her again. Including him.

That had become his greatest fear—that he would hurt Jessie. He didn't know if he could stay, if the nightmares would end, if he could stop looking backward. The other night, Fred had tried to tell him he'd just gotten lucky. Maybe. Ben didn't know about the future. But Jessie was fine and good, and she deserved to be happy. If he couldn't be a whole man, free of shadows, he would leave rather than drag her into his nightmare.

There was a shortcut through the woods, a narrow well-worn path cut among the towering pines. The land curved naturally to form a secret cove. The moment he saw it, Ben knew he'd made a mistake. The cove was too isolated.

Jessie felt his hesitation and wondered what had happened to alter his mood. She turned back to find him studying her with a frown. "Is there something wrong?"

He shook his head. "Let's swim." He peeled off his shirt. His body was long and lean, muscular and tight-knit, without an ounce of spare flesh. Her heart ached at the white scars marking his side. They stood for some part of his life she didn't understand, something he wouldn't share—one of many things. For the time being, he was in her life, but she wasn't allowed to enter his. Perhaps she never would be. Feeling self-conscious at the lack of privacy, Jessie was sorely tempted to duck behind a rock and undress. Instead, she turned and pulled off her T-shirt and shorts. When she turned back, he was staring at her modest navy blue swimsuit, a leftover from school days.

He frowned at her. "You don't usually wear a bathing suit."

"How do you know?"

Ben set his hands on his hips. "Never mind, I just do. What if I said you didn't need one now?"

"I wouldn't believe you," she returned, unblinking.

Did he think she was completely naive? Face flushed, Jessie turned and dived cleanly into the water. Moments later, he dived in beside her. He wasn't wearing swimming trunks. Gasping, she swallowed a mouthful of water. Recovering quickly, she took a deep breath and swam underwater to the opposite shore. A rock rose out of the water. Jessie came up for air and leaned her back against it as she searched the pond for some sign of Ben.

Since their wedding, each hour had been slow torture for her, wondering when he would reach for her, when the impasse would end. It ended when he surfaced in front of her. The water lapped against the shore, like a soft sigh.

"Who taught you to swim like that?" he teased, smiling as his hands closed over her bare shoulders.

"Jared," Jessie whispered, caged in by a pair of strong masculine hands. His thumbs idly traced the curve of her breastbone. She added breathlessly, "He was all-state—"

"Champion," Ben finished for her.

"How did you know?"

He shrugged. "It figures."

Jessie wanted desperately to feel the excitement of his touch again. Ben bent his head and kissed her mouth, not touching her anywhere else. She wanted more contact. When she let her body drift toward him, his long legs locked around her. The intimacy was immediate and shocking. Although her nerves signaled the first sensation of alarm, she couldn't summon the strength to resist—not yet. His arms moved around her, bringing her to him. Locked in his embrace, she drowned in sweet sensation, both new and exquisite. She felt no threat, just a warm slow exploration that soothed her even as it aroused. When his hand slipped between them and fondled her breast, she moaned in pleasure. The wanton sound shocked her.

His husky voice whispering, "Jessie," shocked her even more. "Just let me kiss you, touch you." His voice was full of passion, his kiss drugging. "We won't go any further."

Ben didn't wait for her answer. He untied her swimsuit and lowered the top to reveal her breasts. The shock of cool air felt like a bucket of ice-cold water. Pleasure became mixed with apprehension, fear. Fear of giving herself to a man's passing pleasure and having nothing left—no pride, no resistance. No tomorrow. Ben's deep voice soothed her objections. She saw admiration in his eyes as he looked at her.

"You're perfect, Jessie," he said. "So lovely and delicate." He cupped her breast and gently circled the nipple with his thumb until it was rigid with need. When he stroked it and gently squeezed, the sensation pierced her with shocking sweetness. He kissed her and she became lost. His hands moved to her back and started to roam downward, tracing her spine.

Alarm bells began to go off in her head. He slipped his hands inside her suit. "Ben, stop." She drew away and stared at him. "This is far enough." Her words came out in a rush. Hearing the note of panic, she wanted to find a hole and crawl inside; to her dismay, she sounded like a frightened child.

He drew a deep breath before saying, "We're married." His voice held a note of exasperation.

Jessie couldn't blame his impatience at her drawing back, but it wasn't that simple for her. A piece of paper and a few words spoken in front of witnesses meant nothing. She bowed her head to escape the dark accusation in his gaze. Gathering the ties to her swimsuit, she drew it up to conceal her breasts from his dark, aroused gaze. "Our marriage is only temporary."

His eyes flashed. "What does that mean compared to what we feel right now? How can you deny it?" Brushing her feeble objections aside, he kissed her deeply, reaching into her for a response she ached to give. If only he felt something more, she might silence her doubts, stifle her need for security. He'd never hinted at love. And she couldn't take the risk. When he released her, she drew a ragged breath.

She curled her hands against his chest. "I won't let you use me." Her voice sounded as desperate as she felt.

"Use you!" His face tightening, he started to argue, "Jessie, that's not the way it is. You should know that."

She lifted her chin. "Can you promise you'll stay?"

Something pained flickered in his eyes, as if she'd touched an exposed nerve, a raw wound. Ben dropped his hands. His jaw went rigid. "Ask me something else. Anything else."

Just as she feared, his refusal could only mean one thing—their marriage had no real future. It was only temporary. She'd known all along, but it hurt to have him spell it out so clearly. Why had she asked? Jessie could have lived with the pretense of being a wife a little longer. She shook her head, putting an end to her pathetic little fantasy of a happy, normal marriage. Was there such a thing? "There is nothing else."

Why had she clung to a false dream of love? She could survive without love. She'd survived thus far. But she wanted fidelity, she wanted his promise, she wanted a lifetime. She would settle for nothing less.

"You could come with me," Ben suggested. The words seemed to surprise him almost as much as they surprised her.

To Jessie, the offer sounded forced, as if he felt obligated to make it. After all, they were married, but he could safely assume she wouldn't leave since she was tied to her father and Stone's End. Since he knew she had to refuse, she didn't even consider it seriously. "You know I can't leave."

Ben smiled tightly. "What about when your brother comes home? What then?"

Momentarily confused, she said, "My father will still need me." How long would it take him to realize her brother probably wasn't coming? Even if Jared came, he wouldn't stay.

"Right." His spine rigid, he turned and swam back to the opposite shore as if the devil's own hounds were after him.

Jessie waited until he'd wrapped a towel around his waist before swimming back. She felt cold. She walked out of the shallows, reached for her towel and buried her face in the folds.

"I'm not going to apologize," he said quietly.

Feeling illogically disappointed, she shrugged. "I don't expect you to." Had she wanted him to persuade her, convince her that she had to go with him? That she belonged with him? But no, he would never claim her completely, not totally. He didn't want her heart. She wrapped the towel around her, sarong-style.

"Damn it, Jessie," he said, exploding at her reserve. "You should. You should tell me to go to hell."

He had no idea how tempted she was to do exactly that, but she suspected his experience of hell was a lot more personal than hers. "Would that make you feel better?" she asked curiously.

His lips moved in a taut smile. "No. There's only one thing that will make me feel better, and we both know what that is."

Jessie felt a blush rising from her chest. "Are you always so, so…"

"There is a word for what you're trying to say. I won't shock you with it. Let's just say, I haven't been with a woman in more than two years and leave it at that."

"How can I leave it at that?" She wanted to hide from the raw confession, but couldn't, not if she wanted to know more about the man she'd married. And, heaven help her, she did. When he started to turn away, she said, "Please explain."

Without thinking, she placed her hand on his forearm and felt the muscles ripple in reaction to her light touch.

He looked down at her hand, until she felt as if her fingers must be branded on his skin. Then he slowly raised his eyes and searched her face for a long moment before he said in a voice of steel that somehow failed to hide his anguish, "I haven't felt like being with anyone for a long time." His smile twisted at her sharp gasp. "I want you, Jessie. As shocking as that might seem to an innocent like you, it's a minor miracle to me."

When her gaze wandered to the scars riddling his chest, he added dryly, "And no, I'm not suffering from some old war wound. At least, not physically."

"Ben, I..."

"Don't say it, Jessie. I don't want your pity."

In that moment, he reminded her of a hungry timber wolf. Each year, in the spring, one or two often turned up on her doorstep—half starved after a long hard winter, suspicious of human contact, afraid to accept it. Some starved to death rather than eat the food she left out. Jessie softened at his harsh tone. "I wasn't offering any pity."

"Weren't you?" His cold blue eyes flickered over her.

"No," she said. She wasn't sure what she was going to offer, but it certainly wasn't pity.

Ben's mouth tightened with unreleased tension; he smiled grimly. "Well, at least we agree on one thing."

His words mocked everything she felt.

Hours later, the sun set on another day. Jessie made iced tea and they sat on the porch—rocking. Ben felt like one half of an old married couple. Unfortunately, the other half—his better half, some might argue—wasn't sharing the same sentiment. After day one, marriage was beginning to feel like a lifetime sentence. The honeymoon stage hadn't gotten off the ground before it was over. And yet, oddly enough, he could picture growing old with Jessie by his side.

Fred stopped by. He helped himself to a glass of iced tea. "Sure is humid. Might storm later," he predicted. "You both look hot. Why don't you go for a swim?"

"No." Ben smiled when Jessie's voice overrode his.

"No." She rocked more rapidly.

Fred finished his drink. "Well, I just stopped by to check on Daisy. She's due to drop her calf any time now. It's her first, and you never know what could happen." With a glint in his eye, he fixed a grin on Ben. "Know anything about birthing calves?"

Ben shook his head. "I know horses. That's it."

Fred chuckled. "Looks like you're about to learn. Jessie knows all about cows. If you give her a hand, Daisy will do the rest." Ben couldn't hide his alarm. Fred added, "Night, now."

After he'd left, Ben released a sigh. "How are we supposed to get any sleep worrying about Bessie?"

"Daisy," she corrected—all the cows looked alike to Ben. "We'll set the alarm and take turns checking on her."

Ben set his clock.

At ten, the night was black. He walked out to the barn where a small light was burning. Jessie was there.

She looked startled. Obviously, she wasn't expecting him. "I thought I had first watch."

"So did I," he said ruefully. It looked like they'd done it again—miscommunicated. Lamplit, the barn was inviting, surprisingly clean, sweet-smelling with the scent of new hay, and Jessie in her blue-and-white nightgown. Ben felt a jolt of pleasurable awareness. He swallowed and tried to look away, but each time she moved, the fabric clung to her shape. The fabric wasn't sheer, or sexy; in fact it was quite modest, but with the light behind her, she might as well have been wearing nothing.

Jessie ran her hands over the cow's side. "Position is good. Nothing's happening though, and Daisy looks content."

"For now." Ben leaned against the stall and fought his base instincts. He wanted Jessie's hands on him. "I suppose Jared taught you how to do that."

"Mmm." She smiled, all innocence. How could she not know how she affected him? "He always wanted to be a vet."

"Of course, he would have made a fantastic vet."

She ignored his sarcasm. "The best."

"Now why doesn't that surprise me?" Ben grinned weakly, ignoring a prickle of unease. Was he jealous of her brother? If Jared was such a champion, where the hell was he? Why had he left his sister to cope? Ben was beginning to suspect her brother must be a prize jerk—a spoiled, selfish one at that. One thing was for certain: neither Jared nor Ira deserved her loyalty. And neither did he—her husband. Husband. The word sounded odd when applied to himself. Somehow he'd never thought of himself as belonging to a woman.

"Jared wanted to be a vet—what did you want to be?" he asked, beneath Jessie's questioning gaze.

With a smile that made him want to groan in frustration, she moved to the other side of the cramped stall. His eyes took their fill of her soft curves and shadowed secrets.

"You mean besides star pitcher for the Red Sox?"

He chuckled at her answer. "Besides that."

She shrugged a smooth, tanned shoulder. "I just always wanted to be a farmer. I like the life. Do you?"

"Hmm," he murmured absently. Just as he'd suspected, his chances of separating her from Stone's End were slim if not impossible. "Have you heard from Jared?"

"Um, no." She averted her face.

Her guilty look made him suspicious. A few things started to add up—Jared's bare, empty room, Ira's evasiveness. "Just as a matter of interest, when was the last time Jared came home?"

She left the stall. "More than two years."

Ben said carefully, "When were you planning to tell me?"

"I don't see where it concerns you."

"Don't you? Don't you think I had a right to know that for all practical purposes, Jared isn't coming back?"

Her face closed up. "No."

"Damn it! I almost left you here on your own...."

"But you didn't."

No, he hadn't left. Her simple acceptance of life cut off his temper. If he had left, she would have managed. Quite simply, Jessie didn't need him. The knowledge stunned him.

Thunder cracked in the distance. The lights dimmed.

"We'd better get back," he said, resisting his need for her.

By the time they reached the house, the wind had picked up, scattering large droplets of rain, driving them inside. Now, Jessie's nightgown clung damply to her breasts.

"You can get some sleep," Ben said, knowing he was in for another sleepless night. "I'll check on Bessie first."

"Daisy," she corrected automatically.

He smiled grimly. "Right."

"You're sure? Because I can—"

"Jessie, go to bed," he interrupted. When she walked out, chin held high, he closed his eyes in pain.

Ben couldn't go to bed now. All he could think about was Jessie wearing her pretty nightgown—and his taking it off. There was a blue ribbon and tiny buttons...

Ben ran a shaky hand through his hair. He was going out of his mind. Left alone, he paced. Rain lashed the windows. Lightning lit up the room; each accompanying crack of thunder set his nerves on edge. Out of excuses, Ben went to bed.

Lying awake, he tried to think of something pleasant. Jessie. Moment by moment, he relived her brief sweet surrender at the pond, then her rejection. A roll of thunder sent a shudder through him. When he finally slept, his dreams were filled with her. She was there with the rockets exploding and bodies falling. She held her hand out, as if she could lead him to safety, to the land of the living. But he was struck down, burned up, paralyzed. And yet, she was still there, waiting.

He woke suddenly with her name on his lips. *Jessie.* The erotic episode with her at the pond had been only a prelude. He couldn't spend another solitary night and keep his sanity. Despite every inner warning, he was going to add one more crime to his list—a crime of passion.

In the hall, Bandit went for his ankle.

Chapter Twelve

A shift in the mattress woke Jessie. A firm hand gently massaged her back. She sighed in pleasure. She felt a breath in her ear, a whisper. "Jessie." Ben's voice drifted over her, along with the slow delicious glide of his hand down her spine.

"Hmm?" she murmured into her pillow, wishing he would stop, wishing he wouldn't.

"Are you awake?"

"No."

"You're lying." He was sitting on the edge of her bed. His low masculine laughter melted her insides, like fresh honey on warm bread. She didn't want to move.

Jessie opened one eye. Stifling a yawn, she rolled over. She gulped. Looking no farther than the black mat of hair on his chest, she focused on the throbbing pulse in his jaw; his chiseled mouth; his scar. His dark eyes gleamed down at her.

She swallowed hard. "What time is it? Is something wrong with Daisy?" She'd fallen into an exhausted sleep, her emotions wire-drawn with tension. His presence magnified that vague uneasy feeling a hundredfold.

"It's midnight." He leaned over her. His hand on her waist dropped the comfort level another notch. "The cow's fine, or as fine as she's going to be until she delivers."

"I should get up. She might need me." His hand felt heavy, shifting upward. Jessie couldn't move. Then, she didn't want to move when he took her hand and pressed a kiss to her palm. He trailed a row of kisses up the inside of her arm. "Ben," she said weakly, closing her eyes to ward off the sweet rush of pleasure. "Ben, I don't think we should be doing this...."

"Then don't think." His eyes gleamed with invitation.

His gentle humor softened her resistance. She caught a rare glimpse of the man he'd been before misfortune changed him. He was complex, intelligent, intense at times. He bent over her and found her mouth, teasing her with light kisses until she moaned in defeat and opened to him.

As if granted permission, he sank against her, his weight pressing her into the soft goose-down mattress. She was drowning, lost in a sea of pleasure. She drew a breath when he released her mouth, then promptly lost it when his lips drifted down her throat.

Jessie dragged in another breath. "Ben, about Daisy. She might need me." Her hands pressed against his chest—lost in the sensation of touching him. His male nipples pebbled in response to the accidental scrape of her fingernail.

He groaned, deep in his throat. "She doesn't need you. I do. Jessie, honey, please...I need you," he rasped the urgent plea against her ear. Delicious sensations threatened to drown her common sense. Slowly, his words filtered through.

Ben needed her.

Nearly overwhelmed with needs of her own, Jessie went absolutely still. No one had ever needed her before. She absorbed this new emotion. It felt warm, wonderful and dangerous. It struck at her woman's heart. Oh, he was clever. Despite his urgency, she knew she only had to refuse...but she didn't want to stop his gentle persuasion. His seduction.

Ben took full advantage of her silence. When she didn't object, he drew her nightgown up and over her head. He stared down at her skin tanned to golden perfection. He was a military man. All the softness had been drilled out of him years ago, but just then he wished he were a poet. He wished he could find the words to tell her how beautiful she was, how exquisite.

He hoped his husky murmur, "Jessie," was eloquent enough to describe how much she pleased him. Her breasts were soft and round, peaked and lifting for his touch. He bent his head and lightly kissed one, then the other. Teasing her into submission, he ran his hand down over her flat stomach into the nest of silky curls. Gently, he touched and found her dampness.

Time stopped as he learned the tender secrets of her body, the silk of her skin, the curve of her throat, the sensitive inner flesh of her thigh.

His voice grew ragged. "Tell me you want me or I can't do this." He released a breath when she nodded silently. "Are you sure? I've rushed you into this."

Jessie stared up at him. Although she couldn't see him clearly, she felt his indecision. Every nerve, every living cell in her body screamed in mute protest at his hesitation.

"Ben," she gasped. He couldn't stop now!

"What?"

"Shut up." She sweetly put an end to his soul-searching and second-guessing with down-to-earth practicality. He'd started this seduction—it had been going on forever—and, he had better finish it or she was going to go mad! She drew his head down and felt his surprised laughter drift across her lips. "I want you," she whispered.

"You're beautiful."

Jessie knew she wasn't—but he made her feel beautiful. His touch was sure and gentle and coaxing; he reached inside her for something she didn't know she had to give—herself.

Even as she ached to surrender, she fought the weakness. The rhythm of his touch didn't stop and she couldn't stop her pulse from pounding with each stroke. Then suddenly, without warning, she cried out for release. He eased into her with care that brought tears to her eyes. Filled with him, she felt her last shred of control splinter into fragments of light. The rush in her ears was the sound of his breathing mixed with her sighs. In that moment of rapture, she was totally, irrevocably his.

Ben thought he'd dreamed it; but no, she arched and her voice broke over his moan of satisfaction. He was still terrified of hurting her, disappointing her, letting them both down. She was a virgin. Of course, he'd known. But he hadn't really known; he hadn't felt it—the tightness enveloping him within her body. Her gift brought a warmth to his heart—a soldier's heart, a scarred and battered heart that had known too much agony and defeat to admit any weakness, even love.

Outside, a storm still hovered; wind and rain battered the house. Inside, the room was dark without a moon. He couldn't see her, but he could touch and feel. He could hear and she never once said "stop." Not even when he touched her while they were joined and took intimacies that were new, bringing her to a second powerful climax;

not even when he stole her breath; not even when he claimed her and spilled his seed.

Afterward, she lay damp and spent against him. He rolled over, bringing her with him, holding her close, soothing the tremors that shook her slender form. He kissed her and felt the wetness on her face where a single tear slid down. His lips tasted the saltiness of blood on her lips where she'd clenched down rather than cry out at that first shocking invasion. Remorse bit deep into the pleasure he'd taken. He should have been slower, gentler, easier; and yet he would be lying if he denied a sense of satisfaction. Their marriage was now a fact.

At 2:00 a.m. the alarm went off. Ben groaned and tried to roll over. His left arm—the one close to his heart—was trapped around Jessie. She lay there so sweetly, soundly asleep, obviously unaware of the havoc created by her mere presence.

Feeling guilty, he drew her closer. Would he ever be able to touch her without guilt? He hadn't forced her; he'd seduced her. He knew there would be a price to pay in the morning. She would be furious, no doubt. But for now...

For now, his hands found a softness long forgotten. He shuddered in fierce pleasure when she woke and came alive for him. He marveled at the unique sweetness of a woman's curves, the velvety texture of smooth skin, the scented silkiness of loosened hair. Easy, easy. The message repeated itself over and over in the tender intimacy he sought with her. Within minutes of muted harsh breaths and smothered gasps, he felt her relax against him. He kissed her deeply, stifling her little pleas with lips and tongue. He touched her intimately until her body betrayed its response to what he was doing. She arched in helpless surrender. Her concession was all he needed to lose control of the moment.

Ben was drifting off to sleep when he remembered—the cow.

Shrugging into his clothes, he went out. The rain had stopped. The wind remained, howling between the house and the barn. He struggled to open the barn door. Daisy glanced up at his arrival. "Hey, old girl," he said. She winked a chocolate eye. He hated cows, but she was beginning to get to him. No wonder Beau was smitten.

Ben fetched hay and water before returning to the house and Jessie. With a satisfied smile, he stripped off his clothes and crawled into bed with his wife.

Before daybreak, Jessie turned off the alarm. She scrambled over the male body in her bed, then looked back with something of a shock. Flat on his back, Ben was sound asleep.

Dark stubble covered his chin, reminding her of the menacing stranger she'd met only a few short months ago. Only now, a faint smile touched his lips. She looked away hastily, but a vivid image remained in her mind. A corner of the sheet covered his hips. His chest was exposed. A muscled hairy leg hung over the edge of the bed—as if the bed was too small. She closed her eyes. How could she have welcomed him? The ache she'd felt last night had been assuaged; now she just ached. Ben had discovered nerves and muscles in her body she never knew existed. She felt hot just thinking about some of the things he'd done to her.

She couldn't think of that now. She felt light-headed—with fatigue, she told herself firmly. It couldn't have anything to do with the vital naked male in her bed.

For one wild moment, she wanted to wake Ben with a kiss and begin the incredible, sensuous voluptuous journey all over again. But in the cold light of day, her courage had fled; common sense asserted itself with the morning sun pouring into the room.

A glance in the mirror made her groan. Her long hair was in tangles. For the life of her, she couldn't see what Ben had found so irresistible. She was no beauty queen, nor particularly well-endowed. A nasty little thought invaded what should have been a blissful morning. Of course, just because he'd made love to her once, twice, didn't mean he intended to do it again.

Hadn't he once threatened her with a quick lay?

Her nightgown dangled from the foot of the bed. Jessie hastily shrugged it over her head and crept out of the room. Once downstairs, she realized her choice of clothing wasn't very practical. Too cowardly to return to her room, she grabbed her barn jacket and boots and went out to check on Daisy.

It was barely six when Fred turned up in the kitchen. He raised an eyebrow at her attire. "How's Daisy?"

"Uh, fine." Jessie poured a second cup of coffee and laced it with extra cream and sugar. Her body needed a jolt.

"No calf, huh?"

"Not yet."

"You must have been up half the night with her. Why don't you go back to bed?"

"No!" Rising from the table with too much haste, she spilled the rest of her coffee. "I'm fine."

Her face on fire, she mopped up the spill and rinsed her cup under Fred's thoughtful gaze. How could she go back to her bed? Ben was still in it. She didn't have the vaguest idea how to get him out—if she even wanted him out. She ran a hand through her hair. She was far too exhausted to think straight. Her nerves were frazzled and she had no idea what she wanted. So much for being practical and levelheaded. Her body had turned traitor. No one had told her that a man—not just any man; Ben, she admitted—could make her body crave fulfillment; that sensual pleasure was keener than any appetite; that sleeping with Ben would only make her hunger for more. The inevitable had happened. She paused. Was there an element of relief? Joy? He'd made it easy. There had been no shame, only pleasure. The mere thought made her feel hot. To escape Fred's amusement, she grabbed a broom and tried to look busy.

Half an hour later, Jessie's raised voice shocked Ben awake. "Get out, you good-for-nothing varmint." He sat up. He was still in her bed. "I warned you," she continued. "Next time, I'm getting my gun. I'm through being nice."

He looked—she was nowhere in sight. Her voice drifted in through the open window. Ben grinned. A moment later, he leaned out the window in time to see her take a broom to Beauregard, shooing the bewildered moose out of her garden. Red-faced and obviously annoyed, she looked adorable in thick work boots and a denim jacket thrown over her nightgown. His bride.

"Morning, Jessie," he said, peering down at her.

Flustered, she dropped the broom, mumbled a brisk, "Good morning," and flew inside. She had to come upstairs sometime.

Grinning, Ben lay back and waited. And waited. Finally, he got up. He was half in and half out of his jeans when he heard her footsteps on the stairs. He was on the top landing when she reached it. Waiting.

The dog was whining and scratching at the bathroom door.

"Bandit's locked in the bathroom," she said in confusion, then let the dog out before Ben could object. Teeth bared, Bandit charged.

Grateful for a head start, Ben barely made it to his own

room and slammed the door. "Jessie," he called through it, lifting his voice above the barking. "Get rid of the dog. I want to talk to you."

"You didn't want conversation last night," she snapped.

Like a dash from a bucket of cold water, Ben caught her tone of hurt resentment. Within seconds, he heard her turn the shower on full blast. Hoping she would cool off, he waited until she had time to dress before trying again. When she came out, he opened his door slightly. Ears plastered back, Bandit snarled at him.

Jessie disappeared down the stairs with a tangle of white sheets. "Call off the damn dog!" Ben shouted after her.

She ignored him. She was so cool. It was such classic Jessie—getting him all wound up while she remained immune. Wait a minute. When had their roles switched?

By the time Ben had lured Bandit into his room with an old shoe, showered, dressed, and tracked down Jessie, he was feeling the strain. She was hanging out laundry. The storm had ended; gusts of wind still lingered. Like giant flags of surrender, white sheets billowed in the heavy breeze. Ben didn't think they signaled her surrender, only his. He came up behind her.

"Jessie, about last night."

At the sound of his voice, she spun around. One glimpse of her strained features dissolved his irritation. She looked so fragile. A bright flush crept into her cheeks. He stared in fascination. They'd made love only hours before. Suddenly words seemed inadequate. He simply wanted to kiss the sweet confusion from her eyes, the trembling from her lips. She looked so vulnerable—tangled up in the clothesline, flushed and angry. And so frightened. He couldn't blame her; he was scared as hell—scared of what she made him feel. But it was good. He hadn't felt so alive in years.

"I was looking for you." Ben was determined to penetrate her reserve. "Don't you think we should talk?"

"What is there to say? You had your one-night stand."

He gritted his teeth. "It wasn't a one-night stand. I'll demonstrate right now, if that's what you want."

She glared at him. "You seduced me. I was asleep." She blushed brighter when he raised a skeptical eyebrow. She might have been sleeping when he invaded her bed, but not for long. "I wanted a choice," she insisted.

His face hardened. "You wanted me. Don't deny it."

"I had the right to decide the time and place."

"All right. What do you suggest we do about it now?"

Her eyes rounded. "Why, nothing."

"Nothing! Oh, no, we're not going back."

"And what do you suggest?" she retorted.

Knowing Jessie was in a stubborn mood, he sighed. "You can still have a choice. You choose where we go from here. I can pack my bag and be out of here in fifteen minutes." He felt a trickle of sweat run down his spine at the risk he was taking. "Or I can stay. It's your choice."

Her eyes flashed with temper. "As a temporary lover?"

Out of patience, he reached for her. "Then give me a reason to stay, Jessie. Give me a reason," he rasped against her mouth as his lips bore down. If this was a farewell kiss, he was going to give it everything he had. And he did.

At last, out of breath, he released her. With one last look, which he hoped spoke volumes, he turned and walked away. He reached the driveway before she said, "Ben?"

He stopped. He didn't know how he felt. Relieved? Grateful? Yes, all that. And so many more emotions he couldn't identify; they were all too new.

"Don't go." Her voice trembled.

Slowly, he turned back and walked toward her. She was standing there, her spine rigid as she visibly struggled with indecision. Her emotions were naked; her natural common sense, reserve and distrust were at war with desire. She looked defenseless. He wanted to reassure her, but suddenly he'd run out of inspiration. Yesterday, he'd gone to town and bought her a wedding ring. It was burning a hole in his pocket. Clearly, this was not the time to give it to her.

But soon. "You won't regret it," he vowed.

At the words, Jessie stared at him in dismay. Dear God, she already did. He spoke of regret; she wanted words of love. It was a language she wanted to explore, but not alone.

He bent his head again and kissed her. She couldn't respond. His face was expressionless when he released her with the question, "You're sure?" Dry-mouthed, she nodded. What had she agreed to? "I'll see you later," he said.

Her stomach lurched. She didn't breathe until he was out of sight. She picked up a wet pillowcase and shook it with a snap. Give him a reason to stay? She tacked the pillowcase to the line with a clothespin. Then she paused. When he'd kissed her, she'd felt frozen inside. Even when his kiss grew gentle and persuasive, even when she wanted to wrap her arms around him and cling, she couldn't move. What if she risked her heart, and lost?

So many times she'd given love, but no one had ever loved her back. What if it was too late? Too late to change what she felt for Ben? What if it had been too late from the moment he arrived at Stone's End? Shaking her head in confusion, she reached for the second pillowcase from the laundry basket.

When she returned to the house, she found the mason jar sitting very conspicuously in the middle of the table. Ben had obviously left the jar in plain view for her to find. For one wild moment, she thought he'd actually had the gall to pay her!

In a blaze of hot anger, she picked up the jar, ready to

throw it across the room, then she stared in amazement. A ray of sunshine touched the cheap glass and suddenly it sparkled like fine crystal. Cradling the jar, she slowly sat down, then set it in front of her and stared. Within the thick glass, an ivory rose lay with its creamy white petals spiraling open, its edges blushing a soft rose pink. The leaves still glistened with morning dew. In a trance, she took out the rose.

With the tip of her finger, she traced the petals in wonder. Was this Ben's way of telling her he cared? What did it mean? The rose was so fragile...like love. To grow it needed tender care, a place in the sun. With a soft sigh of defeat, and hope, Jessie fetched the family bible. She pressed the rose between the thin well-worn pages, next to Gran's.

All day, Jessie avoided Ben and kept a close watch on Daisy. To her relief, Ben didn't come near the barn.

Daisy's calf didn't come.

That night, Jessie found Bandit new sleeping quarters in the shed. She left her bedroom door open. If this marriage was going to have a chance, there was no room for games.

Ben didn't come.

At first, she was relieved—he was giving her time to adjust to their new marital status. Then she felt bruised by this new rejection. And finally, she simply felt lonely. Didn't he want her? She closed the door. The latch turned, a final *click* sounded like a shot fired in the dark. Round one. She considered and rejected the impulse to go to his room and crawl into bed. What would that solve? She didn't want just sex. Did she? Well, not really, she admitted, although the idea did tempt her. She wondered how he would react if she seduced him! He would probably be delighted. Men!

She turned her hot cheek into the pillow. But Ben wasn't like other men. He wasn't petty or demanding. He wasn't a user—which didn't solve her problem. After being married all of three days, she wasn't sure what her problem was, exactly. Why had he made an issue of making their marriage real, only to retreat?

Later, when she heard him calling out in his sleep, she wrapped her arms around the spare pillow. He was still having the nightmares. The realization hurt her somehow. Had she naively thought she would be the cure—that one night with her would solve his problem? Apparently not. His ragged voice sent a chill through her. What experience tortured his soul? Sometimes she felt as though she were reliving it with him.

She'd come to recognize the ritual—the sound of fear in his voice, the despair. And the guilt.

She closed her eyes and tried to sleep. Every instinct cried out to offer comfort to him, even if it was only physical. She had no doubt he needed her. When his moans ended and he grew quiet, she stayed in her room. But somehow, his silence was worse. She felt his loneliness, and shared it.

At dawn, she ran into him in the hallway. "It's my turn to check on Daisy," she said. "I'll go."

"Why don't we both go?"

The sun was just edging over the barn. Daisy had reached the panting stage. "This is it," Ben said, as Jessie checked the cow. For the first time, he took a good look at Daisy's black-and-white markings. "Isn't this the cow Beau's been mooning over all summer? Beau isn't... He and Daisy didn't..."

Jessie smiled. "No, he isn't," she assured him.

Nevertheless, Ben was relieved two hours later when Daisy's baby came out looking like a cow and not a moose.

"Isn't she sweet?" Jessie cooed, rubbing the calf down.

"She is sort of cute," Ben had to admit, admiring the

white face and rough black coat. Daisy lurched to her feet, checked out her offspring, then licked it clean.

When Ben placed an arm around Jessie, she relaxed and leaned against his shoulder. Unable to resist her closeness, he turned her into his embrace. He was pleasantly shocked when she didn't raise an objection. He kissed her. They'd made love less than twenty-four hours ago, but that didn't seem to matter. Their kiss became heated within seconds.

He raised his head and looked around the barn—not a bale of hay in sight. "Ever notice there's never a hayloft around when you need one?"

She followed his lighthearted cue. "They're highly overrated, anyway. Full of ticks and fleas..."

Ben shook his head. "Jessie, Jessie, Jessie. There's not a romantic bone in your body." He hoisted her over his shoulder in a fireman's lift.

After a shocked *whoosh,* she giggled. "Put me down."

The laughter in her voice filled him with relief as he carried her back to the house and up the stairs.

There he set her down outside her bedroom door. "I'd like to come in. May I?" He pushed the door wider.

She backed into her room. "It's almost morning."

He started to unbutton his shirt. "I noticed."

She backed away until she encountered the bed and sat down heavily. "You didn't come last night, and I thought..."

"Did you think I'd used up my one-night stand?"

She frowned at his laconic remark. "No, but..."

He pulled off his shirt, then reached for hers. His fingers stopped on the silver concha belt, then moved on. He undressed her slowly, tenderly smiling at her blushes, yet savoring each new revelation. He reached for her hair and freed the constricting knot, slowly unbraiding the fine silky strands until it drifted free in soft waves.

"I've dreamed of doing that," he said huskily. When

she stood before him, he just stared. "You're beautiful, Jessie. Just looking at you makes me ache."

Ben's cooking was improving. Later that morning, he cooked ham and eggs. It was almost edible.

"It's delicious," Jessie assured him. She forked a charred piece of ham into her mouth. She swallowed it.

His eyes twinkled. "Guess I'm not that domestic." He passed her the bottle of catsup, which he'd liberally dumped on his eggs. "Maybe we'll let you do the cooking after all."

"Could be you just need more practice." Had she actually said that?

He lifted a cool eyebrow. "Could be."

Conversation dwindled to nothing. At a knock at the door, Jessie admitted Ramon Morales. He removed his hat.

"Mrs. Harding."

The words shook her. "Jessie," she said hastily, absorbing her new title.

"The men and I want to thank you for arranging for us to come back to work, just as you promised."

"I didn't do anything. Ben did." She glanced at him.

Ben met her gaze. "It was a joint effort."

"Then, we thank you both."

Ben nodded. "I've been meaning to talk to you about a job, Ramon. I could use someone full time. How about it? If it works out, maybe we can make it permanent."

Jessie's spirits sank. Ben still planned to leave—he was training his replacement. Despite the bitter letdown, Jessie endorsed Ben's offer. "It sounds like a good solution."

Ramon nodded. "Then I agree. I'll do a good job for you. Drew won't like it. He cuts a percentage from the workers' pay."

"There are laws to protect farmworkers," Ben said.

Ramon smiled bitterly. "But the Pierces have money. The laws are for them, not us."

Ben wished he could argue with him. The Pierces did control the town. In any case, he was relieved Ramon had agreed to accept the job. He needed a man he could depend on, in case Drew made more trouble.

He spent the day showing Ramon his new reponsibilities.

When he came in from the fields, stillness greeted him, as familiar as the spreading oak tree, the day lilies bordering the walk, Beauregard chomping at the hedge. Stone's End no longer seemed remote. In fact, it felt pretty close to heaven—as close as he would ever get, he thought, as he walked toward the house. The hot day had cooled. A pink sky hovered. The nearest hills were in shadow, dark and sleepy looking. In vivid shades of green, Maine was jewel-like in midsummer. The pine forest remained green all winter. Ben wondered if he would be here to see it.

When he stepped onto the porch, Jessie came to the door, as if she'd been waiting for him. Who was he kidding? The scenery wasn't keeping him here—unless it happened to have wide gray eyes and a winsome smile.

"Oh, it's you." She came out through the screen door.

"Who were you expecting?"

"No one, I guess. I was going to visit my father."

"If you'll wait, I'll go with you."

Her mouth started to form a negative response, then she said, "All right." She'd combed her hair into a coil at the base of her neck. A few wisps of hair had escaped. Now she smoothed back the soft tendrils with a nervous hand.

"Don't do that," he said. She dropped her hand into the patch pocket of her dress. Regretting his abruptness, he said, "Leave it. It looks nice." Nice? That was an understatement.

Bathed in the early-evening light, she looked soft—the

color of her hair, the strange smoky paleness of her eyes, the natural disorder of those small, loose tendrils curling around her face. Her dress was peach-colored—a thin gauzy fabric with a small floral pattern in a deeper shade. Cut in a simple style, it was light and airy and suited her. She looked like summer in her flowered dress. Her delicate white sling-back sandals made her slender legs look long, sleek and sexy.

Jessie touched something in him—the part that still yearned for pretty young girls in soft summer dresses and long hot summer nights that beckoned with all sorts of promises.

Chapter Thirteen

For a timeless moment, they stared at each other. Ben broke the impasse. He walked toward her, easy and unhurried, as if he had all the time in the world to claim her. Jessie felt a shiver of anticipation as he crossed the width of the porch. She backed away, her elbows scraping the rough screen.

Shaking his head, he placed his hands on her waist. "You are such a baby," he drawled, clearly enjoying her discomfort.

"Please, don't patronize me."

"Then don't be so jumpy." He lifted and casually set her to one side. At her gasp, he ran a cool thumb down her warm cheek. "Have a lemonade. You look hot." He went inside.

His laughter continued up the stairs. Moments later, Jessie stood in the kitchen and sipped her drink. Ice cold, the outside of the glass beaded up with moisture. Her hand still shook. How could she adjust? Was he actually flirting with her? What a maddening man. She pressed the cold glass to her flushed cheek.

The relief was only temporary. Ben came back.

In fresh jeans and a white shirt, with his hair damp and slicked back after his shower, he looked rugged and a little untamed. Rakish. The term "macho" didn't apply to him, she realized. His attitude wasn't put on for effect. He was a survivor; he'd earned his status the hard way.

Ben took her glass of lemonade and finished it for her. His simple action of sharing her drink was so intimate, so natural, as if he'd done it a thousand times before. "Ready?" he asked.

No, she wanted to shout. He was slowly, methodically breaking down every last defense. His gaze slid up and down, then back up. Suddenly conscious of her bare shoulders, she took a deep breath to cool the heat in her cheeks. "I'm ready."

He smiled. Did she detect a hint of tenderness? She couldn't be sure. Superimposed was the memory of his facial expression that morning; the naked hunger.

Jessie was alone in the house the following day when she answered a frantic knocking at the door.

"It's Miguel." Rita Morales cradled her small son to her breast. "I have no car. Please, I need a doctor."

Jessie made a phone call. "Dr. Peterson will see him."

Rita's anxious face softened with relief. "Thank you."

The trip to town didn't take long. Prewarned, Dr. Peterson was waiting. "Well, son, let's have a look."

The boy's smile was wan, his dark eyes feverish. "I thought he just had the flu," Rita said. "He is worse today."

Dr. Peterson's murmured, "Hmm," worried Jessie.

"We'll run some tests. Looks like food poisoning. Are any others sick?"

Rita nodded. "Yes, there are many."

Within a week, Miguel got well. Others came down with severe stomach cramps and dehydration. Dr. Peterson visited the camp and diagnosed more cases—several children and adults. Some required hospitalization. Fortunately, all would get well with proper treatment. Work at Stone's End ground to a halt.

Ramon came by; several men were with him. After a polite nod for Jessie, Ramon directed his remarks to Ben. "The doctor traced the infection to contaminated meat from a broken freezer in the camp store." He flushed angrily. "The camp is a health hazard! Will you speak to the authorities for us?"

Ben said simply, "I'm an outsider, just as you are."

Jessie's heart contracted at his words. Ben still felt like an outsider. What would it take to make him belong?

Ramon spoke with passion. "That is why we ask you. No one else will help. The Pierces have too much power."

"What about the police?"

"The law!" Ramon spat. "What law will protect us?"

"I'll see what I can do," Ben said, relieved when the tension eased. "Until then, stay out of trouble." He spoke in Spanish for those who couldn't understand. Except for a few, the men seemed satisfied. As they drove off, Ben discovered he'd lost Jessie's attention. Shading her eyes from the sun, she stared up the road toward a tall, fair-haired man. Ben didn't recognize him. It was probably someone looking for work. With the recent shortage, they could use all the help they could get. Dusty and fatigued, the man didn't appear in any hurry to reach his destination. He was alone.

Jessie took one step, then started to run. The young

man's face broke into a smile when she cried out, "Jared!"

He caught her and spun her around. "You weigh a ton."

Ben smiled. Jessie had started to fill out in all the right places. Jared released her. "You're home," Ben heard her say.

A shadow seemed to cross Jared's face. "Yes," he said soberly. "I'm home." He didn't appear overjoyed.

Recalling Ben's presence, Jessie approached him with her brother in tow. Before she could make the introductions, Jared took the initiative. "I couldn't help noticing, the workers look upset. Looks like we've got a problem."

"A potential one," Ben admitted, taking Jared's measure. He liked what he saw. Jessie's brother was no weakling.

Jared studied him with equal intensity. "I don't think we've met before." He held out his hand. "I'm Jared Carlisle."

Ben left Jessie to make the announcement. She did so haltingly. "This is Ben...my husband."

Jared's hand dropped, his voice lowered a notch. "You never said anything about a husband in your letters."

Jessie glanced nervously at Ben. "It's sort of recent." She cleared her throat. "A few weeks."

Jared's face hardened. "Wasn't that a bit sudden?"

Ben interrupted, "Look, I know this comes as news. Why don't you reserve judgment for a while?"

Making an obvious attempt to end the awkwardness, Jessie asked, "Why didn't you call? I could have picked you up."

"I hitched a ride from town."

Fred came around the corner of the barn. He caught his breath as if winded. "Well, if you ain't a sight for sore eyes."

The two men hugged. Fred's eyes looked watery.

Jared looked around as if surprised. "I have missed this place." He spotted Homer and shook his head. "That old renegade bull is still here. Dad was always threatening to sell him."

Ben said dryly, "Homer became a sacred cow."

There were lots of sacred cows and taboos in the family, he discovered that evening at the hospital.

"Hello, son." No smile accompanied Ira's greeting.

"Dad," Jared said quietly. "I guess it's been a while."

Jessie's brother wasn't what Ben had expected. He was quiet, introspective, serious—and obviously not too pleased to be home. "Two years," Ira said with some bitterness.

Jared shrugged. He was tall but not broad—not as broad as his father. "I'm sorry you're sick. How are you?"

Ira refused to bend. "You took your time getting here."

"I'm here now," Jared returned, squaring his jaw.

Watching them, Ben was curious. Had Ira met his match in his own son? There was a relentless quality in Jared's eyes—gray eyes a shade stormier than Jessie's.

That night, Jessie brought fresh linens to Jared's room. He frowned at the motorcycle boots tucked under the bed. She scooped up a pair of jeans from a chair.

Jared stared. "Don't you share a room with him?"

"He has a name. It's Ben."

"Don't you share a room with Ben?" he returned with a touch of sarcasm. Naturally, Jared was suspicious.

She and Ben were married, even if they didn't share a bedroom, just a bed. "Yes." She blushed. "Yes, of course we share a room." On occasion. Her heart sank. No matter how she tried to disguise it, her marriage was a sham.

Jared folded his arms. "Correct me if I'm wrong, but Dad didn't appear any too fond of your husband. From what I've seen, you and this guy—Ben—don't look exactly cozy.''

Jessie grabbed a box and started to collect Ben's things from around the room. "I'll just get these out of your way."

"Has Dad been up to some of his old tricks?"

"I don't know what you mean." She looked about for more of Ben's belongings. There weren't any; the box was less than half full. He owned so few possessions. He traveled light. If he did decide to leave, she couldn't see him adding a sidecar to his motorcycle. Make that a sidecar and a half. She hadn't been married long, but the suspicion that she was pregnant grew more probable with each day. The thought thrilled her—when she allowed herself to think about it.

Jared said in an exasperated tone, "I'd like an answer."

"All right." She dropped the box. "There was some gossip."

Jared's face looked grim. "Was it true?"

"No," she said, hurt by the skepticism in his eyes.

"But Dad wanted a wedding?"

She couldn't prevent the hurt. "Is it so difficult to believe Ben wanted to marry me?"

Jared looked sheepish. "I'm sorry, Jessie." At that moment, he looked young and unsure. He looked around his old room. His face tightened. "I see Dad got rid of my things."

"I stored them in the attic." She hadn't obeyed her father's orders to throw everything of Jared's away.

"It doesn't matter. He was furious when I left home." Jared hesitated. "Jessie, do you ever think of Mom?"

"No. No, I don't." She denied any recollection, then felt overwhelmed with guilt for denying the woman who'd given her life. Her mother had left and never come back.

Jessie had buried the hurt so long ago. Yet, it still ached. Apparently, some wounds never healed.

"I don't remember much," she admitted after a long silence. "Just bits and pieces." She wrapped her fingers around a bedpost, holding on to something solid. "I remember cinnamon toast. And the color blue."

"Blue was her favorite color. She loved us, Jessie."

Jessie shook her head. "Then why did she leave?"

"She loved you," Jared insisted. "I know she did."

"Do we have to discuss this now? It's late, and—"

"You can't run from it forever."

Jessie picked up the box with Ben's possessions. "I know, but not now." She said good-night and went to her room.

Ben wasn't there. He never spent the night. She placed his things in a corner. The pile didn't take much space. Yet, he filled her life. He'd changed her, made her stronger—in every way but where it came to needing him. Each time he came to her, he broke down her resolve. Each night she promised would be the last, and each night, she lay awake craving his touch, wondering if he would come. Where was he tonight?

And with Jared occupying his old room again, where did Ben expect to sleep? How could they keep up the pretense of a happy marriage if Ben didn't sleep with her? At times she despaired of ever reaching through all the barriers dividing her and Ben, the man she'd married in such haste. She hadn't had the leisure to repent. Until she felt more secure with him, she would never reveal her love. She refused to hold him that way.

For the same reason, she couldn't tell him she suspected she might be pregnant. She sat up and hugged her knees to her chest as she thought of this new impasse. She didn't have to confess anything, but what if…what if…?

Did she have the nerve? Before she could change her

mind, she went downstairs. When she joined Ben on the porch, he put his arm around her, almost as a reflex. She took courage from that small but warm gesture of acknowledgment.

Her courage failed. A southerly wind had risen. Bolts of heat lightning set fire to the sky. Jessie trembled at his nearness.

"Are you frightened of storms?" he asked.

"No, I like them." Excitement made her glow.

He chuckled. "Doesn't anything frighten you?"

He frightened her; what he made her feel. "Why aren't you in bed?" she whispered, amazed at her own daring.

"I couldn't sleep," he said dryly.

She latched on to the distraction. "Don't you think you should talk about your nightmares?"

"No," he said firmly.

"If not to me, then…"

"No."

She sighed. "Then, come to bed."

He stiffened, as if her invitation was the last thing he'd expected. Tilting her chin up, he gazed into her eyes. She hoped they didn't betray the longing in her heart. His voice was husky. "I wasn't sure you wanted me to come."

"I see," she murmured, not seeing at all. She'd made love with this man, taken him inside her, let him take her— take her to the most intimate heights. But she didn't understand him at all. Nevertheless, one issue needed to be resolved. The only way she knew how to deal with a problem was to confront it.

"I'm your wife," she blurted out. "I want to sleep with you—not just have sex."

Ben gritted his teeth. "We don't have sex. We make love."

"Now you're angry. I didn't mean to imply…" She took a deep breath and released it slowly. "Anyway, you didn't ask permission the first time.'' The only time he'd stayed all night.

He frowned. ''That was different.''

''How?'' she asked, genuinely puzzled.

''That's hardly the point. I'm a restless sleeper,'' he said, minimizing his nightmares. ''I don't want to disturb you.''

''You won't disturb me....''

He drew her closer. His eyes crinkled into a wolfish smile. ''I hope that isn't the case.''

She blushed. ''You have to know I'm far from immune. I practically threw myself at you. Besides, I—''

Ben swallowed a groan and whispered, ''Shut up, Jessie.'' He closed her mouth with a deep, drugging kiss. Running his hand up and down her arm, he felt silk. He released her abruptly and stared at her in amazement. She stood there in yards and yards of sheer, delicate, bridal white silk and lace. She looked beautiful, like an angel.

Like an angel.

She also looked unsure. Vulnerable. ''Do I look silly?''

She'd taken an emotional risk. He hoped he was worthy. If there was goodness anywhere on this earth, it resided in Jessie.

''You look like a bride.'' Ben took her hand and led her to her room. Their room. His belongings stood in one corner. He was firmly in her territory now.

Jessie's nerve almost failed as Ben undressed. His tanned shoulders gleamed, like polished teak; his muscles rippled as he unzipped his jeans. His complete lack of inhibition always made her feel tongue-tied and awkward. Her mouth went dry when his last stitch of clothing came off. He slept nude.

She rushed into speech. ''I'm sorry Jared isn't friendlier.''

Lifting an eyebrow, Ben shrugged. "He's only showing brotherly concern. I can respect that."

Jessie hugged her arms around her waist, turning away, trying to ignore the growing, gnawing ache inside. "What do you think of him?" She rearranged a brush on her dresser.

"He's not what I expected."

"What do you mean?"

Coming up behind her, Ben placed his hands on her hips and kissed her neck where wispy little curls settled against her smooth skin. "The golden boy, I suppose."

"He's grown up." Her tilted head allowed him access. In the mirror, she could see him bend over her. His height dwarfed hers. He seemed so large and dark and mysterious. Exciting.

"Jessie." He spoke her name low, in that gravelly deep drawl that invoked pleasure in her. The mere sound could make her want him. He held so much power over her. "It's okay."

She turned, seeking his mouth, melting against him, loving the instant passion between them. "I just wish..."

"Shh." His lips covered hers and stopped the flow of words. "You can't fix everything. Enough about Jared. Let's think about us." He peeled off her negligee, then touched her breasts through the thin silk nightgown. "Think about this."

How could she think at all when he touched her, stroking her passion to life? For now, all she wanted was escape. There would be time to worry about Jared and all the rest tomorrow. Ben stretched her across the bed and joined her. She linked her arms around his neck, aware of his surprise in the lift of his brow. Had she failed to show him that she cared, she loved? The flare of passion in his eyes stopped all her rational thought. There would be time enough to analyze her feelings later.

* * *

Dr. Peterson called—Ira was coming home. Although Jessie had seen her father's strength return, the news came as a surprise. She slowly hung up the phone. Her loyalty was sharply divided. She wanted her father home; she also dreaded it.

Jared already complicated her situation. He tolerated Ben. But the workers weren't quite sure who was boss anymore—Ben or Jared. Jessie bit her lip. She was trying so hard to put the pieces of Ben together, to make a complete whole of the man she'd married. She was trying, Ben was trying; should marriage really be so much work? In any case, her father's return was bound to add tension to an already rocky relationship.

It was just about lunchtime. With sudden decision, she filled a picnic basket with sandwiches, fresh brownies and iced tea and set out to find Ben. A mile down the road, she found a field being worked. She hid her disappointment; Ben wasn't among the workers. Cal Pierce was there—with Serena Morales.

The two separated guiltily. "Hi, Jess." Young and defiant, Cal's expression dared her to disapprove.

While the women worked, Serena watched over Miguel and the other children. The girl's sense of responsibility had impressed Jessie. Cal was a good kid but—like all the Pierces—spoiled.

Jessie hoped their infatuation would wear off, which didn't look likely, considering the secret glances they were sharing. Hopefully no one would get hurt. "I was looking for Ben."

"He's over in the south field."

Jessie left them, aware that her total preoccupation with her husband must be painfully obvious. By now, her clothes were sticking. The thermos of iced tea had grown heavy.

She found Ben at work, mending a stone wall. He lifted

a huge rock as if it were featherweight. He'd removed his shirt. The muscles in his chest and arms rippled and glistened in the sun.

He saw her. "You shouldn't be out here in this heat."

"I won't melt. I brought you a cold drink." She poured two glasses and handed him one. "And lunch."

"Sounds good." He drank deeply, then carefully set his glass aside. "Now, why did you really come?"

How could he read her so well when she still found him so mysterious? "My father's coming home tomorrow."

He took a deep breath and said, "That's good news."

"You will try to get along with him?"

"I have no intention of making things difficult."

"I suppose I'll have to be satisfied with that."

"Jessie…"

"It's all right. I understand." She could only hope for the best. In her role as peacemaker between these two strong-willed men, she might turn out to be the loser. "I just don't want any arguments," she pleaded.

He nodded. He refilled his glass and drank deeply.

Jessie found herself watching the muscles of his throat work, struck by the power of his attraction. Perspiration gleamed. In fascination, she watched a bead of moisture from his skin trickle down his throat toward the hard ridge of bone etching his wide shoulders. Like a tiny drop of dew, it captured the sunlight, then rolled over the edge and disappeared into the thick mat of dark hair covering his chest.

Her finger trapped another drop and wiped it smooth against his vital, tanned flesh. The movement in his throat stopped abruptly. He looked down at her hand now resting against his chest. His eyes darkened. Tossing the cup to the ground, he reached for her and dragged her close against him. He kissed her with a hard, immediate need that drained her and left her wanting more. Jessie wound her arms around his back, pressing into him, feeling his body heat raise hers. She ran her hands across the dampness of his back, kneading the taut muscles urgently, half afraid of what she was doing, yet unable to stop.

For the first time with Ben, she didn't try to control the instantaneous flood of emotion. She moaned and moved against him, silently begging for him to take her.

He wrenched his mouth from hers. "I'll tell Fred I'm taking the rest of the day off. Let's make the most of it."

"Yes," she whispered, barely containing her pleasure. He shared her reluctance to end their idyll.

Ben watched her smile grow. Despite a lack of softness in her life, Jessie's spirit had remained uncrushed. She was proud, idealistic, sensitive. Beneath her practical puritanical front, she hid a hot temper and a stubborn, determined streak—as obstinate as her dad's. It was the first time she'd touched him freely and openly. He'd patiently waited for some sign that she wanted him. He'd ached for her to touch him. Now that she had, why did he feel threatened?

Until his world had blown apart, Ben had thought of himself as coolheaded, efficient, hardened, ruthless if the need arose. With Jessie, he was still discovering needs he'd never known he had. He wanted her to make room for him, to welcome him into her home, her bed, her life. Sometimes he just wanted her to smile.

"Let's go to the pond." Jessie wasn't sure if she'd said it or Ben had, but her response was physical. "Yes." This time, she wouldn't shy away. She knew what she wanted.

He took her hand and they walked across the fields, through dense plants and rich brown cultivated earth, and it felt new, as if they'd never walked this path before. With each step, her heart felt lighter. The distance seemed greater than the last time. This time, she had come to him.

By the time they reached the pine-scented woods, her body felt tight, her clothes constricted her breathing.

Tall ancient trees blocked the sun's blinding force; delicate golden rays filtered through thick branches. Ben held a branch aside. She walked through into a green velvet bower, protected from seeing eyes. He released the branch to enclose them in a private world. Jessie went into his arms willingly. There was more than eager hunger in her kiss; there was desperation. When Ben met and matched it, she felt almost unbearably excited. Time was running out for them.

He brought her down into the green, green grass among long-stemmed daisies that drifted lazily in the soft summer breeze. He kissed her, drawing her emotions into a maelstrom. Then he lifted his mouth to allow her space to breathe. "I want you so badly," he murmured.

The laughter in his eyes was gone.

"I want you, too," she whispered, sharing his need. She needed him like the earth needed rain, like a flower needed sun, like a woman needs a man. She no longer felt like a girl. Love had magically shaken her up, rearranged every molecule in her body and transformed her into Ben Harding's woman. She loved Ben. She admitted the knowledge into the deep, hidden corners of her heart—all those lonely places of her childhood and beyond.

As he undressed, Ben's scars stood out against his tanned skin. Helplessly drawn, she ran the palm of her hand over the puckered flesh. "You were so hurt," she said softly. She moved her hand against his thigh where a long, jagged scar marred the tanned surface. She felt his muscles ripple in response.

"Don't," he murmured, trapping her hand under his.

"Can't I touch you?"

"Please, yes," he groaned. He moved her hand up into the coarse hair on his chest until she felt his male nipples harden. As if he couldn't bear not to touch her in return, he slid her shirt off, tantalizing her with the slow slide of fabric across her breasts. He drew her down against him.

Helplessly aroused, she pressed her naked breasts against him. He let her touch his scars and press her lips to them. With a groan, he turned her then and rested on her, letting his elbows take most of his weight. Desire kindled in his eyes as he looked down at her and touched her intimately. That look set her aflame. She wrapped her hands around him and drew him down.

He kissed her, devouring her mouth as if he was starving for her. He sank into her, slowly, until she surged against him, wanting more of him, wanting much more than gentleness. Losing all restraint, he responded with the same mind-numbing urgency.

Her cries of pleasure mingled with the soft puffs of wind, the lapping of waves on the shore, the flutter of wings as a flock of birds took flight. Jessie felt her heart pound against his; her pulse ran wild and free as she reached the height of passion and felt his body rock against hers. He cried out in satisfaction. His voice sent another thrill of pleasure over her, filling her with the joy of knowing she pleased him. Sated, they lay together.

Gently, she touched his side. "Tell me how you got these scars," she whispered. She needed to know.

She felt him physically withdraw. He moved away from her, but not far. His words sounded as if they came from a distance when he asked, "Why do you want to know?"

"Because it bothers you."

He shot her a quizzical look. "And that matters?"

"Yes," she summoned the courage to say. And that was all. She couldn't tell him she loved him. Not yet.

Chapter Fourteen

"My unit was assigned to rescue a drug informant and his family." Ben spoke slowly at first, then faster, as if he had to get the words out. "The whole town was ruled by a powerful drug cartel. Someone had tipped them off...."

"Who?" Jessie asked in growing horror.

"We never knew." He took a deep breath. "They waited till the copter was full of passengers before they ambushed us." His hands clenched into fists. "There were women and children."

"My God," Jessie cried out in shock. The world he described was far removed from hers, yet it had been all too real for Ben. She could hardly believe he'd inhabited such an alien place. To Jessie, he belonged to the earth and the mountains—not to a cruel, violent world where men shot machines out of the sky.

She'd witnessed his gentleness, and his hardness. Who was he and how did a man of war survive peace?

"I knew it was dangerous," he continued. "There had been leaks before. I should have refused the assignment. The town was a hide-out. A plane was an easy target."

"You had no choice," she insisted, feeling his pain.

"Didn't I?" he said quietly. "I could have argued that a land operation would be safer. It still would have been risky, but it would have saved a few lives." He closed his eyes. "As it turned out, no one stood a chance in hell. Everyone died and I lived."

"Ben, you didn't choose life, it chose you."

He sounded angry. "I can't just forget it and go on with my life as if nothing happened."

She wanted so desperately to help him, to reach him. "You could have died, but you didn't. And I'm glad."

It was as much of an admission as she could make, for now. She wasn't ready to say she loved him; not yet, and probably not until he'd said the words first. He silently reached for her.

But had her words reached him? She prayed they had; that somehow he could find the strength to forgive himself. Until then, their future lay locked in his past. She held nothing back when he made love to her. *Give me a reason to stay,* he'd challenged her after they'd first made love. When they came together, he was everything to her. Was she everything to him?

Was she reason enough for him to stay?

A few days later, Ira came home. "I won't be coddled," he announced. When Jessie tried to send him to bed, he collapsed in his favorite chair. "I'm fine right here."

Later, Jessie informed Ben, "I have to sleep downstairs to keep an eye on Dad. He might have a weak spell."

She avoided his gaze. Ben folded his arms and watched her collect her nightgown and robe. "I see. And whose idea was that? No, let me guess...."

"Please understand, Dad needs me," she said, obviously feeling pressured and hurt by his lack of understanding.

Ben sighed, resigned to the situation. "Of course, you're right." Her father came first; he probably always would.

Perhaps Ira was having second thoughts and feeling threatened by his daughter's allegiance to her husband. That first week, Ben refused to give Ira the satisfaction of knowing he'd succeeded in driving a wedge between them. Jessie was exhausted; she had no time for anything but her father, least of all, a husband. Ben made no demands on her.

At lunch a week later, Ira took a look at the ground turkey and pushed it aside. "Feed that to Bandit. I want real food. And tell Ben I want to see him. Where is he, anyway?"

"He should be here for lunch." Jessie tried to be patient.

Ben came in eventually. Under Ira's grilling, he had to report work was behind. Several workers were still out sick.

"Have you talked to Drew about extra help?" Ira asked.

"According to Drew, there isn't anyone else. This far into the season, they're all committed elsewhere."

"Well, that's just fine. Meantime, my crops rot!"

Jared arrived for lunch. "Sorry, I'm late." He helped himself to the eggplant casserole. "This looks great, Jessie." He looked around when he got no response. "Is something wrong?"

Ira's expression was angry. "Suppose you tell me. Why wasn't I told about the problems at the camp?"

Jared looked from Ben to Jessie. It was Jessie who replied, "We didn't want to worry you while you were ill."

Ben explained the situation, and his involvement. "It had to be reported. I agreed to help."

Ira was adamant. "If you'd asked, I would have said no!"

Ben's mouth went taut. "Then I'm glad I didn't ask."

"Let the migrants settle their own problems—it's got nothing to do with us. We don't need the feds nosing around."

"It's too late for that," Jared spoke up. "The Pierces became wealthy by taking advantage of anyone who works for them."

"Drew said he'd fix everything," Ira interjected.

"Everyone knows he takes his orders from his father."

"The Pierces have political connections," Ira insisted. He glared at Ben. "If you fight them, you'll only lose."

Ben pushed his chair back. "Then I'll lose."

"*I* give the orders around here!" Ira snapped.

While Jessie stared in concern, Jared shoved his chair back and stood. "In case anyone's interested, I agree with Ben."

"Me, too." Jessie met Ben's steady gaze.

"You're both taking his side?" Ira demanded.

Jared said, "I'd rather be part of the solution than the problem. Covering up for the Pierces isn't the answer. They should face up to their mistakes."

Ben added quietly, "There's a second meeting with the authorities the day after tomorrow. I plan to be there."

Jessie and Jared insisted on going with him. For a man who hadn't wanted to get involved, Ben was truly committed.

The day after tomorrow.

Ben had avoided thoughts of tomorrow for so long. Lunch ended with Ira red-faced and blustering. Ben remained withdrawn.

Caught in the middle with her loyalties divided, Jessie soothed her father while her husband left the house.

"That husband of yours is wrong," Ira said. "Drew will cooperate. Ben's just not our kind."

"What do you mean he's not our kind?"

Her father's face became set and hard. "He doesn't belong here."

Jessie gripped the chair back. "You wanted him here."

"All right, I made a mistake. That can be fixed." His mouth tightened. "If you just tell him to go..."

"I won't!" Jessie gasped. "I love you, but you drive everyone away. Everyone I care about. Don't make me choose between you and Ben. I...I love him."

Had she actually said that? Her father turned away without saying a word. Jessie released her grip on the back of the chair. She was so afraid he would drive Ben away.

That night, Jessie slept on the downstairs couch—again. As Ben prepared for bed, he remembered her expression at dinner. She'd seemed upset. Later, he had the dream— screaming bullets mingled with human cries. Jessie was in it, but her image was fading. He woke suddenly, his heart like lead. The room was dark, empty. This was insane. Why was he in bed alone with a wife under the same roof? He tore off the bedcovers and pounded down the stairs. He found her in the darkness, scooped her up, blankets, pillows and all. His mouth on hers cut off her protest, then he held her close.

His voice was hushed in the night, urgent. "I'm not putting up with this a moment longer. You belong in my bed. Whether you like it or not, you're sleeping with me because heaven knows, I can't sleep without you!" Expecting an argument from Jessie—at the very least a debate and a long list of objections, he stared at her, unable to read her expression in the dim moonlight coming through the windows. "Have you got that?" he repeated.

She yawned. "Yes, Ben."

Disarmed by her easy capitulation, he guessed she was too exhausted to fight him. Ben marched upstairs and very gently laid her on her bed. Then he took the empty space beside her and pulled her close, feeling a surge of warm pleasure when she curled up against his chest. Muttering something unintelligible, she reached up. A whisper of a kiss brushed his mouth, and then she subsided. Her breathing was slow and even. Struck by an unexpected wave of tenderness, Ben closed his eyes, content to simply lie there and hold her. He suspected that this was happiness.

Ben confronted Ira the following day. "I hired a nurse."

"I don't need a nurse! I've got Jessie."

"She can't keep up with your demands."

Ira's face flared with resentment. "Just yours?"

Ben flushed. "Jessie may be your daughter, but she's my wife. Nothing you can do will change that."

"Ben," Jessie pleaded. "It's fine. I can manage alone."

Fed up with competing with her father, Ben said firmly, "Well, you won't have to manage alone. She starts today."

Ira clamped his mouth shut.

Ben was relieved when the doctor stopped by later.

Scolding, Dr. Peterson exposed Ira's bouts of weakness. "I told you to exercise. You should be on your feet by now. Not tied to a chair. The nurse has orders to get you up."

Ira retorted, "If I'm doing so great, I don't need a nurse." He wrinkled his brow. "Who is she?"

"Dora Cummings."

"That old harpy!"

Dr. Peterson smiled. "She'll keep you in line. It's natural to be scared, but as long as you take your medicine and follow orders, there's little risk of another attack."

Jessie stared uncomprehendingly from Ben to her father; slowly the facts registered. Her father had used her to get back at Ben. And she had let him.

Dora's arrival created an unexpected new ripple. No matter how much Ira berated the woman, he had put on his new velour robe, Ben noted. He also was wearing what looked and smelled suspiciously like hair gel. Ben hid a smile.

Starch crackling, Dora Cummings took charge. "Ira, now what's this about you not getting out of your chair?" Tall and substantially built, she pulled him to his feet.

He shook her arm off. "I can walk without any help."

Dora stood back with a smile of satisfaction. "Then, please do." She escorted Ira around the yard twice, then helped Jessie serve breakfast.

Later, Jessie could hear her father and brother in the next room, arguing. Their raised voices covered the sound of Ben's approach. Her hands immersed in hot sudsy water with the breakfast dishes, she felt his presence behind her and dropped a slippery plate with a splash. He kissed the back of her neck. She shivered with sensuous pleasure as his breath teased.

"Jessie." He spoke her name low, in that gravelly deep voice of his. Deaf to his actual words, she felt only the effect of his nearness. Drowning in a sea of sensation, she turned to seek his mouth, melting against him, loving the way instant passion flared between them. Loving him.

Did he love her?

Doubts plagued her. Even at the height of passion during their lovemaking, she experienced doubts. Could this be real? Could it last? She didn't know much about love, but she knew it could hurt. It made her vulnerable to needs she hadn't known she had; the need to be touched, to be held and kissed and driven insane with longing. How could anything so agonizing feel so good? She pressed against him, wishing she could leave her imprint on his body as he had marked hers. She carried his child. She was sure of it now. How could she tell him? Would he be pleased? Or would he think she'd deliberately trapped him? Her hands crept up his chest. Ben set her aside with reluctance.

He grinned at the soapy trail she'd left on his shirt. With a rueful smile, she removed suds from his throat.

"I suppose I should get some work done," he said. "Don't let Ira fire Dora. And take it easy today." She had her orders. He reached down and kissed her again, this time with more urgency than before. Finally, he wrenched his mouth from hers. "Later."

Smiling, she watched him leave and wished he'd invited her to go along. She would rather work outside—anything to be with him. If only she could escape. She felt guilty at the thought. How could she leave? Her father's voice clashed with Jared's again.

She groaned. When Jared burst out of the room, she followed him onto the porch. She called to him. He didn't respond, so she called again more sharply. "Jared!"

He was halfway across the yard before he actually stopped. He spun around. "What is it?"

"That's what I'd like to know." She walked toward him, aware of the defensive set of his shoulders. Angering him wouldn't accomplish anything. Determined to get to the bottom of things, she folded her arms. "Dad can't take the stress."

He released a long breath. "I know." He ran a hand through his hair and looked at her, shamefaced. "I know," he said more quietly. "Look, it doesn't concern you."

She glared at him. "I think it does."

After a tense silence, he announced starkly, "I found Mom."

Mom.

Jessie stood as if struck. Something buried deep within stirred. "How?" she whispered, all she could choke out.

"I hired a detective."

"And?" she said impatiently. Dear God, she'd waited twenty years for this day—and she hadn't even known she was waiting. All she knew of her mother was that she'd left. Why? Why would a woman desert her children? Why had her mother deserted her?

He turned toward the fence and stared out across the meadow. His voice seemed to come from a distance as he gathered a few precious memories and shared them. "You were too young when she left, Jessie, but I remember her. She was so pretty, with pale curls and a bright smile. She always smelled like lilacs and she liked to sing. I remember her singing to us," he said, as if he could hold on to that. He swallowed visibly. "I always knew I had to find her. When I turned eighteen, I asked Dad for some information. It was just after Sunny..."

Of course, Jessie remembered how upset he'd been at losing the dog his mother had given him. Apparently the incident had affected him even more than she'd realized. She recalled how he'd gone out with his friends that night. He'd come home alone, he'd been drinking. Her father had been furious.

"Go on," she prodded gently.

He faltered, then admitted, "When he refused to tell me, I went searching through his private papers. I just wanted to find something of hers." He sighed. "There were some old letters. They were unopened, addressed to you and me. She'd written for years before finally giving up. Dad never replied or gave them to us. Instead, he did everything he could to wipe out her memory, as if she never existed. She left us and never came back, but he had no right to hide the letters.'' He swallowed. ''I confronted him. He was furious I'd invaded his things. We fought.'' His face was hard and unforgiving; he was a Jared she no longer knew. ''I lit out of here first thing the next morning. I had to get away, Jessie. Do you understand?''

''Yes.'' Jessie released a sigh. ''But how did you find her?''

''I took the letters with me when I left.''

She placed her hand on his arm. ''And you looked for her.''

''Not at first,'' he admitted. ''For years, I was too angry at both of them, but after I got out of the army, I started looking. I needed to get to the bottom of all the lies. Through a social security number, I found a trail of old addresses and former employers that went nowhere. She moved around a lot. Finally, I traced her to California. She tried to make it in movies. She changed her name. And I thought that was the end of it.''

''But it wasn't?''

He took a deep breath. ''I couldn't let go of it. The last time I came home, Dad still refused to help. Eventually, I saved a little money, enough to hire a private detective. After following several leads, he found her. Ironically, she lived in California, less than four hundred miles from where I was living.''

''Where is she now?'' Jessie whispered. ''I want to see her.''

His face filled with pain and regret, Jared faced her. ''I'm sorry, Jessie. She died six months before I found her.''

Jessie groaned and turned away.

His voice turned her back, made her face the past. ''They gave me her things. She'd kept a snapshot of us. I was five, you were two. Remember the red tricycle you got for your birthday?'' He stumbled over the words, choked and rubbed his reddened eyes.

Overwhelmed with emotion, Jessie couldn't speak for a moment. "Did you tell Dad?" She had so many questions, but for now it was all she needed to know.

His gaze held bitterness. "Yes."

"What did he say?"

"Nothing. I don't think he felt anything." Jared blinked and stared up at the sky. The sun was obscenely bright, but the wind had a cold snap that signaled a turbulent summer. "I pray to God I never get that hard."

Jessie couldn't imagine Jared ever being hard. Perhaps cynical, but not hard. If anything, he was too idealistic. He'd lost respect for his father. Jessie wondered if the rift could be healed. Struggling to cope with her own emotions, she didn't know what to say. "When did you tell him?"

"I called to tell him I'd gotten a job in California."

"Jared, he had a heart attack that night."

They looked at each other. Jared appeared shaken. The news had caused her father's collapse. Jessie recalled how upset he'd been. At the time, she'd blamed Cal's injury and Ben's decision to quit. Her father must still have cared about his wife. For some reason, he'd let bitterness rule his life. She pitied him.

"Can you forgive him?" Even as she said the words, Jessie wondered if *she* could forgive her father's deception. It seemed her mother had loved her after all. "I'm sorry about Mom," she said softly. "The years have been hard on Dad, too. He made a mistake, but he's paid the price." He'd lost his son's love.

"You and your soft heart." He smiled sadly. "What about you? I come home and find you married to some stranger—"

"Ben isn't a stranger to me."

"If you say so." He didn't look convinced. "Anyway, your marriage came as a shock. I know that's not your fault. I should have stayed in closer touch. I got so involved in the past, I forgot the present. I forgot about you. You've changed, Jessie. You've grown up. Can you forgive me?"

She nodded. She had grown up. How could she tell him of all the long, lonely years? She had never felt young, never been kissed. Never felt the earth move with a man's touch. Until Ben. He'd opened up a whole new world for her. The possibility of losing that now left her feeling cold and empty.

Jared shifted uneasily at her long silence. "You deserve some happiness. If that means Ben Harding, don't let anything stand in your way. Dad will come to terms."

Would her father ever come to terms with her marriage?

Jessie had her doubts. She turned back to the house and saw a black crow sitting on the porch rail. She'd lost her mother at the age of three, yet somehow the wound felt fresh. She would never stop mourning the years they'd spent apart—perhaps needlessly—due to her father's unforgiving heart.

Feeling a sick panic, she told Jared she was going for a walk. Ignoring the storm clouds, she didn't realize her destination until she was halfway there. She had to find Ben. When he wasn't in the first field where she'd expected to find him, she went to the next, then the next. She started to run.

Her heart was pounding when she slid to a stop. She'd found him. He was mending a fence. Fear struck her. How she loved him. What if he left, just like her mother? She couldn't survive.

His gaze fastened on her. "What's the matter?"
Everything.

She bit her trembling lip. "Nothing." Meeting his eyes squarely, she didn't look away.

"Your father?"

She shrugged. "I'd rather not talk about it."

He reached forward and gently ran the knuckles of his hand down her face. She held her breath, then released it on a shaky sigh when he whispered, "He'll be all right, Jessie."

"I know," she breathed.

Despite everything, Ben could feel compassion. In that moment, she gave him her heart. She smiled faintly. Of course, she loved him. It explained so much—the instinctive trust, the pain she felt when he was in pain, the need to be with him. She simply hadn't known what love was.

"Come on, let's go home." Ben gathered his tools.

Less than halfway home, a single flash of lightning signaled a downpour. In the woods, just north of the house, Jessie led him to shelter in the old sugar shack. The shack had been abandoned years ago. Part of her still mourned the loss of the large maple-tree grove; they'd sold the trees to the Pierce Logging Company.

Jessie went farther into the dim interior to examine the premises. "There might be mice."

Ben stood in the doorway and watched the dismal rain. He decided Maine had more than its share of both—the dismals and the rain.

Apparently satisfied at the absence of field mice, Jessie turned back to him. "What are you thinking?"

Turning away from the curtain of rain, he let his eyes take in the pleasurable sight of her ruffled composure. She rarely lost her dignity—perhaps due to her rigid upbringing.

"I was remembering the day I came," he said.

She searched his eyes. "A lot has changed since then."

"Yes." He started toward her. The shadows in the dim interior seemed to swallow her up.

Her expression became wary and troubled. "Are you sorry?"

"No. What about you, Jessie?"

She lifted her chin. "No, I'm not sorry."

Ben noticed she'd drawn the line at actually admitting she was happy. He understood her reticence. Happiness was something magical—intended for someone else; something he'd left behind in another life. So far, it had eluded him. Each hour with Jessie was special—stolen moments to be captured before fate played another joke. "I'm glad you feel that way."

Ben wasn't surprised when she hastily changed the subject.

"I forgot they'd predicted rain." She glanced past him, sounding very young and unsure of herself again.

But Jessie had never been that young. He imagined she'd had to grow up fast after her mother had walked out. Jessie fascinated him with her changeable moods. She often stunned him with acts of courage and never flinched when it came to being honest and direct. But she was a coward when it came to dealing with her own emotions. At first it had irritated him; now he found it endearing. One of these days, they were going to have a long discussion on the subject, but not now.

With the rain at his back, he narrowed the gap between them. The small wooden building was windowless. Rain beat down on the tin roof overhead. The air was stifling. Hot.

"It looks as if we'll have to wait it out." She shifted uneasily when he came close.

"Mmm, looks like." He brushed the damp tendrils of fine hair from her cheek, then framed her face with both hands. With satisfaction, he watched her eyes cloud with passion. His mouth slowly descended. She arched against him and sucked in a breath as she felt the hard evidence of his arousal.

At her soft sensuous moan of surrender, he murmured, "In the meantime, where were we?"

They made love before going home.

For the remainder of the day, Jessie tried to dismiss troubling thoughts. No amount of distraction could keep her from the truth. Her father hadn't wasted time on displays of affection; nevertheless, she'd believed in his basic goodness. Now, she couldn't. His treatment of her mother was hard to forgive. He'd allowed pride and bitterness to rule him.

At dinner when Ben tried to talk to her, Jessie didn't hear a word he said. After the meal, the men lingered over coffee. She was glad she didn't have to be alone with Ben. Why should she invest more emotion in a marriage that wouldn't last?

Ben had never hinted at love. Lately, she'd felt his renewed restlessness. Since Jared's return, the workers didn't know who was boss. Her father's interference didn't help the situation. With all the family tension, Ben was probably itching to leave. In a way, she couldn't blame him, but she did. Why did everyone want to leave? Why?

Ben looked at her closed expression and felt his frustration building. He felt left out, as if the Carlisles were closing ranks on him.

"What time is that meeting with the authorities in town tomorrow?" Jared asked, giving Ben an assessing look.

"First thing in the morning," Ben replied, feeling an undercurrent of tension. He knew something was wrong. But what? Ira wasn't saying much. Jared and Jessie had been closemouthed at dinner. Actually, Jessie looked as if she'd received a knockout punch.

"What do you think will happen?" Jessie asked coming into the conversation. She'd hardly eaten a thing, Ben noticed. There were pale violet shadows under her eyes. She looked fragile. In need of protection.

Ben wished she would open up to him. "Let's wait and see."

Ira put an end to the strained meal. "There's going to be a frost." He rose from his chair as if his bones ached.

The summer weather in northern Maine was unpredictable. Days were hot and humid. At night, the temperature dipped low. Jessie looked out the window into the growing darkness.

"I should cover the garden," she murmured.

"I'll help." Ben wanted to offer more. Right then, she seemed unapproachable.

Jessie glanced at him, a question in her eyes. "Thank you," was all she said, but he had a feeling his offer of assistance had somehow surprised her.

Didn't she realize he cared? He would grasp any excuse to be alone with her, away from her father and brother. He felt married to Stone's End and the entire Carlisle clan, when all he wanted was Jessie. He wanted her with every heartbeat, every aching moment of the day or night. She eased his loneliness and restlessness; now he was lonely without her. She was always on his mind, and he suspected she always would be. It was a damnable situation. He wasn't sure he liked it.

"Just tell me what to do." He wished it were that simple. How could he get through to Jessie?

She was wearing the soft raspberry-pink sweater he'd given her recently—at least that was some concession, he noted. She was his wife; he wanted her to have nice things, but he had to be wary of wounding her prickly Yankee pride. Yes, she had her pride, and so did he. From where he stood, knuckling under to Ira for the rest of his life was beginning to look highly unlikely. Jessie would have to choose.

When she grabbed her denim jacket, Ben grabbed his and followed her out the back door. He drew a deep breath of fresh air. Despite all the talk about frost, it was colder than he'd expected. A pale moon rode the banked clouds.

"Who ever heard of a summer frost?" he said absently.

She threw him a surprised look, then smiled. "Anyone who lives this far north."

He smiled back. "Are you casting aspersions on my Southern roots, ma'am?"

"I wouldn't dare."

"It's freezing." He buttoned his jacket against the cold snap. "You'd like Virginia, Jessie. There are green hills, mountains and valleys just like this—only somebody remembered to turn on the heat."

She looked away.

He sighed.

For the next hour or so, Jessie insisted on taking every precaution to protect her large vegetable garden from frost. Ben helped her spread cotton sheets over the exposed plants and anchored the corners with rocks. The moon was full and bright, and the air had a definite nip to it.

When they finished the last row of tomato plants, Ben looked at their handiwork and grinned at the patchwork of colorful pastel sheets, a sight he wouldn't have missed.

They were standing at opposite ends of a long row. And suddenly it seemed too far to Ben. He went to her, fighting the urge to run before she fled. He sensed something had hurt her. He wasn't sure how or why he knew, but he did.

He drew her close, his voice husky. "Now that we've tucked in the garden, let's go to bed." He kissed her.

It was meant to be a short kiss, but somehow things got out of control. With a small moan, she opened her mouth. There was hopelessness, not surrender, in the way she kissed him back. Lately, despite the strain in their relationship, or perhaps because of it, their lovemaking had taken on a frenzied quality.

The sex was great, but it left him feeling uneasy, dissatisfied, and wanting more. He wanted the part of Jessie she was holding back—her heart.

His lips roamed her face. He tasted the salty dampness on her cheek—she was crying. Shocked, he held her away and stared into her eyes. "What's wrong?"

She turned her face into his shoulder. "Nothing."

"Jessie, tell me."

Perhaps his tone convinced her he wouldn't accept an evasion. She told him about her brother, and father, and last of all about her mother. It was all very tragic, an all-too-familiar story of broken lives, parents warring against each other, using their children as ammunition. No matter how much he wished he could make a difference, he couldn't wipe away her past, any more than she could his. But if they could start over, together...

He didn't complete the thought. Perhaps he was expecting too much. "I'm sorry, Jessie," he whispered.

She nodded. "I just wish—" She swallowed hard. "I just wish I remembered the red tricycle."

Oh, God. He winced as her pain ripped through him— the pain of that small, lost, lonely child. What a sad legacy of heartache Avis and Ira had left their children. He hugged her close, binding her to him physically. "I'm just so damn sorry, Jessie. I wish there was more I could say."

She raised her head. "Make love to me."

"Jessie," he groaned.

"Please."

Very gently, he framed her face with his hands and looked at her, feeling a wealth of tenderness for this woman...this woman who ripped his heart to shreds with her baggy pants, muddy boots and soft peach dresses. Her courage left him in awe, and her vulnerability made her real and touchable. At that moment, he'd never loved her more. He could no longer evade the knowledge; he'd loved her for a long, long time. It felt like forever.

They barely made it to their room to bed. That night there were few preliminaries to their lovemaking. Ben struggled out of his jeans while she slipped out of hers.

He caught his breath as the moon filtered into the room and limned her body with a fine delicacy. For a moment, he just looked at her. She was so feminine, her breasts perfect and tipped with mauve. Her legs were long, slender, graceful. Her body was tanned, sleek and smooth, toned with the health of a vigorous life-style.

She shivered. "Oh, it's cold."

"Let me warm you."

She blushed at the husky note in his voice. He gathered her against him and felt her soft sigh of pleasure. Her breasts peaked against his chest. He groaned at the aching pleasure. She was just as aroused; and as they sank onto the bed, she wrapped around him and drew him into her heat.

The suddenness of it stopped him, but then he felt her move and felt his own body catch her rhythm. A fierce need took him in its grip. He couldn't hold back for long. When he felt her climax, he surged against her, matching her pleasure. Suddenly, that sense of urgency was gone. He was going to have time with Jessie. He was going to take time, day by day…if she would have him. He hadn't thought about a future for so long; it felt strange, unmapped.

He loved her—mind, heart, body. Indivisibly. Long moments stretched into an exquisite satiation of the senses. Nothing existed for him but this bed, this room, this woman.

Chapter Fifteen

At midnight, an explosion rocked the farmhouse.

Ben thought he was dreaming. Then he felt Jessie stir against him and heard the shouts. It wasn't a nightmare. This was real. Jared shouted through the door, "It's the Pierce place! I can see the flames from my room."

Ben was out of bed, reaching for his jeans. Jessie scrambled out behind him. "What do you think you're doing?" he asked, his senses alert to her every move.

"I'm going with you." She reached for her jeans.

"No, you're not. I don't want you anywhere near that place." She pulled a sweatshirt over her head. "Jessie." His mouth clamped down at the stubborn set of her chin. He was wasting his breath arguing with her. He dragged her close and kissed her hard. "Be careful." He stared into her eyes. They were burnished silver, like precious antique coins. Everything she meant to him came together in that moment. If he lost her, he couldn't go on living. The knowledge struck him with force.

He didn't have time to analyze the feeling; perhaps it didn't need examining. It had become part of him, just as Jessie had. "Promise you'll stay out of danger." His hands tightened. "Promise me." Her eyes rounded at the raw note of passion in his voice. He did nothing to disguise it. Silently, she nodded.

The truck horn sounded impatient. Jared was driving. "It looks bad," he said when they jumped in.

The truck bounced down the road to the Pierces'. Another explosion lit the night. By the time they arrived, all hell had broken loose. Or so it seemed to Ben. Flames poured from the ruins of the camp store. For a moment, he froze in terror.

Grief struck him, the acid taste of fear, the clutch of dread. He was in a jungle and his plane was a wreckage leaking gas. He could smell it. Gas. Fire. The women and the children. The children. "Oh, God."

Jessie touched his arm. "Ben."

Coming out of an endless dream, Ben grasped her hand and felt the terror recede. He took a breath and barked the order, "Turn the headlights on—over there!"

Ramon came running. "A propane tank exploded. The store was closed, no one was inside when it blew."

Ben checked a broken gas line. Old and corroded, it had probably burst under pressure with added cold-weather demand. "Where's the water supply? Fire extinguishers?"

Ramon stared back helplessly. "The water pump broke."

"Hell! The whole place could blow any minute."

Drew arrived. One of the men went for him and landed several punches. He didn't fight back. By the time his attacker was dragged away, Drew lay on the ground.

Jessie ran to him. "Are you all right?"

Drew stirred. "God, what a mess! Is anyone hurt?"

"Jessie!" Ben roared, from a short distance.

Drew winced. "I think he wants you."

By now, an ambulance and more rescuers had arrived from town. Leaving Drew in capable hands, Jessie returned to Ben.

"I thought I told you to stay close." During the next frantic moments, he kept her by his side, afraid to lose her in the confusion. Black smoke billowed from the camp. Like a pall, ashes and cinder settled, covering everything.

The air was thick and acrid. Just when Ben thought everyone was safe, Rita Morales cried out, "Miguel! *¡Dios mío!* He went back to get the cat!" She ran back toward the campsites.

Swallowing dread, Ben started after her.

Jessie clutched at his arm and physically tried to hold him. "You can't go in there." Her heart squeezed in anguish at the thought of him entering that inferno. She loved him. She had to tell him. "Wait, the fire trucks will be here."

"There isn't time." His eyes were haunted. She felt his muscles tighten as he drew on some inner strength he'd buried along with his men. She knew all about his worst fear.

Losing Ben had become *her* worst fear. Why hadn't she told him before now? Why had she stored all her love inside?

Flames licked at the grassy edge of the compound. The place was going to blow. Jessie knew Ben needed to do this for his own salvation. Maybe he couldn't reach Rita Morales and her son in time, but he had to try.

"Be careful." Her words released him.

Ben stared into her eyes for one long moment, knowing this might be the last time. He kissed her hard. Then, he walked away from her. In the next fiery instant, a dazzling orange light filled his vision. Another explosion! A blast of heat slammed his body backward.

He landed faceup on the ground. Overhead, the sky was impenetrable. *Get up.* He couldn't move. He wasn't sure he wanted to. It hurt too much to live, to be a survivor. He recalled a time in a sweltering jungle when his prayers for a merciful release went unanswered. The memory had grown distant. Jessie. She was his reason for living.

As Ben struggled to his feet, he felt a searing pain. A flying piece of metal had struck his arm. But then a child's scream pierced his own pain. He ran toward the frantic sound. Tearing open a door, he found the boy inside. The cat hissed at Ben.

Ben grabbed a blanket and bundled them both inside. "Don't be afraid. I've got you." The child wrapped his arms around his throat. "Hold on." Ben's chest felt tight. He ran.

His eyes teared. Thick black smoke filled his vision. Another series of explosions went off. Windows burst outward in splinters. Flying glass cut his face. Flames darted right and left. He couldn't see. Then, he heard it…calling to him.

Shielding the child, he homed in on Jessie's voice.

"Ben, Ben… Oh, thank God." Jessie reached for him with all her strength. Someone reached for Miguel. "You're safe," she sobbed against his chest. "It's over."

"Yes, it's over," he said huskily.

She glanced up at the new note of strength in his voice. She met his eyes. The shadows were gone. She smiled through her tears. "You might need a few stitches." Pressing a gauze to his cheek where blood seeped from several cuts, she swallowed hard.

Her heart felt huge, as if it might burst any moment with relief and pride. He'd come through the fire. Somehow, she knew the nightmares were behind him. What lay ahead? She thought of their child. She had to tell him—

soon. She felt so much—love and hope and joy; all the things she'd never dared feel before.

As dawn broke, the distant sky grew brighter. The fire trucks arrived, some with tanks of water drained from the pond. The men turned hoses on the flames.

Cal Pierce pointed to the orange glow in the sky. "The wind's shifted. The fire's spreading."

It was headed west, toward Stone's End.

Jessie whispered, "Dad."

The drive home felt interminable. Despite feelings of dread, Jessie noticed Jared's face was torn with emotion. He felt things deeply—anger, joy, sorrow. At that moment, she felt older than her brother. She squeezed his hand. "He'll be okay."

"I hope so." His voice broke. In that taut moment when time seemed suspended, she felt closer to Jared than she had in years. She glanced up and found Ben watching her.

Along the narrow winding road, only patches of sky were visible. Like fireworks, sparks flew from tree to tree. A tall spindly pine burst into flame right before her eyes.

When the truck turned into Stone's End, her father was standing in the barnyard in his pajamas and robe. He'd let the cows out of the barn. Narrowly missing one, the truck screeched to a stop. Jessie jumped out and threw her arms around her father. "I was so worried about you."

He patted her back awkwardly. "Jessie, I'm okay. Let's get these animals out of the barn."

Ben absorbed the exchange. Despite all their differences, he felt a surge of affection at the sight of the mettlesome old man in striped pajamas. He didn't have time to linger on the thought.

Some men from the camp had left their families to come and help. They ran toward the barn. Before he could stop her, Jessie joined them. Going from stall to stall, they guided the rest of the animals out of the barn to a safe nearby pasture. Homer came out last. He bellowed and rolled his eyes, but cooperated.

Down the road, a produce barn caught fire. Flames flickered here and there throughout the fields. An entire acre was lost in a flash.

Finally, by midmorning, the fire was out. Wisps of smoke curled over the scene. There was nothing more anyone could do.

The smoke cleared. Grimly, Ben surveyed the damage. He found Jessie. Covered in soot and ashes, she looked beautiful to him. With her father and Jared, she looked at the destruction with a dazed, exhausted expression. Several large barns lay in ashes. Ira looked defeated.

He stared at the shell of one barn. "It's gone."

Jared spoke. "We'll just have to rebuild."

The two men exchanged a look. "Yes, we will," Ira said, with a ghost of a smile.

Hands on his hips, Ben looked around. Jessie's garden was still a palette of pretty pastel sheets. A new day had dawned— perhaps a new era at Stone's End, with Ira and Jared working together to rebuild. Ben hoped that would be the case. He had his own future to resolve; his and Jessie's.

Jessie's offer of breakfast was met with enthusiasm. Ben took time for a quick shower. Some women had arrived from town to help. Everyone dug into the large farm breakfast.

Cal stopped by. "Rita Morales was badly hurt in the explosion. She's in the hospital." He looked as if he'd aged ten years. "The authorities are swarming all over the place."

Jessie patted his shoulder. "I'm sorry, Cal."

"The town opened up the school for the migrants."

In a time of need, Henderson had opened its heart.

Jared stood. "Well, there's still work to do. Let's move the animals back to the barn."

Jessie noticed that Ben looked gray with fatigue. After the harrowing night, she wanted to wrap her arms around him and tell him she loved him. And about the baby. Soon...

The main barn had been spared all but some superficial damage. The cattle were skittish. After a taste of freedom, Homer pawed the ground and bellowed rage as the men cautiously circled him. With pitchforks, they prodded him in the right direction, but he kept eluding them.

"Get the gate, Jess," her father ordered.

Jessie hesitated. Homer looked wild-eyed; she'd never seen him so out of control. She swallowed her fear and automatically obeyed. She raced toward the gap in the fence even as everything inside urged her to run in the other direction.

She heard Ben shout, "Watch out, Jessie!"

She glanced over her shoulder. Homer had broken through the men. More than two thousand pounds of hard muscle and bone on the hoof were bearing down on her. She could smell the fury on Homer's breath, see the deadly intent in his eyes. It took every ounce of courage to turn her back on him and run.

Too late, she thought about the baby. She shouldn't have risked it. Her child had suddenly become real. If she could only reach the porch. Homer was gaining on her. She would never make it. The earth thundered beneath his weight. The roar of Ben's motorcycle mingled with the roar in her ears. She felt a rush of air as she tripped. She fell to the ground and screamed.

Ben shuddered at the sound. Shifting to full throttle, he aimed the bike at Homer. At the very last second, the bull veered away from Jessie. The motorcycle caught Homer with a glancing blow to the hind quarter. The bull exploded with rage and turned on Ben. Regaining his balance, Ben swerved the bike around, darting in and out of Homer's path. A horn caught and tore off a fender, missing Ben's thigh by an inch.

Homer retreated and pawed at the ground. His head dipped and swerved, then he charged the bike again. Ben played him, losing track of time as he locked wills with the rogue bull. Homer hung in there, coming back again and again. Trying to tire the animal, Ben rode in circles until the massive bull stood, head down, panting and confused.

The other men moved in and herded him into the barn. Jared quickly closed and secured the gate. Ben ran to Jessie's side, kneeling on the ground beside her. Her face was ashen.

"Jessie," he groaned, gently smoothing the tumbled hair from her face. He took her hand. Her pulse felt weak, her breathing seemed almost suspended. Her eyelids fluttered to reveal a leaden expression, her mind obviously still locked in terror.

At the sound of Ben's frightened voice, Jessie tried to sit up and reassure him she was all right. But she wasn't sure how she felt. Terrified, for one thing. What if something had gone wrong with her unborn baby? Had she fallen, or been struck down by the bull? She couldn't even recall. It was all a nightmare. Ben's hands held her like a vice. She watched his face darken to a graven mask.

"What did you think you were doing?" His eyes burned into hers. "You could have been killed."

"Dad called me," she said weakly.

"Ah, yes, I should have known."

She opened her mouth to speak, but he cut her off. "Don't say a word, Jessie. I'm not in the mood for your excuses." He lifted her in his arms and headed toward the house. "Any normal female would have stayed put. But not you. You are the most stubborn—"

Regaining some of her spirit, she gasped. "Why, of all the…" To her embarrassment, they had a full audience.

Cal looked shaken. "The bull slipped past me." He ran his hand over his face.

Ira caught up with them. "Is she all right?"

Ben snarled, "She'll live—no thanks to you."

"Now hold on," Jared interrupted. "What happened was no one's fault."

"Besides," Jessie inserted, "nothing happened. I'm perfectly fine and—" Her voice wobbled when she recalled her pregnancy. She prayed everything was all right. It had to be. Life wouldn't be so cruel. Would it? Suddenly, she felt frightened. Thus, she was slow to react when Ben stopped and abruptly set her down on her feet.

"Is that so?" Ben reacted. His fear had subsided. Now he just felt furious as he resumed the argument. "Nothing happened!" He'd just risked his life to save hers, and she thought it was nothing! "If you Carlisles tried applying some common sense occasionally, you wouldn't need rescuing every time I turn around!"

Ringed in by her father and brother, Jessie drew in a wounded breath. "That's, that's…" she sputtered.

"That's the honest truth and you know it, Jessie! I've been bailing you out of one mess after another since the day I got here. I'm fed up with the whole damn setup."

That much was painfully obvious. He was fed up with her.

"Well, you needn't bail me out any longer," Jessie snapped. Fed up with feeling young, inept, and out of her depth, she wanted to be his equal, not a yoke around her neck. Damn him! "I can take care of myself."

Ira's voice held triumph. "Jessie's right. We got by before you came. We'll get along fine after you're gone."

Jessie gasped in dismay. She hadn't said any such thing! Her blow for equality had fallen short. Before she could explain, Ben exploded, his anger directed at her father—leaving her out, as usual. "You're right, Ira. Stone's End belongs to the Carlisles, lock, stock and barrel. You can have it. I quit. And this time I mean it! I'm sorry, Jessie. I tried."

With a hard parting glance at her, he turned and walked back to his bike. Jessie stared in disbelief. He'd tried? He was sorry? That was it?

"Damn his blasted hide," Jared swore as Ben drove off.

Too numb to move, Jessie heard her father's satisfaction. "He's gone."

Ben was gone. Sounds and sights swirled around her. She'd come full circle. How many times had she stood in this spot and watched someone leave—her mother, Jared, now Ben?

Was she destined to relive the same scene over and over? When would she learn not to care? Like a self-fulfilling prophecy, Ben was gone, just as she'd expected. She'd thought herself prepared. The emptiness was overwhelming. Much worse than anything that had gone before.

"But what about Jessie?" Jared asked.

Ira huffed, "She'll get over him."

Jared shook her out of her stupor. "Go after him, Jessie. He can't have gotten far."

She shook her head. "I wouldn't know where to start."

"He'll be in touch," Jared insisted.

Her father looked doubtful. "I'm sorry, Jessie." For the first time in her memory he appeared lost for words.

Pain threatened to shatter her control. How could she have been so blind? Her life had never been easy, but she'd faced each day with renewed determination. Her loneliness had ended when Ben Harding roared into her life. She'd failed to recognize it; she'd fallen in love so timidly, afraid she would lose it....

Well, now she had.

The knowledge came too late. She turned and walked away. Jared and her father were still arguing, but somehow there wasn't the same rancor. At least, some good had come of this destructive night.

She couldn't return to the house, not yet. Instead, she walked toward the pond. When she reached the clearing, she stared at the devastation. The tops of the trees were gone, the lower branches were charred black. A bulldozer had plowed a rough track to the water's edge, where the fire trucks had filled their tanks. The pond was nearly drained. Miraculously, a small green patch of ground remained. She sat down—and her inner reserves collapsed. She wanted to cry, but couldn't.

Ben had made love to her here among the cathedral pines. Now they were all gone. Destruction and ruin lay where love had found its roots. She was bound by it, but Ben felt no such ties. He'd never spoken of love. Just as she'd feared, the emotional ties had all been one-sided.

The other day, Jared had spoken of their father's hardness—was she hard and unbending? So many times, she could have told Ben she loved him. Instead, she'd kept it locked inside, buried deep within her heart where it couldn't come to light and flourish. She'd been afraid of rejection. But her coldness had only earned more rejection. She'd let her fear of abandonment keep her from telling Ben how she felt.

Give me a reason to stay. She recalled how he'd challenged her the morning after they'd made love. He'd reached out to her from the loneliness of his soul and asked for her love. She'd given her body—when all he'd wanted was her heart.

She might have slept, she wasn't sure.

When a noise alerted her, she sat up abruptly. Ben stood across the clearing from her. Jessie scrambled to her feet, shocked, delighted, frightened. She wanted to run to him, but her legs felt like lead. Her stomach churned. What a time for morning sickness! She wanted to laugh, but her throat felt thick with tears—tears she hadn't shed.

His words shocked her. "I hope you're saying goodbye to this place," he snarled, angry passion darkening his blue eyes. "Because if you're hiding..."

"I thought you'd left," she whispered in confusion.

"Not without you." His face grew taut, his lips firm with determination. "I went to town to arrange for a van to move your things. I'm not leaving without you."

Her heart skipped a rapid beat. From opposing sides, they faced each other. She took a tiny step forward, then stopped. Once again, she was ready to accept Ben on any terms. He had come back. No. He'd never left! He'd gone to town. The knowledge gave her courage to demand more. This time, she had to be sure; this time, he had to say the words.

Ben spoke again. "I'm not asking you to change your life—just let me into it. I want us to be partners."

"I thought you were leaving. You said you didn't want any part of the Carlisles or Stone's End."

"Ah, but you're not a Carlisle. You're my wife." He smiled. "Are you going to make me beg?"

There it was again, that small tug-of-war. Their love was a battle of wills, starting with a contest over the bedsheets the first night he arrived. They were two opposing forces, a push-me pull-me kind of love that tugged at her heartstrings. A battle she intended to win. Jessie took another step. She smiled, seeing, at last; seeing the depth of yearning in him, as strong as her own. "But you didn't choose me." That still hurt.

"Didn't I?" His eyes grew tender with amusement.

"You only stayed for my father," she reminded him.

"Your father and I have our differences. I respect him. Hell, I even like Ira on his good days. But that isn't why I married you." He started toward her.

In dawning wonder, Jessie watched him dig something out of his pocket, something small and shiny. A ring, a simple gold wedding band. When he held it out to her, it became more precious than diamonds.

"I've been carrying this around for weeks," Ben said. "I didn't know how to give it to you. Will you take it?"

"What are you asking?" She felt her heart pounding.

"I want you to be my wife." He stood and offered her everything, everything she'd ever dreamed of. "I want you to forgive me for not courting you the way I should have. I want you to come with me. I want you to love me."

"I do...I will. I love you." Tears of joy sparkled in her eyes. Jessie held out her hand. When he slipped the ring on her finger, she held it out and just looked at it.

One tug of her hand brought her into his arms. "I love you so much, Jessie." That note of possession transferred to his lips as he swept her into a bone-crushing demonstration of ownership. She kissed him back in helpless hunger, unable to deny her need. Ben whispered against the corner of her lips, "Come with me. Trust me."

"You're sure?"

"I'm sure of one thing—we belong together. If you can think of anything that matters more than that, then tell me. Because I can't think of anything but you." Ben watched as her soft gray eyes shimmered, then cleared to reveal a gleam of joy. "We can come back here often," he reassured her. "But for now, I think we should start fresh somewhere. We can start a new life."

"We already have." Feeling ridiculously shy after all they'd been to each other, Jessie placed his hand on the gentle mound of her stomach where their unborn child fluttered like a tiny winged butterfly trapped beneath her heart. A heart was a funny thing, she'd discovered. She could risk it after all; give it away and get one back. Ben's heart.

His eyes devoured her. "When?"

"Come spring."

His smile was slow. "Our child," he whispered.

Unzipping her jeans, Ben slipped his fingers into the gap and caressed his child. He felt Jessie's pulse quicken and slid his fingers farther down. She drew in a sharp breath at the intimate invasion. All the passion came rushing back, along with the mutual need to be one. He undressed her, slowly revealing every tender inch of her. She was rounder in places; fuller, more sensitive in others. The signs of their child growing filled him with wonder as he touched her gently. There was acceptance in her eyes. Love for their child.

Ben thought of her garden—how she'd nurtured it—and knew that any child of Jessie's would be blessed. He kissed her, wanting to share the emotion with her. His touch was sure, arousing her to an excited pitch that left no room for hesitation. She needed him, as he needed her. With clothing removed, with no barriers, nothing hidden, nothing between them but sun and sky and wind, his body covered hers in one swift motion. He claimed her with purpose— hungry, needful—and with what he hoped was the utmost mutual pleasure. They made love as if it were the first time.

As the sun reached high into a cloudless powder blue sky, they walked back to the farmhouse. Jessie asked, "Where are we going?" Somehow, saying the words wasn't as painful as she'd expected. She loved Stone's End and would miss it, but leaving was the only solution for everyone. She'd always known Ben was too independent to remain at her father's beck and call.

Besides, Jared was staying. He and her father would resolve their differences. Her place was with Ben; whenever, wherever he went, whatever he did, she planned to be there.

"I was wondering when you'd ask." He smiled wryly. "About that farm in Virginia—did I ever mention it's a horse farm? My grandparents are waiting for me to come back and take over so they can retire." A horse farm.

She tilted her head to look at him. "No, I don't believe you did." Could it really be so simple?

"They're going to love you. It's time I went back."

He didn't have to say he'd stopped running. Jessie looked into Ben's eyes and saw tomorrow and tomorrow. The shadows were gone. He was promising "forever." When he drew her against him, she felt "forever" in his touch, the whisper of his kiss on her lips. At last, Jessie had found love.

At the gate, Ben glanced at the weatherbeaten sign hanging at a crooked angle from the old fence-post. Stone's End. When Jessie's gaze followed his, he saw sadness, but no sign of reluctance. Her trust and loyalty humbled him as nothing else could. It was something he'd tried to earn. In the end, she'd simply granted it as a gift. That was Jessie—no half measures, no conditions. Ben looked out over the farm with affection.

Like this northern land, love was for all seasons, like a mountain stream that thaws at the end of winter and runs strong like a river in spring. At the touch of his hand to her cheek, Jessie gave him a radiant smile. The smile transformed her face from pretty to beautiful. She was his; his to touch, to hold, to keep.

He smiled. Yes, she was definitely a keeper. The road ahead might be full of twists and turns, but for Ben and Jessie, it wasn't the end; it was only the beginning.

Epilogue

It was Ira's birthday. He sat on the porch, rocking, waiting. Jared had warned him they might not come for hours, but Ira wanted to be there when Ben and Jessie arrived.

When a van pulled into the driveway, he felt a fullness in his chest. A feeling of gladness swept over him as he watched Ben help Jessie out of the passenger side. She walked slowly up the walk and up the porch steps. After the birth of her baby less than two months ago, she looked slim again, like a girl. She looked so pretty in her pale blue dress, with her fair hair and soft smile, just like her ma. A wave of emotion threatened his composure, but he held on—until she lay the baby in his arms. A tear rolled down Ira's cheek.

Jessie said softly. "Meet your grandson—Nathaniel."

After a long moment, Ira cleared his throat. "Poor little scrap—he's got Ben's black hair," he said gruffly, unable to express what he really felt inside. "But he's got Jessie's far-seeing eyes."

Ben chuckled. "That he does." He placed a hand on Jessie's waist and brought her back against him.

Ira caught the movement. He looked at his son-in-law. Ben Harding had the look of a contented man—a man who had gone to hell and back and found heaven. Yes, he was the right man for Jessie. With a glance at the loaded van, Ira asked, "You planning on staying awhile?"

Jessie answered. "We're going to stay part of the summer."

Ira nodded. "Good."

The migrant camp was closed. As a result, Stone's End was short of help. Jessie hadn't needed to ask—Ben had offered to come north for the summer season. His grandfather had gladly agreed to manage the horse farm for a few months. Ben's family had become Jessie's; they'd welcomed her without reserve, grateful to her for bringing Ben back where he belonged.

"While we're here," Ben said. "I thought we could look into buying a vacation house."

Amazed at the announcement, Jessie smiled at him in delight. "A summer place. You never said anything."

Ben smiled back. "I wanted to surprise you."

Surprising them both, Ira offered, "Reckon there's an acre or two right here at Stone's End to build, if you'd like.

Jessie held her breath, waiting for Ben's answer. She released it when he said, "That sounds just fine."

She loved her new home in Virginia and never tired of the green hills and rich red earth, but she loved this place, too. She loved Ben even more for giving her a piece of it back.

The baby stirred. His tiny fists waved in the air, until Ira caught one. Nathaniel wrapped his fingers around a thumb and hung on. "He's got quite a grip for a young one," Ira said.

Jared came around the corner. "Jessie!" A wide grin split his face; he grabbed her around the waist and hugged her. He shook hands with Ben.

"Hey, what have we here?" Sobering abruptly, Jared bent towards the baby nestled against Ira.

Ben introduced him. "Meet your nephew."

Jessie stood back. Her heart swelled with love and pride as she leaned against the porch rail and watched the three men huddle around one tiny baby. She smiled, content in this precious moment—one of the many Ben had given her. As she looked at his dark head bent over their baby, she thought her heart would burst. She loved both her husband and her son with a depth that still frightened her at times. Just then, as if aware of her thoughts, Ben glanced toward her. Their gazes locked for a brief moment. That's all it took and she felt connected, a part of Ben, just as he was part of her forever.

That night, Ben sat in Jessie's rocking chair in her old room and watched her prepare herself and the baby for bed.

Between bathtime and feeding, it was quite a production. Finally, Jessie stood before him, with the infant in her arms. She was freshly scrubbed, sweet and innocent in her long white cotton nightgown.

"Are you sure you want to build here?" she said hesitantly.

"Yes, I'm sure. I want our children to know this place. It's part of their heritage." When she smiled in relief, he drew her onto his lap and wrapped his arms around her and the baby. Jessie's strength, courage, and goodness were bred in this place. He wanted that for his children, and himself.

He felt her sigh and settle against him more comfortably.

When the baby nuzzled against her breast, she opened her nightgown and let him nurse. Jessie had taken to mothering as naturally as she did everything else. That small dark head nestled against the pale curve of her breast sent a visceral feeling of possession coursing through Ben. Jessie had given him so much. First, herself, then a son. At times, Ben felt awed and humbled at her capacity to give. He'd never known so much peace, joy, and contentment existed. Like a fresh breath of spring, she brought renewal, love.

"Sometimes, I can't believe a baby could be so perfect," Jessie's voice penetrated his thoughts.

Ben smiled at the wonder in her voice. He felt it too.

"He's your son, Jessie."

"Our son," she whispered.

Jessie ran a light finger down the infant's downy cheek. In response, Nathaniel stopped feeding for a moment. He smiled and gazed at his parents with those far-seeing eyes. That early vision of love would guide him through his life.

Rocking gently, Ben held his wife close to his heart and felt her breathing slow to a gentle rhythm. Nathaniel yawned. A breeze whispered through the open window. With a few creaks and groans, the house settled down for the night. Ben leaned his head back and closed his eyes, not in any hurry to end the tender moment.

He'd traveled a far distance to get to this place. A year ago, he'd found Jessie waiting at the end of that long lonely road. In her, he'd found love—a love that grew and flourished despite the odds; a love that grew in stony ground.

* * * * *

Daniel MacGregor is at it again...

New York Times bestselling author

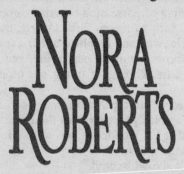

NORA ROBERTS

introduces us to a new generation of MacGregors
as the lovable patriarch of the illustrious MacGregor
clan plays matchmaker again, this time to his three
gorgeous granddaughters in

THE
MACGREGOR BRIDES

From Silhouette Books

Don't miss this brand-new continuation of Nora Roberts's
enormously popular *MacGregor* miniseries.

Available November 1997 at your favorite retail outlet.

Silhouette
SPECIAL EDITION™
That SPECIAL Woman!

**These delightful titles are coming soon to
THAT SPECIAL WOMAN!—only from
Silhouette Special Edition!**

**September 1997   THE SECRET WIFE
                    by Susan Mallery (SE#1123)**
Five years ago Elissa's dreams came true when she married
her true love—but their honeymoon was short-lived. Could
she and Cole Stephenson get a second shot at happiness?

**November 1997   WHITE WOLF
                    by Lindsay McKenna (SE#1135)**
Hard-core cynic Dain Phillips turned to mystical medicine
woman Erin Wolf for a "miracle" cure. But he never suspected
that Erin's spiritual healing would alter him—body and soul!

**January 1998   TENDERLY
                    by Cheryl Reavis (SE#1147)**
Socialite Eden Trevoy was powerfully drawn to Navajo
policeman Ben Toomey when he helped her uncover her half-
Navajo roots. Could her journey of self-discovery lead to full-
fledged love?

**IT TAKES A VERY SPECIAL MAN TO WIN THAT
SPECIAL WOMAN....** Don't miss THAT SPECIAL WOMAN!
every other month from some of your favorite authors!

SILHOUETTE WOMEN KNOW ROMANCE WHEN THEY SEE IT.

And they'll see it on **ROMANCE CLASSICS**, the new 24-hour TV channel devoted to romantic movies and original programs like the special **Romantically Speaking—Harlequin™ Goes Prime Time.**

Romantically Speaking—Harlequin™ Goes Prime Time introduces you to many of your favorite romance authors in a program developed exclusively for Harlequin® and Silhouette® readers.

Watch for **Romantically Speaking—Harlequin™ Goes Prime Time** beginning in the summer of 1997.

If you're not receiving ROMANCE CLASSICS, call your local cable operator or satellite provider and ask for it today!

Escape to the network of your dreams.

See Ingrid Bergman and Gregory Peck in *Spellbound* **on Romance Classics.**

ROMANCE CLASSICS

©1997 American Movie Classics Co. "Romance Classics" is a service mark of American Movie Classics Co.
Harlequin is a trademark of Harlequin Enterprises Ltd.
Silhouette is a registered trademark of Harlequin Books, S.A.   RMCLS-S-R2

**SHARON
SALA**

**Continues the twelve-book
series—36 HOURS—
in October 1997
with Book Four**

FOR HER EYES ONLY

The storm was over. The mayor was dead. Jessica Hanson
had an aching head...and sinister visions of murder.
And only one man was willing to take her seriously—
Detective Stone Richardson. He knew that unlocking
Jessica's secrets would put him in danger, but the rugged
cop had never expected to fall for her, too. Danger he could
handle. But love...?

For Stone and Jessica and *all* the residents of Grand Springs,
Colorado, the storm-induced blackout was just the beginning
of 36 Hours that changed *everything!* You won't want to miss a
single book.

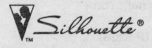

COMING NEXT MONTH

#1135 WHITE WOLF—Lindsay McKenna
That Special Woman!
Hardened corporate raider Dain Phillips turned to mystical medicine woman Erin Wolf for a "miracle" cure. But he never expected to care so deeply for Erin—or that her spiritual healing would forever alter him body and soul!

#1136 THE RANCHER AND THE SCHOOLMARM—
Penny Richards
Switched at Birth
Schoolteacher Georgia Williams was stunned when her fiancé passed her in the airport, got attacked and suffered amnesia. How would she handle the revelation that this riveting man who stole her heart was *not* her groom-to-be—but instead his long-lost identical twin?

#1137 A COWBOY'S TEARS—Anne McAllister
Code of the West
Mace and Jenny Nichols had the *perfect* marriage—until Mace discovered some sad news. Jenny was determined to convince her brooding cowboy of her unfaltering love—and that there was more than one way to capture their dreams....

#1138 THE PATERNITY TEST—Pamela Toth
Powerful Nick Kincaid could handle anything—except his mischievous twins. His new nanny, Cassie Wainright, could handle everything—except her attraction to Nick. Now Cassie was pregnant, and Nick was being put to the *ultimate* test.

#1139 HUSBAND: BOUGHT AND PAID FOR—Laurie Paige
Fearing for her life, heiress Jessica Lockhart hired P.I. Brody Smith—and then proposed marriage. Her aloof bodyguard agreed to a platonic union, but that didn't mean the lovely lady had the right to wiggle her way into his heart.

#1140 MOUNTAIN MAN—Doris Rangel
Gloria Pellman was a single mom, raising her young son, Jamey—alone, thank you very much! She didn't need a husband! But when Hank Mason rescued them from his rugged mountain, Jamey discovered a friend...and Gloria discovered her heart was in danger!

Share in the joy of yuletide romance with brand-new
stories by two of the genre's most beloved writers

DIANA PALMER

and

JOAN JOHNSTON

in

LONE STAR CHRISTMAS

Diana Palmer and Joan Johnston share their favorite
Christmas anecdotes and personal stories in this
special hardbound edition.

Diana Palmer delivers an irresistible spin-off of her
LONG, TALL TEXANS series and Joan Johnston crafts an
unforgettable new chapter to **HAWK'S WAY** in this wonderful
keepsake edition celebrating the holiday season. So
perfect for gift giving, you'll want one for yourself...and
one to give to a special friend!

Available in November at your favorite retail outlet!

Only from

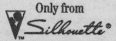